Legends from the kingdom of Alba

Legends From the Kingdom of Alba

What readers say

A sweet world of magic, family, and love.
******* Reviewed in the United States**

I truly enjoyed the story of Avery. The story of her finding her true self and all the magical creatures that will forever be part of her life. I loved all the magical creatures that came to live and fight with Avery and her friends to bring the light back into a Dark world.

Rheeah **I enjoyed this novel**
****** Reviewed in the United Kingdom**

I do not normally write reviews but felt I should in this instance. Why? Well, this book which is the first in a long time that took me back to the novels of my younger years. It is, to me, a book that adults and children will both enjoy. Full of interesting characters, a few of whom you will want to have further adventures with. But most importantly and simply, the fact is I just really enjoyed the read.

Stephen McSporran

Mythical Scotland
******* Reviewed in Germany**

I myself do not know the fantasy genre, but I bought this book as a gift on recommendation, and it was a great success. The recipient was absolutely enthusiastic-both by the imaginative and entertaining story, as well as by the lively writing style and the ability of the author to take the reader to a mythical medieval Scotland on the first pages. This shows once again that you should give even lesser-known writers a chance.

Gaby

It's well worth the read.
****** Reviewed in the UK**

The story really gets you indulged in another realm of reality. As someone who reads a lot, I must admit that I don't regularly come across writing as descriptive as this very often.

I felt very content long before I even finished it. It's well worth the read.

Cover and interior Artwork Ursula Williams
Images used:
www: shutterstock.com, /Depositphoto.com

The Sword of Light

Volume I

By Ursula Williams

Legends from the kingdom of Alba

CONTENTS

Legends from the kingdom of Alba

Legends from the Kingdom of Alba

If you believe in legends and magic, then come with me into a time that is long gone or never was.

All you have to bring is your imagination and the willingness to dream.

Let us travel back to the year 1223 and visit Mackenzie's Inn near the small village of Dallmally in Argyll & Bute. Visit lochs, rivers, mountains, and the realm of the Seelie Fae, as we accompany four friends on their quest.

1 BAD NEWS

Avery felt a shiver run down her spine. She quickly pulled the featherbed right up to her nose, buried her head deep into the soft pillow, and wondered if it was time to get up. It was market day, which meant lots of early guests, news, and a visit from Ursula's best friend. She opened her eyes and glanced around her room. Her windows were covered with ice flowers that sparkled in the morning sun, and the remaining embers from last night's fire filled her room with a soft golden glow.

'Avery, Mo Leannan, get up. Remember, it's market day. The first travellers should be here soon. We have to get the fires going!'

'Oh no, Granny, please let me sleep a little longer. The sun is only just coming up.'

'No, Avery, we have to get the hall warmed up and prepare the food. Out of bed, lazy head.

'Avery sat up and felt goosebumps creeping up her legs. It's no use I better dress and make my way to the kitchen. At least it should be warmed up by now. With that thought, she slid out of bed, dressed, and washed her face. The water was ice cold, but it did the job. She was awake now and ran down the steps, taking two at a time.

'Take it easy, you could fall, and I might not be able to catch you. You are so big now,' chuckled William, who stood at the bottom of the staircase. Aye, but you manage to carry a cask of ale all by yourself, don't you? Avery thought as she skipped the last two steps and leapt into his arms.

'See, you can. I knew it,' Avery whispered in his ear, ruffling his blonde locks and giving him a smacking kiss on his cheek.

'Well, I say you are in a good mood! Is there something that I should know about?'

'Aye Da, don't you smell it? Granny is making pancakes, and I am sure they are for me,' she said with a grin.

'Am I right, Granny?' called Avery, letting go of her father dashing into the kitchen. The kitchen was Avery's favourite place, especially during the winter month. It was always warm and filled with goodies. Smoked ham, bacon and sausages hung from the ceiling, and the shelves along the walls were stacked with jars of honey, jams, and jellies. Granny was busy sweeping ashes and wood chips away from the hearth. She only noticed Avery as she lifted her head to brush back some long, silver strands of hair that had come undone from her bun.

'Well, good morning, sleepyhead. Your breakfast is almost ready,' her Grandmother said, smiling. 'But before you sit down to eat, go and start the fire in the hall for me. Please,' she added, handing her a clay pot filled with glowing peat from the kitchen fire.

The tab room was Dark and cold as Avery rushed to the fireplace, placed the glowing peat on the flagstone, and covered it with straw, twigs, and some small branches. The fire flared up with a roar, and soon its flames began to Dance between the logs sending sparks up into the chimney like wild bees. Warmth and light spread far out across the room. Avery lit a few candles and placed them on the wooden tables before stepping outside. The sun had reached the top of the hills by now and made the freshly fallen snow glisten like diamonds. She made her way through the knee-deep snow while keeping close to the wall to avoid the ice-cold wind, opened the shutters and rushed back inside.

'Granny, I am finished. Are the pancakes ready yet?'

'Aye, my bonny lass, they are on the table near the hearth. Go sit down. I'll bring you a cup of tea and some blueberry jam,' replied granny while filling a cup with steaming herb tea.

Granny loved to cook and eat, which showed on her hips, but she had a good sense of humour about it. The people from the surrounding villages travelling merchants and tradespeople came to enjoy her cooking and never missed her special stew on market Days.

'There you are, sweetheart, enjoy but don't linger. I believe I hear a carriage,' said Granny as she went into the hall.

Avery sat down on a stool near the fire, warmed her hands, and lifted her skirt to dry the seam. She was in no hurry; she thought it was much too early for guests. Took a large spoonful of blueberry jam, picked up her tea and savoured her breakfast before entering the hall to help her Grandmother. So, Granny was right. There is a carriage, Avery thought when she saw four men sitting at the fireplace.

'Oh, there you are, Avery,' Grandmother said when she saw Avery entering the hall.

'Go on, get some hot broth and bannocks for these poor men. They must be frozen to the bone! And set these cloaks near the fire to dry,' she said, handing her the wet cloaks and closing the door behind her.

'What's the rush, and why is she closing the door? Avery wondered as she placed the cloaks over a rack near the fire. She could not resist returning to the door to open it just a crack, listening to the conversation. 'Oh, dear Avery, the kippers are burning,' shouted her father as he stepped through the back door with a stack of firewood in his arms!

'What is going on? Why did mother leave the kitchen with food on the fire? And why, for goodness sakes, is the door closed?' William mumbled, dropping the wood and rushing to the hearth to pull the pan from the fire.

'I don't know, Da. Granny wanted it this way,' Avery shrugged her shoulders and reached for the handle to open the door when her Grandmother stepped in.

'Oh William, I am glad that you are back. Could you please help me get some food ready for our guests?' Granny's voice was shaky, and she looked pale and very nervous.

'Of course,' William responded before adding with hesitation,' why is the door closed?'

'Never mind that. I will tell you later,' Granny said, tightening her apron and beginning to chop some onions. Avery placed four bowls on the table and picked up a scoop to get the broth for the men when Granny called over to her.

'Never mind, lass, I'll handle that. Go and fetch me a bucket of water.'

Startled Avery, rested the scoop back on the table, picked up the bucket, and stepped into the garden. Clearly, Granny wants me out of the kitchen so she can talk to Da without me listening in. What's the big secret, and what could these four men have to do with it?

'Crivens!' she shouted as she tried to regain her balance. The ground underneath her was frozen solid and slippery under the freshly fallen snow. Her hope to return quickly, to pick up some of the news Granny was sharing with her father, were squashed. She had no other choice than to stroll to avoid falling, and the heavy bucket she was trying to balance didn't make it any easier. It took her a long time to get back to the house. When she finally reached it and knocked the snow off her shoes, she noticed that she was alone. The door to the hall was still closed. Before she tiptoed to the door, she set the bucket down very carefully so as not to make any noise, opening it slightly to overhear the ongoing conversation.

'Ar ye telling me that the stranger returned?'

'Aye William, he was seen at the market last Saturday.'

'Have more girls disappeared?' Her father's voice sounded hoarse and very concerned.

'Aye, Grace and Dallis, we are all anxious. We thought we better come to warn ya' before anything happened.'

Avery didn't recognise the voice and couldn't see anyone from where she stood.

What stranger, and how could Grace and Dallis just disappear? She wondered as she opened the door a bit more to get a glimpse of the men sitting at the fire.

'This is bad news. We hoped the stranger had stopped coming. No one had caught sight of him in Ardteale for a long time,' Granny said with quiet intensity making eye contact with each of the visitors.

'Oh no, Maighread's, he was always around, and every time he appeared, one or two girls would go missing. It's terrible. Ten are gone so far.'

The man that spoke sounded familiar, but Avery couldn't place his voice.

'William, we must get to the market and warn the other villagers. Quick get our cloaks. We don't have time.'

The man that had spoken got up. As he turned, Avery saw him clearly. It was Harris, the peddler from the neighbouring village. She would always recognise him by his height and the richly decorated green hat. I must get away from the door. Da will enter the kitchen any moment to fetch the cloaks, she thought. She barely made it to the other end of the kitchen when her father stepped in.

'Avery, come, lass, help me with the cloaks. Our guests are ready to leave,' he said, picked up the cloaks and handed two of them to her.

'Sure, Da, but why are they leaving so soon? Their cloaks are still wet!' Avery asked, hoping to coax some information out of him. He left back into the hall without answering. Avery followed him quickly, eager to see the men that came to warn the villagers.

'Oh, guid mornin me bonnie lass, how are you?' Harris addressed her with a big smile. 'It's been such a long time since last I saw you. I believe it was last spring when you bought some pretty ribbons from me.'

'Aye, right you are! Did you bring some with you today? I would love to take a look!' Avery replied, hoping he would stay a little longer to answer some of the questions swirling through her head.

'I am afraid, not, my dear. I am not here to sell anything today. But I shall be back soon, and then I will show you the beautiful laces I got in Brussels.' Harris swung the cloak over his shoulders with these words and walked out, followed by the other three men. Avery swung around to face her family as soon as they had gone.

'What was that all about, and what stranger did they all talk about? Please do not try to tell me that it is not my business.'

'Avery, calm down. We'll explain everything in time,' her father responded in a low voice, disturbed by the news.

'It is time now! Dallis and Grace are my friends. It is my business to know!' She was not about to give in and looked her father straight in the eye. Seeing that he wouldn't budge, she left the hall, ran up the stairs and straight into her room, slamming the door shut behind her. Her head was pounding from the hundreds of questions going through her mind.

In time, it is time now. How long do Da and Granny want to wait before telling me? Could I be in Danger, and who is this stranger? What does he want from Dallis and Grace? Where are they? She felt angry and frightened, so she lay down on her bed, closed her eyes and fell into a restless sleep. It was already past midday when she woke to the sound of excited voices coming from the great hall. Oh dear, I slept all mornin! Grandmother will need my help in the kitchen. She thought, splashing cold water on her face before she ran downstairs. The tab hall was filled with people returning from the market by now. As Avery walked through the crowd, she noticed the farmer John slumped on a bench near the door. His broad shoulders and flaming red hair stood out in the crowd. Avery hurried over to greet him and find out if his Daughter Ursula was with him today.

'Guid Dai Farmer John, hou are ye? And where is Ursula? I don't see her anywhere. Did she not accompany you to the market today?'

'Oh, guid Dai Avery. No, Ursula had to stay back. I am afraid the weather being bad as it is, I did not want her to leave the house. But don't fret. You will see her as soon as the snow stops,' replied John in a soft voice. Something about his voice didn't seem very convincing.

'I don't mind the snow. May I come along when you leave? I must speak to her. It is important,' she urged, hoping he would agree.

'I do not think it is wise, and surely your Da wouldn't want you away from home now,' John said, looking over to the kitchen door, where her father had just entered the hall.

'Avery, you had us worried', he exclaimed when he saw her. Now go and help Granny in the kitchen, would you?'

Avery and Granny had lots to do until late in the evening. Only after all the dishes were washed, and the kitchen cleaned was Avery able to join her father in the tab hall, where she found him sitting by the fire. Next to him sat a woman with hair as white as snow dressed in a colourful robe.

Avery recognised the woman right away. It was Adelaide, the weaver who lived near the forest's edge. Avery loved her dearly and visited whenever she could to help her spin the wool from her sheep and watch her weave the most fantastic cloth. She cherished their walks through the forest, collecting barks, flowers, and berries to make beautiful dyes. It was rumoured throughout the villages that her cloth could protect the wearer against Dark magic and spirits. Avery loved these stories of magic but did not honestly believe them.

'It is nice to see you, Adelaide,' she greeted her. 'I was planning to visit you tomorrow and bring you a cake Granny made for you.'

'Oh, my bonnie lass, you can bring it along when we are leaving. Your Da asked me to keep you at my home until it is safe for you to return,' replied Adelaide.

'Da, why didn't you tell me? Why do you want me to leave, and why would I not be safe at home?' Avery asked, surprised.

'You will be all right. My sons and I will look in on you regularly, do not be afraid!' Avery spun around and saw Bhaltair, the miller. She had not noticed him before but was glad to see him.

'I would like that, Bhaltair, but why all these secrets? And why do I have to leave?' her voice sounded frightened.

'The village elders agreed that all lassies your age should be taken in by childless people to keep them safe from the stranger. He seems to be responsible for the disappearance of more than ten so far. We cannot prove it, but one or two will vanish every time he is seen,' Bhaltair responded.

Avery looked at him in disbelief. She felt that her knees were about to buckle, so she leaned against the wall and shook her head. Her father rushed over to her.

'Avery, I want you safe, and Adelaide offered to take you in. You were always happy to go to her, so we thought it best you stay at her home. Let's go and get the bag Granny packed for you. Bhaltair is taking you to Adelaide's home,' said William, putting his arm around Avery's shoulder and walking her to the kitchen. She did not know what to think. Her heart pounded like a drum in her chest, and she began to cry.

'Granny, I don't want to go. No one will see me if I stay in my room,' Avery pleaded. Granny held a heavy travelling bag near the back door and was visibly shaken.

'It is hard for all of us, Mo Leannan, but we have no choice. You are not safe here at the inn,' said Granny in a quivering voice. 'It is time to go. The carriage is behind the house. Adelaide and Bhaltair are waiting.'

Avery climbed onto the carriage and waved to her Grandmother just as Bhaltair cracked the whip. The two brown horses fell into a trot, pulling the carriage away from the small inn that was Avery's home.

2 Adelaide's Cottage

It was a cold starry night. Flurries of snow Danced in the moonlight, and the frozen ground cracked under the wheels as they passed. The wobbling of the carriage and the fresh night air had made Avery drowsy. She fought hard to stay awake by looking at Adelaide and Bhaltair, trying to read their expressions. That's when she noticed that Bhaltair's eyes were scanning the surrounding trees. 'What is it, Bhaltair? Do you see something?

'No, don't fret, I was just looking for Adelaide's house. We should be close by now.'

'Aye, it's just around the next bend, Bhaltair,' Adelaide answered. 'Soon, we'll all sit by the fire enjoying mulled wine. It's not often that I have visitors, so I am glad of the chance to sit and chat with you for a while.'

'I can hardly wait,' he said with a smile.

'I think we all could do with a hot drink by now. I just hope I will be able to let go of the reins! My fingers are so cold I can barely move them.'

'Goodness, why don't you wear your mittens!'

'I forgot them at your house when I dropped the lads. But never mind, it's not so bad, and in any case, we've almost arrived. Giddy up, fellas!' shouted Bhaltair to the horses. Adelaide's cottage stood peacefully in the distance, its thatched roof and stained-glass windows drawing them in from the cold. Avery pushed back her hood and grabbed her bag as the carriage rattled over the small bridge leading to Adelaide's cottage. Just as the carriage stopped in front of the threshold, the door opened to Bhaltair's two sons, Hugh, and Glen, who ran out shouting to Avery.

'Hiya, lass, mighty fine to see ya again! It's been such a long time since you came to the woods!'

'That's not true. It has been only a month or two. I can't help it that you weren't around,' Avery teased.

'Never mind, let me give you a hand with that bag! Glen, you'd better pick her up so she doesn't have to walk through the snow and wet her boots.'

'Aye, right, Hugh, just as soon as you get out of my way,' his brother responded. 'Come on, Avery, jump on my back. I'll carry you.'

'Are you sure? I am pretty heavy, you know.'

'Oh, come on, you are light as a feather compared to the sacks of flour I lug around all day.'

'If you insist,' she replied with a grin as she jumped onto Glen's back. He indeed had no problem carrying her. The work at the mill made him very strong. He brought her to the cottage, stooped through the doorway and safely sat her down near the fireplace.

'Thank you, Glen, though I'll admit the comparison with the sack of flour was not all that flattering,' she laughed as she kissed him on the forehead.

'Aye, my dear brother is a real charmer, and he even gets a kiss. What about me! I carried your heavy bag all the way to your bedroom!'

'Oh, come here, Hugh,' said Avery with a big smile, hugging and kissing him just the same.

'Goodness, lads, that's enough hugging and kissing for one night! Let's sit by the fire and enjoy Adelaide's famous mulled wine before we have to go,' said Bhaltair as he ushered the three of them to the fireplace. The wine was delicious, and Adelaide had even found some gingerbread, nuts, and dried fruits to go with it. The group enjoyed each other's company very much, sharing the food and many great stories till late into the night. As the fire began to die down, many hours later, Bhaltair spoke up. 'Oh, goodness me, lads, it's very late. Your mother must be worried stiff. Let's get on, shall we? Hurry, along now.' with that, he bid goodbye to Adelaide and Avery and pushed his sons through the door, just leaving them enough time to pick up their cloaks and give a quick wave. After the men had left, Adelaide turned to Avery.

'That was a long day, my dear. I am tired, and I am sure so are you. Leave everything as it is, and let's go to bed.'

'Aye, Adelaide, you go ahead. I'll check the fire and close the shutters. Guid nuit!'

'Guid nuit, Avery and sweet dreams,' Adelaide said as she made her way to her bedchamber. Avery stepped outside to close the storm shutters. She was captivated by the bright night sky. The moon looked like a silver disk on black velvet, surrounded by a sea of diamonds. She was so mesmerised that she didn't notice the wind blowing snow from the treetops towards her. Just before the whirl of snow reached her, she felt a shiver. She looked around, barely avoiding getting engulfed in a shroud of icy crystals. Goodness, that was close, she thought, pulled her shawl up over her head, and closed the last shutter. On her way back to the door, she turned around one more time to take a last look. At that moment, she noticed the shadow of a man in a whirling snow cloud. After a moment of hesitation, she spoke up, taking a deep breath to steady herself for what might come.

'Who are you? What do you want?' she called over to the edge of the forest. She stood perfectly still as if she was frozen to the ground and listened intently for a reply. But the snow cloud and the shadow had disappeared. I must have been dreaming. She concluded—no wonder after all the excitement of today. Adelaide can give me some answers tomorrow. She is always well informed and wise. She is not blinded by fear or rumours, she thought, as she locked the door and made her way to her bedroom.

3 The Truth

The sun stood high in the sky when Avery was awoken the next Day by the busy click-clack of Adelaide's loom. Adelaide had covered her straw mattress with soft sheepskins, and she felt so comfortable she could have stayed in her bed all day. It is so nice not to have to rush out of bed. Avery thought, stretching her arms over her head as she let her eyes wander through the sunlit room. The reflection of the stained-glass windows looked like-coloured lights floating in the air. Avery would have loved to look at it all day. But she wanted answers to her many questions, so she got up, readied herself and went straight to Adelaide's workroom.

'Guid mornin Adelaide, hou are ye?' 'I'm fine. I hope I did not wake you, but I have to finish this plaid today. I trust you had a guid nicht,' said Adelaide.

'Aye, I always do when I am here. The sheepskins are so soft. It feels like sleeping on a cloud,' Avery replied with a smile. 'But tell me, who is this plaid for? It must be a big woman judging by its size.'

'Well, she is not that big, she just wants it to wrap around comfortably, but enough of that, it is high time to get food in you. I baked some scones and laid the table in front of the fire in the sitting room. We can talk there. I am sure that you have many questions.'

'Aye, I do, and I hope you will tell me the truth. Please don't keep anything from me. I want to know if I might be in Danger.'

'Of course, Avery, I promise. But let's have some breakfast first. I am starving.'

They went into the sitting room, sat down in front of the fireplace, and enjoyed their scones with honey and a cup of tea. Avery had always loved the relaxed and peaceful atmosphere at Adelaide's cottage. It was so much calmer than the inn. No noise from rowdy guests. No rushing around preparing the meals and making beds. But it was time to find out what was going on, so she broke the morning silence.

'Adelaide, tell me. Who is this stranger everyone is talking about? Where is he from? And why do the people from Dallmally and Ardteale believe he is responsible for the disappearance of the lassies?'

'Oh, dear, one question at the time,' said Adelaide. I have to tell you so much that it might disturb and even frighten you. But I promise it is the truth,' she looked at Avery before continuing.

'Almost seventeen years ago, your mother came to me to order a baby blanket. She brought her own wool, which was so soft and fine, unlike anything I had ever seen.'

'You knew my mother? Avery asked in disbelieve. What was she like? Da never told me anything about her, and Granny only cries when I ask.'

'Aye, Avery, I know her.'

'What do you mean, you know her? She is dead. She died the day I was born,' Avery protested.

Adelaide took a deep breath before replying.

'That's what you were told. But it is not so.'

Avery stopped chewing the scone that was in her cheeks.

'No, no, that can't be true, Da would have told me. Why should he lie about something like that?'

'Avery, William is not your Da. He swore an oath to look after you, to keep you safe and to never tell anyone,' whispered Adelaide. She rested her hand on Avery's knee and continued.

'My dear, your real Da is Gregor, the son of Jonathan, the fisherman. The villagers believe that he drowned in a storm almost twenty years ago.'

Avery's head started to spin as she tried to take in everything she was hearing.

'So, are you saying that Jonathan is my Grand Da?' Avery urged.

'Aye, Avery, but he doesn't know that. No one knows. They all believe William had gotten married while studying law in Edinburgh and that his wife had died in childbirth.' Adelaide got up and went to her bedroom, leaving Avery by the fire. Moments later, she returned, carrying a small basket.

'This is the basket William found you in, under the old oak tree, near the lake.'

'What do you mean he found me?' Are you saying that my real parents just left me in the woods?' whispered Avery. She got up and began to pace as if she was about to run out any second.

'Avery, please, Mo Leannan, calm down. It's not like that. You will understand when I tell you what happened.' Adelaide urged, getting up to put her arm around Avery's shoulders and leading her back to the fireplace.

'Sit down. I'll make us a cup of tea before I continue. Some lavender with honey will help you calm down,' Adelaide said softly, kissing Avery on the cheek before she walked out. Avery found herself sitting alone, staring at the flames as they Danced in the fireplace. She felt more confused than she had in her entire life as her whole world had just crumbled in ten minutes. The man she loved and believed to be her Da was, in fact, a stranger who found her in the woods. Her own parents had abandoned her. Has there ever been any truth in my life? Whom can I trust? Is Adelaide telling me the truth, or is this just another deception? The thoughts raced through her mind, each one faster than the last. She took a deep breath to steady herself for what might be revealed today. Moments later, Adelaide came back into the room, carrying a tray of tea and cake.

'Be careful, my dear. It is boiling,' Adelaide said, handing Avery a cup. 'I also brought you a few slices of Maighread's cake to calm your mind. Are you sure you want me to tell the rest? Or do you want us to take a break before we continue?'

'I am fine, please don't stop! I need to know everything about my parents,'

Avery urged, moving her chair closer. Adelaide looked at her with a look Avery couldn't quite place and continued.

'Very well. It all began twenty years ago. The fishermen kept returning with empty nets. Many lives were threatened. That's when Gregor decided to row out every morning, long before the sun was up, trying to catch anything he could, returning late at night.

One Day the weather was so bad that none of the fishermen Dared to go out in fear of a storm. So, they pulled their boats out of the water and secured their nets. Only Gregor braved the weather. But he never made it back. Two days later, his boat washed up on the shore, laden with fish. And ever since that day, the boat has been filled with fish every morning. Jonathan blames the Seelie Fae for Gregor's disappearance. He is convinced that the fish is restitution for the loss of his son.'

'Seelie Fae, Adelaide, this makes no sense. These are old wives' tales,' Avery replied in disbelief when she finished.

'Avery, he is right. Even if you have never seen any, elves exist and so do many other magical beings. Do you want to hear the truth, or do you want to continue to live in ignorance? Adelaide asked, running her hand through her long white hair.

'Of course. I want the truth, Adelaide. But what you are telling me is so hard to believe.'

'It may be hard for you to believe, Avery, but every word is true. So, let me continue and please open your mind. There is so much in our world that you don't know,' she said, looking at Avery solemnly.

'Remember how I told you that your mother came to me to order a baby blanket?'

'Aye, Adelaide, I do. Please forgive me for doubting you, you never lied to me, and I know that. But it's all just so confusing,' Avery replied and hid her face in her hands.

'I understand, Avery, and I know that it must feel as if the world has turned upside down, but the time for the truth has come. Your mother expected you to be born around the summer solstice. She came to me asking me to spin the wool, weave the blanket for you and dye it with rose hips and Elderberries. She then handed me a feather from her golden eagle and told me that she would receive any message I write using this feather the moment I write it. So naturally, I wrote a note as soon as I had finished your blanket, and to my amazement, she arrived the same day to pick it up. She offered to pay me with a beautiful jewel, but I told her no and that I felt honoured by her trust. She smiled, telling me that any cloth woven on my loom will be protected, from now on, against Dark magic and evil spirits, because of the magic left by the wool I used to make your blanket. Before she left, she revealed to me how she met your Da and how much they look forward to the birth of their daughter. They will name Avery.

'So how did she meet my Da?' 'Gregor's boat had capsized in the storm, and he was drowning. When he had no more strength to fight the waves, he sunk to the bottom of the loch. At that moment, your mother came, pulled him to safety and brought him to her Island. She healed all his injuries and nursed him until he had regained his strength. When the time came for Gregor to return to his father, she told him that she had watched over him for many years and wished he would stay. He, too, had strong feelings for her and didn't want to leave, but he could not stay because of his elderly father, who could no longer fish and would surely starve without him. So, with a heavy heart, Gregor said goodbye and held her one last time before pushing his boat away from the shore and starting to row. He didn't turn around because it was too painful, so he stared at the floating islands of bonnets and water lilies, and that's when he saw her, gliding effortlessly through the crystal-clear water next to his boat. Before Jonathan could make sense of it, she surfaced right next to him and told him she was Murigen, the Goddess of the loch. She promised him his father would be cared for if he married her and lived with her in her kingdom. He accepted at once, and they got married on the night of Beltane. Since then, your father has gone out fishing every morning, and the Ashrays pushed the boat filled with the most excellent fish up to our beach before sunrise,' Adelaide continued.

'If they wanted me so much and if they loved each other so strongly, why did they leave me all alone in the forest?' Avery urged, grabbing Adelaide's shoulders.
'That I don't know, mo ghràdh. All I know is that something terrible must have happened on the Island so that the golden eagle had to bring you to safety under the old oak tree. You were wrapped in the plaid with another eagle feather and a message to the one who would find you, asking to keep you safe, raise you as their own, and never to tell anyone how they found you. Thank heavens that William saw the eagle and followed him to the oak tree. He took you home and told everyone that he had gotten married in Edinburgh and that his wife died giving birth to their Daughter. The moment I heard about it, I went to offer them my help, but when William showed me the basket with the blanket and the feather, I knew who you truly were. Since that day, I have kept this secret and made sure that you have been safe. I decided to keep the basket with the blanket and the feather here at my home until you were old enough to know the truth or in case you needed its protection. I am afraid the time has come,' said Adelaide handing Avery the ruby red blanket and the eagle feather.

Imbolc

Two days had passed since Avery learned the truth about her parents and that magic was not only all around but a part of her. The thought that her parents might be in Danger kept her up all night and even erased her fear of the stranger. She was the first to wake up that morning. Adelaide had worked on the loom till late and was still sleeping soundly. Adelaide will be surprised when she gets up. I just hope she likes my baking. Avery thought as she took the shortbread and bannocks out of the oven, placing them in a large basket covered with a cloth. Okay then, that's done. I better go and check the fire in the sitting room again and fix our breakfast. It will not be long until Adelaide gets up, and then we will be busy as bees. There is still so much to do for tomorrow's celebration, she thought as she began to set the table in front of the hearth.

'Madainn mhath Avery. When did you get up,' Adelaide called out, entering the kitchen? Her greeting gave Avery such a fright that she almost dropped the milk jug she was carrying.

'Goodness, you startled me, Adelaide. I just thought about what else I could do before you get up.

'Well, lass, I am up and ready to go on with the preparations. Sorry to have startled you.' Adelaide said and broke out laughing.

'Aye right, you go ahead keep on laughing. I'll just wait till the next mouse runs through the kitchen. Let's see who will be laughing then,' Avery teased and gave Adelaide a wink.

'Fair enough, but let's have a quick bite before we start. We should finish the cleaning and start with the decorations later today.'

'Aye, Adelaide, we will. I removed my sheets and put them to soak early this morning. I'll go and get yours now while you fix breakfast,' Avery announced and was gone in a flash.

'Alright, but don't linger,' Adelaide shouted behind her and started to prepare breakfast.

Avery and Adelaide went straight back to work after breakfast, but when cleaning the windows, Avery pondered what to use.

'Adelaide, what do I use to wash the windows?'

'Well, water Mo Leannan, add a wee bit of vinegar and use a soft cloth,' Adelaide explained, reaching Avery a small bottle of vinegar.

'Are you sure? Wouldn't the vinegar remove the colours,' Avery wondered?'

'Nay, silly lass. The panes are made from finely sliced stones like Quartz, Amethyst, Amber, Beryl, and Aquamarine. They were a gift from the Drows. It is said that they dispel black magic and protect the people within from any kind of negative attack on body, heart, mind, and spirit.'

'Who are the Drows? And where do they live?'

'They are mountain elves and live in caves in the highlands. Drows are gifted crafters and blacksmiths. Their metalwork is said to have magical powers.'

'Really,' Avery under her breath, intrigued by the workmanship. 'How did you meet them, and why have they given you such a precious gift?'

'Well, I met them many years ago when I moved into this house. Three of them were chained to a blacksmith forge down by the brook and forced to work for the laird who used to own this land. I freed them, destroyed the forge, and thereby broke the spell binding them to this land,' Adelaide explained. 'They were so grateful that they returned a month later with their brothers, built my windows and exchanged all of the hinges and locks on this cottage. Thanks to them, no one with ill intent can open or break the windows and doors, nor can they enter the cottage.'

'What a fantastic gift, no wonder that I feel so at ease when I am in your home. Have you ever seen them again,' Avery inquired, hungry for every scrap of information about this newfound magical world?

'No, Avery, but I know they come around now and then,' Adelaide responded with a smile and added. 'Talking about coming around, let's make sure we have enough food for tomorrow. We will have at least seven guests!'

'Well, I baked a basket each of scones, shortbread, and bannocks this morning. The Bonnach bride and the apple fruschie should be about ready now,' Avery responded and left the pantry. Adelaide remained in the pantry to look through the shelves for blackberry jam, dried fruits, and nuts. *It's time for winter to end. Our stocks are getting low. We could do with some neeps and carrots*, Adelaide thought, putting the third jar of blackberry jam in her basket.

'Adelaide, I hear a carriage! Are you expecting anyone,' Avery inquired and hurried to the door to look at the approaching guests? And was surprised to see farmer John and Ursula. Thrilled about their visit, she picked up her skirt and ran as fast as she could to the bridge to meet them.

'I am so happy to see you, Ursula. I have so much to tell you.'

'That's nice, but what about me, lass? Am I invisible,' John asked, stopping the carriage for Ursula to get off? The two girls hugged and ran into the cottage.

'It is farmer John, and he brought Ursula! I am so happy, Adelaide! We are going up to my bedroom. We'll not stay long, I promise,' Avery called out, pulling Ursula up the stairs and into her bedroom. Just as they were about to make themselves comfortable on Avery's bed, the door opened, and Adelaide stepped in.

'I am very sorry to disturb you, my sweets. I need your help, but don't fret. You can talk all night. Ursula is staying with us for a while.'

'That's brilliant news. Go ahead, Adelaide. We will be right down. Ursula just needs to change.'

'Alright, but don't linger! I'll go and help John unload the carriage in the meantime. See you in the kitchen,' Adelaide responded and went back downstairs and nearly ran into John as he walked through the door holding a basket filled to the brim with eggs.

'Crivens Adelaide, we almost had a calamity here!'

'Aye, you are right, John. That would have been a lot of scrambled eggs,' Adelaide responded, bending over laughing. Hearing the commotion, the girls poked their heads out of their room.

'What's so funny? Did we miss something,' Avery shouted, leaning over the bannister?

'Well, we almost made scrambled eggs right here on the threshold,' John replied with a guffaw.

'Ursula. Come help me with the milk, and Avery, you can get the cheese. I'll carry the butter and the vegetables,' John exclaimed, picked up a large basket and returned to the pantry.

'Oh dear, John, I don't know how to thank you,' Adelaide sighed, looking at the basket in his arms.

'We were almost out of neeps, carrots and onions, but now, thanks to you, I can prepare a nice stew for tomorrow.'

'Aye, you most certainly can. Look what I got,' John replied, lifting up the back leg from a wild boar.

'This fellow made a mistake to come into my barn trying to steal the food from my hogs. Well, now he is a roast. I can't wait to taste your stew tomorrow, but I must hurry back home before my wife puts me out. See you tomorrow morning Adelaide!'

'Goodbye, John. Give my love to Anette!'

After securely storing the food in the pantry, the three women tightened their aprons and returned to work. It was already afternoon when they decided to take a break and sit down in front of the fire, enjoying a cup of tea and some shortbread.

'I think we are just about done,' Adelaide said with a satisfied sigh. 'The stew is cooking, and all the linens are washed. The only thing left to do is to decorate the cottage. Talking about decorating, did you bring the straw, Ursula?'

'Aye, Adelaide, I put it to soak in the barrel outside. It should be nice and soft by now.'

'Fine, then you two can weave Brigid's cross and pick some heather when you are done. I will keep an eye on the stew and finish up the kitchen,' Adelaide suggested.

'Alright, but wouldn't it better if we got the heather now? We'll make sure to be back by nightfall,' Avery and Ursula said in one voice, picked up their shawls and baskets and ran out of the house.

Avery and Ursula were happy to be alone and finally have the chance to talk about everything that happened since last they saw about a month ago. They discussed Grace and Dallas's disappearance and Avery's rushed departure from the inn until the light faded.

'We will talk tonight,' Avery shouted out of breath, trying to catch up with Ursula.

'My goodness, Avery, look, isn't this magical,' Ursula exclaimed, grabbing Avery's hand and pulling her up. The glen with its heather covered banks glowed like a purple sea in the light of the setting sun.

'Aye, it is magnificent, Ursula, but let's get the heather now. We must make it back before Dark.'

Avery and Ursula hurried back as soon as their baskets were filled. By then, the sky had darkened, and the moon began to spread his silver light across fields and forest when the cottage finally came into sight.

'Oh, thank the Goddess, we are almost there. I am so hungry. My tummy is growling like an angry bear,' Ursula giggled as they rounded the corner and were about to step onto the small bridge across the brook in front of Adelaide's cottage.

'Stop and be still!' Avery whispered, grabbing Ursula's hand and pulling her down.

'What is it? What did you see?'

'Don't you see the shadow near the barn? I swear it's the same one I saw the night I arrived at Adelaide's cottage.'

Avery and Ursula crouched low and walked cautiously across the bridge and up to the barn.

'Do you think it is a good idea to look for him? Shouldn't go and tell Adelaide about it?' She will know what to do!'

'Oh, don't be such a coward, Ursula.'

'I am not a coward,' Ursula protested! 'But what do we do if he attacks? Hit him with the heather,' she chuckled, lifting the basket, and spinning it around as if she was going to knock out an invisible assailant. Ursula and Avery bent over laughing when suddenly a hooded man appeared from the dark and addressed them

'Guid evenin, lassies. You should not be out so late. It is not safe for you to roam the woods at this hour.'

Ursula and Avery felt as if their limbs had turned to stone. Their hearts and minds screamed for flight, but they could not move or even breathe until Avery finally gathered some strength and spoke.

'Who are you? Why are you following us? And why do you sneak around the cottage at night?'

'My name is Darion. You do not have to fear me, Avery,' he answered in a voice as soft as velvet. 'Lady Murigen asked me to guard you and keep you safe. I am sorry if I startled you and your friend, but I think it is best if you return to the cottage now. We can talk tomorrow at sunrise. I will be waiting for you in the barn,' he whispered and disappeared in the darkness of the night.

'Goodness, where is he gone? I didn't see him move. He just vanished.' Ursula shouted, spinning around scanning the surroundings.

'Well then, let's not wait for him to reappear,' Avery replied, picking up her skirt. Grabbed Ursula's hand and began to run.

'Ursula, you must promise that you are not going to say a word to Adelaide about this,' Avery insisted before opening the door.

Ursula looked at her friend in hesitation but then agreed. 'Aye, I promise.'

'Adelaide, we are back and hungry as a pack of wolves. What's for supper' Avery called out as they entered the cottage?

'My goodness, I am so glad that you are home. You had me worried,' Adelaide sighed, drying her hands on her apron.

'The heather is gorgeous. Thank you. We will put it up with Brigid's cross tomorrow, right after breakfast. But it's time for some food now. Come on, you two, the pottage is ready, and I even have some stewed blackberries for you.'

'That sounds yummy! We just go to freshen up a bit,' Avery called out as she and Ursula ran up the stairs. 'We will be back in a flash!'

Avery and Ursula enjoyed the sumptuous supper and felt quite tired after finishing their bowl of blackberries.

'Adelaide, the supper was great. Thank you so much,' sighed Ursula rubbing her tummy.

'Aye, I am stuffed as well and could fall asleep, right here and now,' Avery added, stretched, and got up. 'Would you like us to do anything else, or can we go up now?'

'Of course not, You can go to your bedroom, my dears. You worked so hard all day. I'll take care of the kitchen. See you tomorrow, have a guid nuit.'

Avery and Ursula ran up the stairs as fast as they could. It was finally time to talk things over and share the latest news.

5 Darion

Avery and Ursula didn't sleep a wink that night. All the exciting news and the prospect of finally getting some answers had made them restless.

'In the name of the wee man Avery, come back to bed. You could see the rising sun from right here. The window is facing directly to the east,' Ursula protested as Avery got out of bed for the fifth time.

'I think he is already in the barn. We should get down there now. Come, get out of bed and dress,' Avery urged, pulling back Ursula's duvet.

'What gives you that idea? You can't even see the barn from here.'

'I don't have to see the barn to know it. I have a strong feeling Darion is there.'

'Yeah, right,' Ursula growled, rolling her eyes, getting out of bed, and dressing quickly.

'Oh, come on, Ursula, a snail, moves faster than you.'

'Blimey Avery, can I at least wash my face and run the brush through my hair?'

'Aye, do that if you must, but then let's go. and watch your step. We don't want to wake Adelaide,' Avery demanded. She opened the door slowly to stop it from creaking, just as she had done countless times before. They squeezed through the narrow opening, tip-toed downstairs, and stepped out.

'Crivens, it's Baltic. Why did you agree to meet this early? I bet not even the chickens are up at this hour,' Ursula complained as they stepped out into the cold?

'Och, stop fussing, Ursula. The barn is just there. Walk faster if you feel cold.'

After a few steps through the freshly fallen snow, they had reached the barn, and Avery tried to open the large door.

'Ursula, can you give me a hand to open the door. The snow is blocking it.'

'Sure, just step aside and let me handle this, sweetie,' Ursula replied as she leaned against the barn door and gave a strong push.

'There you go. Let's get in there to meet your protector, shall we? I bet he is not even here.'

'Are you talking about me, lass? I am right here.'

'Och, must you always do that? Why can't you just walk up to people like a normal man,' Ursula snapped.

'Sorry lass, that I can't do. I am not what you call a normal man.'

'Aye right, so then what are you?'

'I am a Pict,' replied Darion with a big smile and bowing to Ursula.

Choosing her words very carefully not to offend him, Avery asked.

'You are a Pict? I have never heard of a Pict before. Are you an elf?'

'Sort of. My father is an Elf, my mother a mortal, which makes me part mortal. But let's not waste time talking about me,' Darion insisted, taking off his cloak and giving Avery a smile that would melt a glacier.

Avery and Ursula were startled by his looks. He was very handsome with long hair as black as a raven's feather and mystifying dark brown eyes. Avery was spellbound and unable to move or take her eyes off him, which reminded her of the night when she saw him in a whirl of snow for the first time. Just as she would ask if she was in Danger, Darion spun around and disappeared like a flash of lightning.

'Wow, did you see that? He is as fast as a shooting star,' Avery exclaimed in wonder!

' Well, that might be so, but I was more impressed by his armour and his weapons.'

'Don't be silly, Ursula.'

'I am not silly. I am dead serious, Avery. The Elf looks as if he has emptied the Laird's armoury. But I bet the only thing you saw was his eyes,' Ursula said with a frown.' He carries a dirk in each boot, a sword, a bow, and enough arrows to wipe out our entire village.'

Avery blushed and nodded. 'You are right, but you must agree that he is truly fascinating. And yes, the only thing I saw were his eyes,' she added with a grin.

'Who is fascinating,' Darion inquired as he returned?

'Goodness, you nearly made me faint! I wished you could stop doing that,' Avery letting herself drop onto a heap of straw.

'What is the matter? What did you see' Ursula urged, looking around nervously?

'No need to fret. it was Adelaide who had gone to the well to fetch some water.'

'Oh dear, she is up. Let's hope she thinks we are still in our beds. Darion, let's not waste time.

Tell me if I am in Danger. Where you met my mother, and why she did not come with you?' Darion nodded and leaned against the barn wall as he began his story.

'Two years ago, the golden eagle Ioroth brought me a message from your mother, Lady Murigen, asking me to watch over you and keep you safe. She wrote that a man who calls himself Lord MacNab is looking for you. So yes, Avery, you are in Danger. He has taken your friends and is holding them captive in his caves. Lady Murigen is bound to her Island kingdom by a curse, so we can only communicate through Ioroth or her Ashray warriors,' Darion explained. 'I'll tell you more tonight. Still, for now, you better return to the cottage before Adelaide notices you left. Meet me in her workshop around midnight,' he concluded, pulling the hood deep into his face and disappearing.

Avery and Ursula were relieved that they had made it back into the cottage and their bedroom unnoticed.

'Well, this was interesting,' Ursula said, kicking off her boots and laying down on her bed.

'We still don't know much. I hope Darion will clear it all up tonight. I am not going to let him get away this time before he has answered all of my questions.'

'Aye, right. But you better count me out this time, Avery. I can't make it one more night without sleep. I am truly sorry.'

'No problem, Ursula, you can stay and sleep. I will not leave the cottage, but now is not the time to get comfortable. We have to go down before Adelaide starts to get worried.' Avery urged, pulling Ursula back up.

'Right, but first, you have to brush the straw off your skirt, or Adelaide may think you busted the mattress,' Ursula giggled, pulling bits of straw out of Avery's auburn hair.

'Maidin math' you two! I thought you would stay in bed all day. Come on and grab a scone. There is no time to sit. You can eat while you are setting the table. I'll set up the kitchen, Harris should be here soon, and I am sure the others will not be far behind,' Adelaide declared, rushing to the kitchen

Avery and Ursula picked up the scones Adelaide laid out for them and began setting the table, taking a bite now and then. In no time, the table was beautifully decorated with heather and well stacked with baskets of all sorts of cakes, pies, scones, loaves of bread, and even a giant wheel of cheese.

'Well done, you two, we are almost set. All that's missing are bowls, and tankards get them quick. I think I hear Harris's drum!' Adelaide laughed and rushed out.

' I think Adelaide is right. Can you hear it too, Ursula?'

'Aye, now, I do! Come on, we get the tankards later!' Avery called, took Ursula's hands, and pulled her out of the cottage. The sound grew louder, and moments later, three beautifully decorated carriages came around the bend and over the small bridge. Bhaltair, Hugh, and Glen played the pipes, and Harris accompanied them on his drum.

'I wish you all a blessed Imbolc! Welcome to my humble home. 'I am so happy you are here so early,' Adelaide greeted the guests warmly.

'Blessed Imbolc Adelaide! We had to come early. John couldn't wait any longer to try your stew. He has been talking of nothing else since last night,' Annett said, laughing ruffling John's hair.

Avery and Ursula stood in the doorway, holding hands and listening to the music.

'Oie lassies, stop holding hands and get over here. Help us unload,' Bhaltair called out. 'And you lads, stop the racket and get the ale in the kitchen. I am thirsty!'

'Aye, Da, that is a bloody brilliant idea. Let's get to it, Glen!'

'Sure thing, Hugh. Lassies step away from the door. The ale is about to roll in!'

' Oh, and when you are done, come for the wine, lads!'

'Don't fret, Harris. We will get to it right away.'

Suddenly, the serenity in the cottage was replaced by excitement and a happy bustle. Everybody was rushing back and forth to get things in place for the celebration, which was about to start. Hugh and Glen rolled the heavy casks of ale and wine into the pantry, where Harris and Bhaltair propped them on short stools and knocked in the tabs. Adelaide and Annett carried the cauldron with the stew to the heart and placed it on the cast iron hook over the fire while Ursula added more wood.

I wonder how Da and Granny are coping. The inn will be packed with people from the villages by now. How will they handle all the work without me, Avery thought? She felt sad and had to get away from the excitement to make sense of what had happened. She pulled her shawl tied around and sat down on a rock under an old Rowan tree.

'Why are you so sad, Avery? You are surrounded by people who truly love you and care for you.'

Avery turned around to see who had spoken, though she was pretty sure it was Darion. And there he was, right behind her, reaching out his hands to pull her up.

'Everything is going to be alright. We will find a way to lift the curse binding your mother and free your friends,' he said.

'I hope so, Darion. But what will happen to Granny and my Da? I mean, Maighread and William? They are all alone now. The work at the inn is too much for the two people.'

'Don't fret. They are not alone. I asked a group of Brownies to move in and stay as long as needed.'

'Thank you, Darion!' Avery exclaimed. You must forgive me. I am struggling to make sense of what happened. Not even a month ago, I thought Elves and Fairies only existed in tales, and now, here you are. You must tell me what you know about Lord MacNab. My parents, and why he is looking for me. But right now, I think it is best to return to the cottage before being missed. See you tonight,' Avery whispered and walked back to the cottage in the hope nobody had noticed her absence.

'Come have some stew, Avery. It's delicious,' Glen called when he saw her. 'Adelaide is a true master when it comes to seasoning. Do you think she would be willing to share her secret ingredients? By the way, where were you, Glen urged?'

'I just checked on the animals,' Avery lied. And yes, I would love some stew. I am starving. All I had so far was a dry scone for breakfast.'

'Well, that's no good. Let's go and have some ale and stew.' Glen giggled, placing his arm around Avery's shoulders, ushering her back to the cottage. The celebration was now in full swing. Bhaltair played the pipes, and Harris beat the drum as if there was no tomorrow. Everybody danced and sang praises for Brigid and the return of spring.

'Avery, Ursula, come along. We are about to light the bonfire!' Hugh and Glen called from the field behind the cottage.

'Aye, we will be right there! We'll just have to fetch some ale. Don't start without us, Avery and Ursula shouted back!'

'Right then, but don't take long. The sun is about to set,' Hugh called and added more logs to the already towering stack of wood. Avery and Ursula had reached the kitchen and pushed the door open, almost knocking over Annett.

'Blimey, watch it,' Annette cried out, struggling to regain her balance and keep the Bonnach bride from falling.

'Sorry, Annett. We were in such a hurry to get the ale and head back to the bonfire that we did not see you,'

'No harm was done. I am heading there myself. Everyone else is already there, so hurry.'

Avery and Ursula filled the jugs and rushed over to the bonfire.

'Put the jugs down and join the circle! Blessed, be everyone,' John announced as he lowered his torch and lit the fire.

The celebration lasted well into the night and ended with last year's Bridges cross burning. It was close to midnight when the house finally fell silent. Adelaide and Ursula had turned in and were fast asleep when Avery quietly walked down the steps to meet Darion in Adelaide's workshop. She cautiously placed her steps to avoid the creaking floorboard and any furniture. Knowing Adelaide was a light sleeper and would wake at the faintest sound. She was relieved when she finally made it to the workshop, took a deep breath and closed the door. Only now did she notice how cold it was. Her hands and feet felt like ice, so she hurried to the fireplace ran her hands over the mantle, searching for the flint, when she heard a rustling noise near the window behind her.

'Darion, is that you,' Avery whispered while trying to adjust her eyes to the darkness of the room? She held her breath, listening, but the only thing she could hear was the faint gurgling of *the brook.*

I am hearing ghosts now. This is getting ridiculous. I must hold it together, Avery thought and continued searching for the flint. She breathed a sigh of relief when she finally found it and tried to strike it, but her hands were so cold and numb that she dropped it twice. Avery began to rub her hands until the feeling in her fingers returned, and she was able to make the flint spark. It did not take long before the fire caught, and soon, its warmth and brightness helped her regain her courage and clear away her fear. But it did not stop her mind from racing.

I wonder what's keeping Darion. It has to be past midnight. I hope nothing happened to him. He is the only connection to my parents. What if the mysterious Lord MacNab has caught him too? I can't just sit here by the fire and do nothing. I have to go and look for him. What if he needs my help, Avery thought? She got up and walked to the door leading into the garden when she heard the rustling sound again and felt a cold breeze on the back of her neck.

'Where you think you're going,' Darion asked as he entered through the window.

'Well, as a matter of fact, looking for you! I thought something happened to you since it is long past midnight,' Avery said, placing her hands on her hips.

'Forgive me. I didn't mean to be late. But I had to make certain we were alone, and your presence remains unknown.'

'Very well, I forgive you. Just don't do it again!'

'Aye, I'll try my utmost best, Avery.'

'Oh, and one more thing,' she added. 'When you next approach me or enter a room, knock! My heart always skips a beat when you just suddenly appear out of thin air like that.'

'I promise,' he replied with a smile. 'But it might not always be possible.'

'Fair enough,' she consented. 'I am freezing. Let's sit by the fire while we talk.'

'I can see that. You are shivering, and your lips are blue. Why don't you use your plaid to keep warm?' Darion said, wondering, picking up the plaid and placing it around her shoulders.

'It is not mine. Adelaide made it for some noblewoman,' Avery responded. 'But wait, come to think of it, why hasn't she picked it up yet? Adelaide was in such a hurry to finish it. She worked on it throughout the night.'

'I am sure there will be no harm done if you wear it for one night. It will keep you warm and comfortable while we talk,' Darion suggested pulling Avery closer to the fire. Both of them sat in silence, staring into the fire before Avery turned to Darion.

'Darion, tell me about my parents, Lord MacNab', and what you are planning to do to lift the curse.'

Darion turned to face her, his eyes filled with warmth and mystery.

'Your mother, Lady Murigen, is the Lady of Loch Awe and the Island Kingdom. She is very loving, beautiful, and just,' he explained, taking Avery's hands

'What about my father? Do you know anything about him?'

'I never met him, but your mother told me he is very courageous. It seems to me you have inherited this trait from him along with your beautiful auburn hair and your gentle hazel eyes.'

'Now I understand. I always wondered why my hair was not blond like William's. But let's not talk about looks,' she pushed on, not wanting to get side-tracked. 'It is far more important to talk about what has happened and what we can do to lift the curse.'

'I am afraid I can't tell you that. I don't know what happened on the island. We must try to find out from your mother.'

'How can we do that? You told me she is bound to the island and that there is no way to communicate with her directly.'

'There is one way. We should try to talk to her during the night of the next full moon. We'll walk to the middle of the lake and call her name. She might be able to talk to us if we get close enough to the island kingdom.'

'Why not tomorrow night! Why wait so long,' Avery urged?

'We need the protection of Lady Arianrhod, the Goddess of the Moon. Her silver light will guide us and make us invisible to all malevolent entities. For now, let's plan how we get you out of the cottage unnoticed.'

'Now, that is no problem at all,' Avery chuckled.

'Ursula sleeps like a stone, and I know my way around the cottage in the dark. No one is going to know I am gone as long as I return before sunrise.'

'You will be back long before then, trust me,' Darion said with confidence. 'But there is one more thing. You must tell no one about our plan. Not even your best friends or Adelaide. Do you promise?'

'I don't understand why not,' she protested. But the look of seriousness in Darion's eyes made her stop. 'Aye, alright, I promise.'

'Very well, Avery, I hold you to your promise. But I think it is high time for you to get some sleep. I will be around if you need me, even if you don't see me. Guid nuit Avery,' he whispered, squeezing her hand, and disappearing into the night. *The room suddenly feels so much colder*, Avery thought, pulling the plaid tighter around her shoulder scanning the room. *Well, no wonder the window is wide open. Why can't he use the door like any normal human being? Oh right, he is not a normal human being. He is half-Elf,* Avery thought, smiling silently, closing the window, and returning to the fire, where she remained for many more hours to think about her conversation with Darion and the upcoming journey.

Why am I not allowed to share this information with my friends? I would feel much safer if they came along. After all, they say there is safety in number, not that I don't feel safe when I am with Darion. I most certainly do. It actually feels as if I have known him all my life and that we belong together. I miss him and long for his return when he leaves, which is truly strange, keeping in mind we only met yesterday. she thought, smiling inwardly, glancing at the window. *Crivens, it is time to go to bed. The sun will be up soon, and so will Adelaide. How would I explain being in her workshop at this early hour?* With this thought, Avery got up and rushed back to her bedroom.

6 The Plan

Ursula was still fast asleep and snoring loudly as Avery climbed into her bed. *I desperately need a few hours' sleep* to slow my mind, she thought as countless thoughts buzzed through her head. And then, just before she dropped off, she felt a strange sensation opened her eyes, sat up and saw that the new morning was already downing. Its bright light shone through the window and painted a rainbow on the floor, which grew steadily and moved closer with the sun's rising. Avery was mesmerised and soon found herself in a cocoon of brilliant light. She felt as if she was floating in a sea of warmth and serenity. All her anxiety and questions gave way to tranquillity. She closed her eyes and fell into a deep, dreamless sleep.

When she woke, the sun stood high in the sky, and she felt refreshed and full of energy as if she had slept for days. She stretched like a cat in the sun, jumped out of bed, and walked to the window to pour water into the small basin and wash her face. The cold water felt wonderfully refreshing and soothing on her burning eyes. These long nights and all the secrets have to stop, she decided. There is no reason to continue whispering like this and hiding the truth. It is time to share what I have learned with Ursula, Glen, Hugh, and Adelaide. She dressed and headed to the kitchen, determined to tell Adelaide and Ursula all about last night's talk with Darion. She was amazed and a bit worried when she found the kitchen empty and silent.

'Adelaide, Ursula, where are you?' she called, walking out into the garden.

'Oh, good afternoon, Avery. We thought you might sleep through the rest of winter like your little friends, the squirrels. Come on over,' called Adelaide from the workshop window.

'Will do. Just let me have some breakfast. I am starving.'

'Well, better make it lunch,' giggled Adelaide.

'There is a bit of stew left from yesterday, and fresh bread is in the oven.'

'Thanks, Adelaide,' Avery replied, helping herself to a bowl of stew and a large chunk of the freshly baked bread before she sat down on the bench near the hearth. Hugh is right. Adelaide is a master when it comes to seasoning. I wonder where she finds all these spices, Avery thought while enjoying the savoury taste of the stew.

'Are you done yet, Avery? Hurry up. We could do with your help!'

'I will be right there, Adelaide, just fetching some water,' she replied, trying to buy some time as she walked up to the well, looking for Darion. He has to be here somewhere. He said that he would always stay close. But where is he? She thought, scanning the surroundings intensely. Seeing nothing, she went back inside.

'What would you like me to do, Adelaide?' Avery asked as she entered the workshop.

'Add some logs to the fire. It is getting kind of nippy in here, which is strange, considering that the fire burned all through the night, don't you think?'

'I supposed so,' Avery replied. 'But what makes you think that the fire burned throughout the night?'

'Well, there were some embers left this morning,' Adelaide replied. 'Though none of us remembers lighting it yesterday, isn't that strange? 'Avery nervously cleared her throat.

'Aye, very strange indeed,' she looked away, trying to change the subject. 'What else can I do to help?'

'Get me some spools of the brown and green yarn so that I can finish before the light goes. They are on the shelf next to Ursula.'

Avery placed another log into the fire before she went to the shelves near the window where Ursula sat at the spinning wheel.

'I need to talk to you,' mouthed Avery as she picked up a basket full of spools. Ursula looked up and nodded with a broad smile on her face.

'What's funny?' Avery inquired, narrowing her eyes.

'I'll tell you later when we are alone.' 'What are you weaving, Adelaide? Is it another plaid?' Avery inquired as she

placed the basket near the loom.

'Aye, Mo Lennan, it is. I have two more to do when I am done with this one.'

'Goodness, this is a big order! Who are they for?' Avery exclaimed as she admired the cloth.

'Why did they choose such Dark colours? They look almost like the forest floor.'

'Well, that's the whole idea! They are meant to blend in with the colours of the forest.'

'So, they are for a group of hunters!' Avery exclaimed.

'Precisely,' she responded with a smile.

The women worked the whole afternoon, stopping only as the sun began to set and the light in the workshop was fading.

'Come on, lassies. It's time for a cupa. We got a good bit done today,' Adelaide said.

'If we keep on working like this, we should be finished by Sunday.'

'I'll say! My back is killing me!' Ursula complained. 'How do you manage to do this every day?'

'Well, I don't weave every Day. I spend a lot of time in my garden and collecting roots, plants, and berries in the forest,' Adelaide replied. 'You'll see when you come along. We'll take a walk as soon as the snow has melted.'

'But I will be home helping Ma and Da in the field,' Ursula affirmed.

'Hmm, actually, you will not be able to do that, at least not this year.'

'I'm afraid you wouldn't be able to,' Adelaide said softly. 'At least not this year.'

'What do you mean, I wouldn't be able to? Da is picking me up in three Days,' she said louder this time.

'I am sorry, lass, but he wouldn't be. He asked me to keep you here together with Avery until it is safe for the two of you to return,' Adelaide said, looking at the girls with a look of concern. 'Please don't get upset. Let's have some supper and sit by the fire.'

Avery saw the frustration in Ursula's face. I can imagine what is going through her mind. I was right there when her father told her that he would be back before Sunday to take her home, she thought as they made their way to the sitting room. I am sure that she was happy to spend some time with us, but she certainly didn't plan to spend weeks or months away from home.

'My sweets help yourselves to some food while I pour the wine,' Adelaide said gently. 'I am sure we all could do with a drink right now.'

'Thank you, but I am not hungry,' Ursula responded with her arms crossed.

'Come on, Ursula, you have to eat something. It will make you feel better,' Avery tried to calm her. 'It's not Adelaide's fault that you have to hide out here with me. It is because of me, and for that, I am truly sorry. Darion told us that Lord MacNab is searching for me and that my age is the only thing he knows about me. This must be why he has abducted all the girls in the village. And now we are the only ones left.'

Ursula looked to her friend weakly. 'But I didn't think for a moment that he would be looking for me.'

'So, you met the elf, did you?' Adelaide spoke from behind them, overhearing the conversation.

'And what did the Elf tell you exactly?' her voice sounded angry.

'He told me things about my parents that you didn't know,' Avery replied. 'He believes that there is a way to contact my mother and to find out what happened the day she had to send me away. and he knows how we could lift the curse binding her to the island.'

'What curse?' Adelaide stopped, clearly confused. 'I don't know about any curse. All I know is that Lady Murigen never responded to any of the messages I wrote.'

'Well, you can ask the elf when he chooses to show his face next. I know that he is close by and can hear us,' Avery said, looking around the room for something she couldn't see.

'He is most likely upset because I broke the promise not to tell you anything.'

'So how do you plan to contact Lady Murigen? And what will you do to lift this curse?' Adelaide asked, caught between anger and intrigue.

'We plan to row out to the middle of the loch during the next full moon. Darion believes that my mother has the power to bring us close enough to the island to talk to us.'

'Maybe she can,' Adelaide said softly. 'But you can't go alone. You need protection.'

'Darion knows that. That's why he has chosen the night of the full moon so Arianrhod can protect us. And I am certain that Hugh and Glen will come with us. I'll send them a message tomorrow morning and ask them to meet me here.'

'What about me,' Ursula spoke up. 'Do you think that I am useless?'

'Of course not!' Avery turned to her friend. 'I never doubted for a moment that you would come with me.'

'You're Damn right. I will.'

'So, how are you planning to get the message to the lads?' Adelaide asked. 'You can't very well send Darion.'

'That's no bother. I know a way that has never failed. You'll see, I have done it for many years but kept it my little secret,' Avery said. 'Say speaking of secrets - who are you weaving these plaids for? Nobody came to the cottage. How did you get the order?' Adelaide looked at Avery, impressed by her cleverness. 'You are right. There is no order. The plaids are for you and Ursula. They will keep you safe whenever you leave the cottage. The third one is for me if Lord MacNab tries to get you through me. He is desperate and would not hesitate for a moment to do whatever he feels necessary to get hold of you. These plaids will make you invisible. They keep you warm, dry, and safe from Dark magic.'

Avery looked at Adelaide, moved by her kindness.

'Adelaide, how can we ever thank you for all you have done for us?' she asked.

'My bonnie lass, there is no need. Keeping you safe is the most important thing for me to do.' Avery felt that the words gave her a strength she did not recognise.

'Adelaide, do you think that there is enough yarn left to make two more?'

'Of course. I should have just enough. But I'll need your help, so let's not talk any longer. We have to get up early tomorrow if we want to finish it. Up to bed, lassies, have a guid nuit and sweet dreams!'

'Guid nuit,' Avery replied while pushing Ursula up the stairs. Once they were back in the bedroom, the girls exchanged stories from the Day.

'What was the grin all about this afternoon?' Avery asked. 'You said you would tell me once we are alone. 'Well, we are alone now, so spit it out.'

'It was nothing, Ursula laughed. 'I just loved how you played the Innocent when Adelaide mentioned last night's fire. She knew all along that you lit it during the night. She also knew that you met Darion, of course, but she wanted to hear it from you.'

'Oh dear, she must be very disappointed in me,' Avery said with dismay. 'Only I did not want to upset her. I'll explain everything to her in the morning. But for now, let's go to bed,' she sighed.' Yes, you need your beauty sleep. I don't want you in a grumpy mood tomorrow.'

Avery blew out the candles as Ursula curled up in her bed. She couldn't help walking up to the window to look one last time into the Dark, hoping to catch a glimpse of Darion. But all she could see was the night sky and the black silhouettes of the forest

7 The Message

Avery and Ursula got up made their way down to the kitchen long before sunrise. They were surprised to find the fires lit and breakfast with freshly baked scones and steaming hot milk on the table near the hearth.

'My goodness, Adelaide must be up for hours,' Avery exclaimed. 'I thought she was so tired last night that she would sleep a little longer today.'

'Really come on, Avery, did you not hear the click-clack of the loom last night? Maybe she did not sleep at all.'

'I didn't hear a thing. I must have slept like a stone. But where is Adelaide?'

'She must be in the workshop,' Ursula answered. I think I hear the taping of the spinning wheel..., hang on, I go and take a look,' she turned to open the door to the workshop, but it did not move. What's wrong? Why is it stuck? It was fine last night. That's strange, she thought, puzzled. She leaned against it with all her weight, but the door did not budge.

'Avery, can you give me a hand? The door is jamming. I can't open it.'

Joining her, both of the girls pushed with all their might until the door swung open with a bang. They stumbled into the workshop, surprised to see all candles lit and the spinning wheel turning, but no sign of Adelaide.

'Oh, wow, this is spooky. Pinch me, Avery. I must be dreaming.'

'You are not. I see it too.'

'Seeing what?' they heard Adelaide calling from the kitchen. 'What is going on?'

'How on earth did you do that?' Avery said, startled. 'We just heard you in the workshop. The spinning wheel is still moving, and you are in the kitchen,' Avery said and hesitated a minute before asking. 'Are you an elf too?'

'No, Avery, I am not,' Adelaide replied. 'Come back and sit with me, you two. I'll explain everything over breakfast.' The women made their way back to the kitchen, sitting around the hearth.

'Years ago, a family of Brownies came to my cottage asking for shelter,' Adelaide began. 'They had been living and working in the kitchen of Kilchurn Castle but could no longer bear the cruelty of the Laird. I offered them my barn, and since that day, they have cared for my animals and helped me in the workshop.'

'Oh, please, can I see them, Adelaide! Darion told me that a group of Brownies moved in with William and Maighread to help them run the inn. I would love to speak to them,' Avery pleaded.

'I am sorry, my dear, but that will not be possible. Brownies are extremely shy and do not trust mortals. Maybe they will show themselves to you after they got used to you being around.'

'It's not the Brownies that interest me. We have some of them helping us when it is time for the harvest,' Ursula interrupted. 'The story about the Laird, I want to know. Da told me that he is an evil man.'

'He is not. He is a good friend of my Da. I mean William,' Avery said. 'He made him the justice of the peace for Ardteale, Auchtermally and Edendoich.'

'Well, that may be so, but Ursula's Da is right. He is a very sly and dishonest man. He tried to take the cottage and all the land from me after his father had bequeathed it to me shortly before he died. He would have succeeded if it had not been for William's help. But apparently, he did not want to risk their friendship, so he gave in. But enough of this, it is time to start working. Let's go, lassies.' Adelaide said and walked into the workshop.

'You go ahead. I will join you soon,' Avery said. 'I just have to get the message on the way to Glen and Hugh.'

'How are you going to do that? Sending a pigeon with a letter?' Ursula asked.

'No, I send it by water. The brook is my messenger. Tell Adelaide that we will be with her just now, and meet me under the bridge,' Avery said. 'Hurry!'

She ran up to her bedroom, pulled a wax-coated piece of red cloth from her travelling bag and hurried down to the brook.

'Ursula, where are you?' Avery whispered and looked under the small bridge for her friend.

'I am right here. What are you planning to do with that old thing?'

'That is my message, I throw it into the brook, and the current will carry it right up to the mill, where it will get caught in the wheel and stop it,' Avery explained.

'Don't fret. Glen and Hugh know the procedure. Come up here as soon as they free the wheel. You will see.'

'That will not work,' said Ursula, full of doubt. 'The cloth is going to sink to the bottom as soon as it is wet!'

'Aye, it will. I have done it hundreds of times. I coated the cloth with wax so it cannot sink,' Avery retorted and let go of the cloth, which floated on the water like a leaf.

'Believe me now? Let's go back to Adelaide. The lads will be here soon.'

'That is pure dead brilliant Avery,' Ursula laughed, taking Avery's hand and pulling her up onto the bridge.

'Let's go. Adelaide is waiting. We have a lot to do if we want to finish the plaids in time for the next full moon.'

8 Getting Ready

'Avery, did you get your message on the way?' Adelaide asked.

'Aye, it should not take long. The brook is flowing fast today. The snow on Ben Croachan must be melting.'

'Alright, let's get to work, lassies. Ursula, can you please comb the fleece and Avery? I need you to do some spinning so that we will have enough yarn to get the plaids done in time for the next full moon.'

'Aye, Adelaide. But please, tell us a bit more about the Drows and the magic of your windows while we work. I have never seen anything like them,' pleaded Ursula as she picked up a basket with the fleece.

'Alright then,' Adelaide conceded with a smile. She sat down at her loom and started to throw the shuttle, telling the girls stories as they worked. The rhythmic and hushed tapping sounds from Avery's spinning wheel and the click-clack of the loom created a dreamlike atmosphere that seemed to carry Avery and Ursula away into the mythical world of the Drows.

The hours passed by like clouds in the wind, and it was already afternoon when the workshop door opened.

'Guid efternuin, lassies!' The sound of Hugh's voice echoed as he stepped over the threshold.

'We tried knocking, but I guess you didn't hear us over all that click-clack. Anyhow here we are. So, what's the reason for the red flag you sent?'

'I am so happy you are here,' Avery said, stopping the wheel to greet her friends. 'We have so much to talk about!'

'I am so sorry for causing you this much trouble,' she added. 'We tried to get here earlier, but the brook is running strong today, so we decided to get as much grinding done as possible. That is until some cursed piece of red cloth got caught in the wheel,' Glen explained. It was a real task to get it out of the gears this time.'

'Well then, let's call it a Day, girls!' Adelaide said. 'Nice to have you here, lads. To be honest, I did not believe that your message would work, but I was proven wrong. I reckon it's time for some good food, wine and talks, so let's pick up the candles and move over to the sitting room.'

'Brilliant idea, we are starving! What's for tea Adelaide?'

'Bread, cheese and ham, lads. The stew is all done, but there is some broth in the cauldron if you'd like something hot. Avery and Ursula, lassies, get some wine and ale for us. And you lads take care of the fire while I get the food.' It was not long before they all sat comfortably in front of the fire and enjoyed the food and drinks. Avery and Adelaide could finally share all the long-held secrets with the men in the calm. Hugh and Glen were stunned by all that was revealed. They looked at Avery as if they saw her for the first time.

'This is incredible. Of course, we've always believed in magic ourselves,' Glen exclaimed. 'After all, we have a load of Brownies helping us at the mill. But we have never met an elf before. Are you sure this Darion is truly an elf?' he asked, raising his eyebrows.

'I am half-human,' to be more precise.' Darion appeared as if out of nowhere.

'Darion, you did it again!' Avery exclaimed. You promised me you would make yourselves known whenever you enter a room!'

'And you promise not to tell your friends about me and our plan,' Darion responded. 'So, we are even.'

'Dear me, don't argue it is better this way,' Adelaide jumped in. 'There has to be an end to all the secrets, at least among us. I am delighted to see you again, Darion. It has been a very long time.'

'I was always around Adelaide but could not show myself to you. I am glad that all this hiding is finally over.' 'How long you have known each other?' Avery asked, confused.

'From the Day Adelaide came to this cottage and freed the Drows.'

'That can't be!' she exclaimed. 'That was at least thirty years ago. You were not even born then.'

'Do you remember me telling you that I am a part elf?' Darion explained to her. 'Well, we do not age like you mortals do.'

Avery was thunderstruck by this revelation and looked bewildered at Adelaide and Darion.

'Never mind your age,' interjected Hugh. 'All we should be talking about is what you are planning, see as to do since we only have ten days left till full moon.'

'How long would we be gone? And do we need to arm ourselves?' asked Glen, walking over to Darion and embracing him like a good old friend.

'We should be back before sunrise,' Darion replied. 'And no, you don't have to arm yourselves. All you need is warm clothes and good control of your senses, so that strange sounds or visions wouldn't fool you.'

'We can do that, no problem. We spent many nights hunting in Eredine Forest since we were small,' Hugh said. 'The real problem is finding warm clothes for the lassies.'

'I think that they should dress like us. I'll get the lassies proper buckskin truis and lambskin boots,' added Glen.

'I like that,' Avery agreed. 'And Adelaide is making thick woollen plaids for all of us that look like the forest floor and will make us almost invisible.'

'Good, but keep in mind that it will still be Dangerous,' Darion said. 'We have to be vigilant and keep what we are about to do a secret. I'll go and talk to my brother about our plans and ask him to be our guardians for that night. Take good care, my friends,' he said and vanished.

'Goodness, which is magical. I wish that I could do that.'

'Aye, right, and leave me with all the work. I can just see that happening, my dear brother,' chuckled Hugh and slapped Glen on the shoulder.

'Come on, lads, settle down. I think it is time to find a place for you to sleep,' Adelaide said. 'I gather that you are going to spend the night with us.'

'Aye, it's Saturday, so Da would not need us tomorrow. We'll sleep in the barn, don't fret yourself,' said Glen stood up and winked at his brother to follow him.

'Oh well, yes, guid nuit,' grumbled Hugh as he stood up and followed his brother.

'The lads are right. I think we should go to bed as well,' Adelaide said. 'The night is short, and we have to get up early if we want to finish the plaids in time. Guit nuit lassies, see you tomorrow and Avery, promise me not to come down if you hear the loom tonight. You'll frighten the Brownies, and we need their help now more than ever before,' she looked sternly at Avery and left. 'I can't sleep now. I am too excited! I think we should make a cup of tea and bring it up with us,' Ursula said after Adelaide had disappeared.

'Good idea. What do you think about lavender tea with a big scoop of honey?' Avery replied with a smile.

'That sounds like my kinda cup of tea, and we can surely do with something hot when we go up.'

'Why is that?'

'Well, because we forgot to restock the fire in our bedroom. I am sure that it has burned out long ago.'

'Oh no, don't tell me that. I was so looking forward to our cosy little room! It will take half the night before it gets warmed up,' Avery groaned. 'Let's take some of the glowing peat with us, so it won't take that long for the fire to start,' she handed Ursula a bucket with peat, picked up her cup and a candle as she left the kitchen.

'Don't forget your tea. You will need it,' Avery added.

'Oh no, I wouldn't. Let's go and face our icy chamber, brr,' chuckled Ursula and gave a shiver. The house was dark and quiet except for the creaking of the staircase. The girls had decided to spend the night in a freezing bedroom but were startled when they opened the door and found the fire blazing.

'Crivens who lit the fire! We were downstairs the whole Day?' Avery exclaimed in surprise.

'I am sure the Brownies did it. They are an accommodating bunch.'

'Oh, yes. Speaking of the Brownies, how come that you never told me about them, Ursula?'

'Well, you have always been so adamant that magic beings do not exist that I did not see the point in arguing with you.'

'What makes you think that I would have argued with you?' Avery protested.

'Let's just say that I had a strong feeling, and anyway, it no longer matters because now you know that magic does exist.'

The Days passed quickly, and tonight was the long-awaited night of the full moon and the start of a great adventure. Hugh and Glen had arrived before sunrise and were sitting in the kitchen, enjoying a hearty breakfast while talking excitedly about the upcoming journey. Adelaide had not slept all night and was still busy trying to finish up the seams and edges on the last two plaids when she heard Avery and Ursula coming down the steps and into the kitchen.

'Oh dear, what are you doing here this early in the morning? We are not leaving before Dark. You must have smelled our breakfast right up to the mill, am I right?'

'Yup, I guess we did, Avery, but we left some for you lassies. After all, we are no scoundrels,' replied Glen as he jumped up and embraced the two girls.

'Crivens Glen, don't frighten the lassies, you unkempt, wild man!' called Hugh, pushing his brother aside. 'Guid mornin ladies, I hope you had a good rest. Your knights are ready to accompany you on your journey.'

'Come on, you noble knights, try your plaids and leave the lassie alone so that they can grab a bite too,' called Adelaide from the workshop.

'Aye, fair lady Adelaide, as you command. We are at your service,' giggled Glen, nudging his brother with his elbow and walking into the workshop.

'These plaids are huge, Adelaide! Thank you, they will keep us warm even on the coldest nights.'

'You are welcome, lads. Just make sure you fasten your belts correctly so that they don't slip.'

'Come on, lassie, it's your time now to try on your gear for tonight. I made some heavy tunics for you to go with your truis.'

'Oh, that's terrific, Adelaide, we're coming,' shouted Ursula excitedly and came running into the workshop, pulling Avery behind her.

'You look even better as lads,' teased Glen and walked around them to fully appraise their looks. 'Hugh, you have to see this. The lassies can truly pass as one of us - that is after they hide their long locks, of course.'

'Oh yes, Adelaide, we have to braid our hair and find a way to cover it,' Ursula urged.

'Don't fret. I already have a plan,' said Adelaide picking up some strands of wool.

Glen and Hugh decided to walk up to the lake to check the path for the night and try out their new plaids while the girls were busy in the workshop.

It had been snowing for days, so the old familiar path lay hidden under a thick layer of snow. Hugh and Glen had no choice but to search for a new way down to the lake, which could quickly be followed at night. They tied strips of cloth onto lower branches and laid twigs on the ground wherever the path changed its direction. It was freezing even though the sun was sending her rays through the treetops, making the glazed branches and ferns sparkle in her golden light. Glen and Hugh struggled on through this crystal forest until they finally saw the azure blue of the frozen lake through an archway of snow-covered willows.

'I am so glad we got here without any frostbites. We would not have made it if it wasn't for Adelaide's plaids. There are simply no words that can express how grateful I am,' said Hugh in a hushed voice. His eyebrows were encrusted with ice, and his lips cracked, but he felt pretty warm under his thick plaid.

'You're right. These plaids are magical, but even though we have to go back, have something to eat, meet with Darion and discuss our next steps, so let's go.'

As they made their way back, Hugh and Glen re-checked all their marks and ensured the strips of cloth were tied correctly. Exhausted but satisfied, they walked into the cottage in the late afternoon, took off their plaids, and slumped down in front of the fireplace in the sitting room.

'Goodness lads, I am so relieved you are back; you were gone for such a long time.'

'Well Adelaide, the old path was buried under a deep layer of frozen snow and blocked by branches that had broken under the heavyweight of the snow, so that we had to find and mark a new one.'

'Oh, dear lads, why didn't you leave your boots outside! Get up and go into the kitchen and have something to eat while I take care of that mess. Avery, sweetie, bring some rags and woollen socks for the lads so that they can dry and warm their feet.'

'Sorry, Adelaide, we forgot. All we wanted to do was to rest and warm our feet. They feel like lumps of ice.'

'I can well imagine. I'll place your boots near the fire so that they will be dry by tonight, and when you are ready to go, make sure that they are properly stuffed with the fresh straw that should keep your feet warm.'

'Thank you, Adelaide, you always know what to do.' 'Enough with the compliments! Now go eat and rest. You need your strength later. Darion will be here before sunset to ensure you are ready for your quest.'

'Somethings smells good lassies. I hope it is ready. We are famished!' said Glen as he went straight to the hearth and picked up a ladle. He was just about to help himself when Ursula took the scoop from him and slapped his hand.

'Just what do you think you are doing? Go and sit down. I'll bring you a bowl in a moment. Have some bread in the meantime.' Glen smiled at Ursula and threw her a kiss before he sat down next to Hugh, who was slumped over the table, his head resting on his folded arms.

'What's so funny? Come on, if you have something to say, say it,' hissed Ursula and curled her lips.

'I was just admiring your colourful new hairdo,' responded Glen, bending over laughing as he looked at Ursula.

'You can laugh all you want. It is warm and comfortable,' said Ursula, throwing her head back as she left the kitchen.

'What is the racket all about?' asked Hugh, lifting his head from the table and rubbing his eyes.

'Well, you would have noticed if you weren't sleeping all the time. The lassies have braided their hair with strands of green and brown yarn,' Glen laughed. 'It looks as if they were wearing a big woollen cap.'

'Well, that's a good way to keep warm! You are just jealous because your hair is not long enough to do it.'

'Yeah, right, let's go and have some food. It smells like pottage, and knowing Adelaide's cooking, it will have a good bit of meat in it,' said Glen and picked up his spoon. At that moment, the back door swung open with a bang, and Darion bolted into the kitchen.

'What on earth were you thinking, didn't I tell you to keep what we are about to do a secret?' shouted Darion furiously, throwing off his cloak.

'What is your problem? We didn't tell anyone, not even our parents, so what are you on about?'

'You trampled through the forest and left a trail in the snow worse than a herd of wild boars! And to make things worse, you tied bloody strips of cloth to the trees. Even a blind man could follow your trail. You could have gotten us all killed,' Darion raged. He was breathing hard, trying to control his anger.

'We thought it would make it easier to follow the path,' answered Glen in a trembling voice.

'Yes, you did, for Lord MacNab' and his Red Caps! We are lucky that a group of Dryads followed you and erased any sign of your presence, foolish mortals.'

'Oh dear, please forgive them, Darion. They meant well!' Adelaide said. 'Do you think that Lord MacNab' would be looking for the lassies here at Teatle Water?'

'He has his spies everywhere, especially around the loch, so we have to be extremely vigilant,' said Darion calming down as he embraced Adelaide. 'Don't fret. We will be safe Ghilli Duh asked Laratbogh and Faerydae to remove all of our footprints. My brother Asanopirh and my sister Sorcha will be our wardens tonight.'

'Good, that gives me peace of mind. Now shake hands with the two lads to make peace, please. They are still very young and can act foolish sometimes,' whispered Adelaide looking deep into Darion's eyes.

9 Eridine Forest

'Dryads, what are they exactly, Adelaide? Are they elves like Darion?' whispered Avery, pulling Adelaide closer.

'Not quite, Dryads are female fairies that live in the treetops of the forest. They have the most beautiful voices I have ever heard.' Adelaide responded.

'Have you met any of them? What do they look like?' 'These fairies are as beautiful as their voices,' she said.

'Their clothes are made from feathers, ferns, and flowers, and their long hair glows like the morning sun.'

'Oh, I would love to meet them, Adelaide. Do they show themselves to mortals?' Avery responded dreamily.

'Seldom, but even if they don't, they will always help you if you ask politely and may even share some of their secrets of divination with you. Laratbogh, which means the Gem Falcon and her sister Faerydae, the Dark Child, are the only ones I have ever met. They are the guardians of Eredine Forest and live in the Willow Grove near the lake. I'll tell you more about them when you return, but now it is time to dress,' said Adelaide. She took Avery's hand

and walked with her to the hearth, where her friends were getting ready.

'What did you do to our boots, Adelaide? They look so different,' the men said as she came in.

'I smeared them with hot wax and sealed the stitches so that they keep your feet dry. But you should stuff them with a bit of straw before you put them on so they will keep warm as well.'

'Aye right, Adelaide, which is a brilliant idea, thanks,' said Glen and began to stuff his boots with straw.

'Well, then, my sweets, it seems that you are all set, but wait a moment before you go so I can say a prayer to Arianrhod asking for her protection.' She closed her eyes and began to sing in a melodic voice.

'Fair Lady of the silver moon, Watch over yer bairns tonight. Send them your wisdom and your shining light. Return them safely to my side.'

'Don't fret, Adelaide. I will make sure that they stay safe and return to you by morning,' said Darion, kissing her on the forehead before he stepped outside.

'Keep safe, my bonnie bairns,' called Adelaide from the kitchen as Avery and her friends left the cottage.

The moon had not yet risen, so the woods were still shrouded in Darkness, which provided a perfect cover for the group of friends as they followed Darion, slipping and stumbling through the snow. The forest looked so different this way. It appeared almost to be alive. The frozen leaves on the forest floor cracked like crystals under their feet, and bits of snow fell softly from the treetops. Avery felt uneasy, as if eyes were on her back while they walked ever deeper into the forest. Shadows were Dancing above them in the faint light of the rising moon, and there were strange sounds like whispers in the shrubs and trees. Something or someone is following us, she thought.

'Hush be still,' whispered Darion. He signalled them to hide under a large fir tree with shallow branches.

'What's the matter, Darion, are we followed?' mouthed Avery.

'I am not sure, but you better take cover. You should be safe here under the tree,' Darion replied. 'Your plaids will hide you well. Wait here until the moon has fully risen and you can see the loch. Tell your friends to keep perfectly still until I come back.'

'Aye, Darion, but how are we supposed to see the loch from here? We are not anywhere near it yet!'

'Trust me, Avery, you will. But for now, join your friends and wait,' he whispered and disappeared into the dark forest.

The ground under the ancient tree felt like a soft carpet made from layers of pine needles and moss. Its low branches supplied a perfect shelter from the cold and prying eyes.

'This is a fantastic hideaway. I could stay here all night! How come that we have never noticed it before,' murmured Hugh as he lay down and curled up in his plaid. 'Hugh, come on, it is no time to sleep, you lazy head. We can't stay here all night,' said Ursula. She nudged him in his side before she crawled over to sit with Glen and Avery.

'What are you looking at, Avery?' 'The rising moon, Glen. Don't you see its growing light on the snow? It wouldn't be long before we can get back on our way,' she replied.

'Aye, you are right,' said Glen, parting the branches to get a better view.

Moments later, Darion appeared and spoke in a hushed voice.

'Come on. The moon is up. We can now step onto the loch safely.'

'We have to get to it first, don't we?' replied Avery as she stepped out from under the tree, brushing some pine needles from her plaid before looking up. The loch lay inexplicably in front of her. How is this possible? She thought and took a deep breath while staring at the snow-covered loch that lay before her in the brilliant light of the moon.

'It's magic, she whispered as she stepped onto the ice.

'Be careful, don't be fooled by the snow, Avery. It is just a thin layer. You will be fine as long as you do not lift your feet, slide them over the ice and try to keep your balance! Let's go, Ursula, and you lads, close your mouths and follow us. We have no time to waste,' Darion stated with a twinkle in his eyes. This was undoubtedly his realm, and he was happy to be back. Moments after the friends had left the shore, a gust of wind swept the powdery snow from the lake's icy surface towards the edge of the forest like a wall of icy mist. With the snow gone, the lake now looked like a mirror that reflected the night sky with a myriad of glittering stars and the bright full moon, giving the group of friends the feeling of being suspended and transported into another world.

'This is some mighty magic, Darion,' said Avery in amazement.

'It's the magic of the Moon Goddess. We are now under her protection until we re-enter the forest.'

'This is wonderful, and I am certainly very grateful, but how will it help me to find my mother?' Avery asked. 'All I see is the sky and the loch. There is no sign of an island anywhere.

'All you have to do is call her, and she will show you the way.'

'How?' asked Avery, looking pleadingly at Darion.

He nodded, looked at her with a gentle smile, then raised his arms to the sky and called out.

'Fair Lady Murigen, hear our plea. Open the sky and show us the way As we bring your Daughter to thee!'

When he spoke and lowered his hands, the sky lit up in the most vibrant colours.

'Is this the sign from my mother, Darion?' implored Avery anxiously. She turned around slowly, trying to understand what had just happened.

'Dear me, look at the beautiful northern light!' exclaimed Ursula in admiration.

'They are moving! Shall we follow them, Darion?' Glen asked.

'Aye, the light is our guide to Lady Murigen.' The group of friends followed the band of light.

They were gliding effortlessly across the ice until it suddenly stopped and descended onto the icy surface. The friends held their breath gazing at this beautiful apparition, when they heard an ethereal chorus of elven voices reverberating from the cloud of light. Avery closed her eyes and felt how the voices lifted her into a world flooded with a brilliant light and the scent of thousands of flowers. As she floated through this otherworldly realm, she heard a soft voice calling her name. Somehow, she knew that it was the voice of her mother.

'Avery mo ghràdh, I missed you so much that I thought my heart would break, and now you are standing before me so beautiful and brave. My beloved Daughter, it grieves me that I must ask you to accept tremendous challenges and face extreme Danger to defeat Lord MacNab' so that we can be reunited again. Lord MacNab' has taken your father from my side and vowed to kill you if I did not relinquish my power and thereby accept the annihilation of my kingdom. I could not yield as it would have meant sacrificing my folk and losing you and your father forever. Lord MacNab is mortal but draws magic powers from a Sapphire he had stolen from my sister Cailleach. To break his power and defeat him, you must return the Sapphire to the Blue Glacier of Ben Nevis. You will find Lord MacNab and the Sapphire in the mines of Wemyss, where he keeps your father and the girls from your villages as slaves. If you accept this quest, all the Elven clans, warriors, and white light spirits will fight on your side and protect you with all their might against anyone that means to harm you. Choose wisely, my Daughter, but whatever you decide, Darion will be your counsel and guardian throughout your life. But you must now return Adelaide, the wise crone of the forest, as my sister Arianrhod has to make way for the rising sun. Farewell, mo ghràdh,' Lady Murigen's voice fainted away, taking the beautiful sound and the Northern Light with her into the Darkness of the night.

'Where have the lights gone? And where are the beautiful voices?' Ursula asked, looking crestfallen at Darion.

'Why have they just vanished, Darion? Weren't they meant to show us the way to the island and Lady Murigen?' Glen asked.

'They have. Everything is as it should be. Let's return to Adelaide before the sun begins to rise.'

'How do you mean everything is as it should be? Hugh shouted. 'We did not hear a word from Avery's mother, nor did we see the island!'

'Calm down, Hugh. I will explain everything as soon as we are back in the cottage.'

10 The Ultimatum

The way back to the cottage was arduous. No one had the energy to speak. Everyone seemed lost in their thoughts. The forest was black and lifeless, as if every living thing was holding its breath. The friends felt relieved when the lights from Adelaide's cottage appeared in the distance.

'Oh, dear, I am so glad to be back. All I want to do now is sleep for Days,' sighed Hugh quickening his steps.

'Wait, something is not right. Let me take a closer look,' Darion said, lifting his arm to stop Hugh.

'I know that you need rest, but believe me, it is not wise to let our guard down now,' he whispered, pulling his hood deeper into his face and disappearing in an instant.

'What's the matter, Hugh? Where has Darion gone?' Avery asked, looking around nervously.

'To the cottage. Darion said that something is not right and that he wanted to have a closer look before we approach.'

Avery felt her breath fasten and a sense of Danger rising in her chest. She crouched low to the ground, hid in the tall cotton grass, and crawled slowly towards the cottage. As she came closer, she noticed that the barn door was ajar and made a run for it.

'Are you perfectly mad, Avery? You were supposed to wait until I told you that it is safe to step out in the open,' Darion hissed angrily, pulling Avery behind the well.

'No, I am perfectly sane, but we are talking about Adelaide here, and in case you didn't know, I love her and will not sit idly hidden behind bushes while she might be in Danger. So, what did you see?' replied Avery defiantly as she shook off his grip.'

Darion looked at her in admiration for a moment before conceding. 'Alright, let's get into the barn, and I will show you.'

Darion and Avery stayed low to the ground and slipped into the barn hidden by the shadows of passing clouds.

'What is John doing here at this time? Something bad must have happened,' whispered Avery, her eyes wide with terror.

'We'll find out, but we must wait while my brother makes sure that no one is lurking in the bushes before we walk up to the cottage.'

'Your brother? I haven't seen anyone near the cottage. Where is he?'

'That's because my brother and sister are invisible to the ordinary human.'

Avery wanted to protest and give Darion a piece of her mind when she felt a presence behind her. She spun around and almost choked on her breath when she looked into a pair of green eyes.

'Forgive me, your majesty. I did not mean to startle you. I am here to escort you to the cottage where you and your companions will be safe.'

Avery found herself lost for words. She stood frozen, staring at this luminous elven warrior waiting for Darion to break this awkward silence.

'Avery, may I introduce you to my brother, Asanopirh. He and my sister Sorcha guarded us throughout the night and are about to leave, so let's not waste any more time, the sun is rising, and we need to get you safely into the cottage.'

'Yes, sure, thank you, Asanopirh,' stammered Avery as she followed him and Darion to the cottage.

'Oh, Avery, I am so happy that you are back unharmed. Sit down, my bonnie lass and rest. You must be exhausted, cold and hungry,' Adelaide greeted them with a heavy sigh as the group walked through the door. She pushed Avery in a chair near the fire, covered her with a thick quilt and ran off to the kitchen to get her a cup of hot broth.

'Thank you, Adelaide. Yes, I am freezing,' Avery replied with chattering teeth, pulling the quilt up to her shoulders and stretching her feet towards the fire.

'Avery, my parents are here. You won't believe what's happened!' shouted Ursula

'I know, Ursula, Avery answered. 'I saw your father's carriage in the barn! Tell me what's happened!' Ursula's father spoke up from the corner of the room.

'The young Laird and his men came to our farm looking for you two,' he said in a trembling voice. 'They turned everything upside down, and when they could not find you, they took all of our livestock and threatened to burn down the farm if you don't show up at the castle before the next full moon. I tried to stop them by telling them that you lassies had gone to visit family in Edinburg, but they did not believe me and told me to swallow my lies, or I will end up like William and Maighread,' He sobbed, embracing Ursula and Anette.

'Why?' Shouted Avery as she threw off the quilt and jumped up.

'What does he have to do with anything, and what did they mean when they said you would end up like William and Maighread?'

'We will know in a while, Avery. Calm yourself,' said Darion, 'Hugh and Glen are on their way to the inn to make a delivery and check on William and Maighread. No one suspects them. We were able to bring them back to the mill unseen. You all should go and rest. The cottage is impregnable and surrounded by white spirits. No one can harm you while you are in here.' he said in a soft voice before he took the bow from his shoulder and left the cottage.

'Darion is right. You are safe here, go and rest. I have set up bedsteads for you in my workshop. We all need to calm ourselves and gather strength for what might come,' Adelaide agreed while ushering John and his family into her workshop before she returned to look after Avery.

As she entered the sitting room and walked over to the fireplace, she found Avery all curled up in the armchair, fast asleep. Adelaide picked up the quilt and started to tug it around her when two brownies stepped out from behind the chair and spoke.

'Do not fret, mistress. We will look after her. You go and sleep. We keep watching.'

Adelaide was exhausted. She had not slept for the last two days and nights, and the recent events began to wear her down. She sunk on her cot and closed her eyes when she heard the gentle and familiar voice of the Goddess Momu speaking to her.

'Adelaide, me bonnie lass, everything is going to be alright. We are at your site. Do not despair. Sleep, my love. We'll take care.'

The cottage lay silent in the rising sun as the Goddesses Coventina and Momu appeared, raised their hands and placed a shielding enchantment over the cottage, and all its inhabitants, repelling any ill intent and Dark magic.

~

At the mill, Glen and Hugh had just loaded two sacks of flour and an empty ale barrel onto the carriage and were ready to leave when they heard their mother calling from the barn.

'Wait, you two. You must take a sack of oats as well! I am certain Maighread could do with some!'

'Oh Ma, we just brought her one last week,' quarrelled Hugh as he entered the barn.

'Look at me, Hugh, and listen. If anyone asks you to open the sack, do it from the end with the loose loop and leave the two last stitches intact. I tied a message to the other end before I filled the sack. Maighread will find it as soon as she pours the oats into the box.'

'That's brilliant, Ma! Don't fret. I'll be careful,' replied Hugh.

'Let's go, Glen. Da wants us back before midday.'

'Aye right, hang on, here we go,' Glen called out as he cracked the whip in the air.

'What do you think they have done to William and Maighread?' Hugh asked once they were on their way.

'Nothing, I reckon. After all, William is a close friend of the Laird. I believe they just wanted to intimidate John.'

'Well, we are about to find out,' Hugh replied with a chuckle.

The brothers fell silent, paying close attention to their surroundings as they drove up to the inn and saw about twenty horses tied to the nearby trees.

'Just as Ma expected, the Laird sent his men to the inn to watch William so that he has no chance to warn the lassies.'

'Aye, right, but he thought wrong, didn't he?' chuckled Glen as he jumped off the carriage.

'Damn right he did, come on and let's announce ourselves,' whispered Hugh with a big smile on his face and opened the door to the inn.

'Guid mornin William, where do you want your flour to go?' shouted Hugh. He walked straight up to the counter where William was busy pouring ale for some soldiers.

'Well, you are busy this morning. Is the Laird holding a tournament? Good morning noble knights, gentlemen,' called Glen, bowing to the men at arms.

'Oh, guid mornin lads, you can bring it straight into the pantry and then go to the kitchen. My Ma will fix you something to eat,' replied William.

'Hold it right there, lads. Two of my men have to inspect the sacks first,' shouted one of the higher ranks. He waved two of the soldiers to follow Hugh and Glen.

'As you wish, Sir,' answered Hugh, leaving the inn followed by two armed men.

'Hang on, gentlemen, that's a dusty business. I don't want the flour to make a mess of your beautiful uniforms,' said Glen winked at his brother and let the sack hit the ground hard, sending a cloud of flour up in the air.

'Oi, look out, you eejit!' screamed one of the soldiers.

'I am sorry, but you can't say he didn't warn you,' Hugh replied as he placed the sack on his shoulder and headed into the pantry.

'We would be done much faster if you give us a hand. Look, why don't you take the sack of oats? It isn't that heavy,' said Glen and handing the sack of oats to one of the soldiers.

'Open them up, lads, so that I can have a look.'

'As you command my man, just look out, or you get powdered with flour,' Hugh replied and opened the stitching of the two sacks of flour while the second soldier placed the bag of oats next to the door and sat down on it. The armed soldier drew his sword and ran it into the flour several times, then nodded, satisfied, and left the pantry, followed by his comrade.

'Oh Glen, don't ever do that again! I thought that I'd drop dead right on the spot.'

'What? It worked, didn't it? They are too Daft for their own good,' laughed Glen and went into the kitchen.

'Where do you want the oats, Maighread,' asked Glen and winked.

'Oh, if you could be so kind as to pour them into this box, my lad, this will make it so much easier for me,' Maighread answered with a big smile and a nod.

'Aye will do, but then I'm afraid we have to go. Da wants us back before midday. All that is left for us to do is to fetch a barrel of ale from William.' Glen explained politely.

'No need. William already loaded it for you. Take good care, lads, and give my love to your Ma and Da,' Maighread responded, hastily waved goodbye and closed the door.

'Well, that was short and sweet. I wonder why Maighread was in such a hurry to get rid of us.' Glen said to his brother with raised eyebrows as they left.

'Let's check the barrel as soon as we reach the forest, Glen. I have a funny feeling that she somehow hid a message for us.'

'Aye, but we have to be careful, just in case they send somebody to follow us. It'd be best if you check Bessie's huff while I inspect the barrel.'

'Pure dead brilliant,' murmured Hugh as re-tied the barrel and got back on his seat. 'She must have dropped something in it. The cork is wrapped with something and feels kinda loose. Let's hurry home and find out.'

'So how did it go? How is Maighread?' called Bhaltair as he saw his lads drive into the yard.

'Fine, Da and Ma were right! Maighread was waiting for the oats. Where do you want the ale to go, Da?' called Glen tilting his head in the direction of the carriage.

'Ah, I think you better bring it in the cellar so it keeps cool. And while you are at it, why don't you open it just a smidge? I am thirsty. Madge, my mo chridhe, bring us the tankards and have a drink with us.'

'Aye, Bhaltair, I will be right there.'

Moments later, the men looked anxiously at Madge as she removed the strip of cloth from the cork and pulled it out.

'Maighread is a smart lady. Look at that, lads. She placed a message in a vile and tied it to the cork. No wonder that William was so quick in loading it.'

'What does it say, Ma? Come on. don't keep us hanging here.' Hugh urged impatiently, leaning over her shoulder.

Dear friends,

I hope you all are safe and well when this message reaches you. William and I have been held captive at the inn since the young Laird had raided it last night. He was desperately trying to find Avery and Ursula and threatened to throw us in the dungeons if the lassies didn't turn themselves in before the next full moon.

Dear John,

I beg you to take Annette and seek shelter at Adelaide's home. The Laird has given the order to burn down your farm and everything in it.

Bhaltair,

It seems that the Laird is still unaware of your family's involvement, but I think that you would be wise to plan your escape in case the situation changes.

Adelaide,

My wise friend and mentor, please provide shelter for our friends and seek help from your elven guardians. I fear that we will not survive this Dark time without their protection.

Blessed be)O(

'Oh dear, this is far worse than I thought,' Madge said. 'We have to tell John and get his valuables out of his home before it is too late.'

'But how are we going to do this without leading the Laird's men straight to Adelaide?' Bhaltair asked through concerned eyes.

'I am going to ask the Brownies for their help. After all, they also have a family at the farm that needs to be alerted.' Madge replied as she hurried out of the house and straight into the mill to warn her little helpers.

'Oh dear, this is far worse than I thought,' Madge said. 'We have to tell John and get his valuables out of his home before it is too late.'

'But how are we going to do this without leading the Laird's men straight to Adelaide?' Bhaltair asked through concerned eyes.

'I am going to ask the Brownies for their help. After all, they also have a family at the farm that needs to be alerted.' Madge replied as she hurried out of the house and straight into the mill to warn her little helpers

11 The Laird's Secrete

Avery was woken up by the rumble of thunder and the patter of rain against the window. She felt exhausted even though she knew she must have slept for hours. She rubbed her eyes and looked dreamily into the smouldering fire when her memory brought back the events from the morning. Oh dear, I hope Hugh and Glen made it to William and Maighread. In that kind of weather, where is everyone? She thought as she walked down to the kitchen, hoping that Adelaide or Ursula would be up.

'Oh, you are up! Did you have a good rest, Avery?' Adelaide greeted her. 'How do you feel?'

'Stiff, the chair is not as comfortable as my bed. But how are you? You look exhausted.'

'I'll be fine, don't you fret me, lass. Come to sit with me and have something to eat.'

'Where is everyone?' Avery Asked. 'Did you hear anything from Hugh and Glen?'

'Not yet, and I do not expect any news before nightfall. Ursula, John, and Annette are still sleeping. We should not wake them till we've heard from the lads.'

'You're right. The three have gone through so much and need all the rest they can get.'

'So, tell me about your journey. Did you see the island and speak to your mother?' Adelaide's eyes shone with curiosity despite herself.

'We did not see the island, but we saw the most beautiful northern light.'

'Are you telling Adelaide about last night, Avery?' asked Ursula in a sleepy voice as she and her parents entered the kitchen.

'Yes, I was just about to do that.' 'How did you all sleep? Are you

feeling a bit better now?' Adelaide inquired.

'A bit, but we are anxious about what the Laird might do next,' answered John sinking on the bench near the hearth.

'Did you hear anything from the lads?' asked Annette. 'No, and I do not believe we will do it before Dark. But Avery was telling us about their journey last night. Come sit with us, Annette, and have some tea.'

'Come on, Avery, tell us what happened!' Ursula urged impatiently.

'Part of it, I know, but I have no idea what happened while the lights and the beautiful voices engulfed us.'

'That is strange, didn't you hear what my mother said? It was loud and clear.'

'Nope, not a word. So come on, let's hear it.'

'It was like a dream.' Avery started, her eyes gazing out the window. 'I was floating in bright white light and was bathed in the fragrance of thousands of flowers when I heard my mother's voice.'

'What did she tell you, Avery?' asked John moving closer.

'She told me that Lord MacNab' had taken my father and vowed to kill him and me if my mother would not relinquish her power and accept the destruction of her kingdom. She also told me that Lord MacNab' is mortal and that he gets his magic powers from a Sapphire he had stolen from the Goddess Cailleach.'

'Crivens,' John exclaimed and added. 'What can we do?'

'She told me that we could break his power and vanquish him by returning the Sapphire to the Blue Glacier of Ben Nevis.'

'Brilliant, but how do we get the Sapphire? He will not give it to us, and we don't even know where to find him.'

'I do,' Avery said with determination in her voice. He is hiding in the caves of Wemyss, where he keeps my father and the girls as his slaves.'

'Blood bas! So, when do we leave?' Ursula jumped up.

'After you have learned how to fight,' replied Darion, who had again appeared without warning. Avery was about to say something concerning his disregard of their agreement but was too relieved to see him.

'After we've learned to fight?'

'Yes, Ursula, fight. He will not hand us the stone and give up his strive for the island kingdom. He commands an army of Red Caps and controls the men at arms from Laird Duane, not to mention the Boobrie.'

'Aye right, and the five of us will triumph over them,' remarked Avery and shook her head.

'With what, may I ask?' Ursula asked, her voice thick with scepticism. Unless you call a rake and a spade weapons, we have no weapons.'

'Not quite, but Glen very is skilled with the staff and knows how to set fires. Hugh is a very good bowman, and as far as I know, you are a master with the slingshot.'

'Ah, and what am I good at, throwing a tantrum?' asked Avery and stemmed her fist in her hips.

'No, my fair princess, you are going to use the sword. Two of them, you have swordsmanship in your blood. After all, you are the Daughter of the Goddess Murigen.'

'I don't know what is in my blood, but I never held a sword in my life,' giggled Avery, picked up the fire poker and spun around like a skilled swordsman.

'Damn. Avery, he is right! I don't want to see you with a sword in your hand,' said Hugh, who had just entered the cottage through the back door.

'Goodness lad, you are drenched. Hang on. I'll fetch you some dry clothes from John,' exclaimed Annette and disappeared into the workshop.

'Did you swim? Why are you so wet?' teased Ursula nudging his shoulder.

'Go and change, lad. I placed dry clothes on John's cot. And hurry! We want to hear about William and Maighread,' said Annette. She pushed Hugh into the workshop before she went to the hearth and filled a bowl of hot pottage for him.

'That feels better, thanks for the clothes,' said Hugh. He sat down next to the hearth and enjoyed his food before sharing the news.

'Well, the Laird has gone mad. Why else is he doing this? What does he have to do with any of this?'

'Lord MacNab' threatened to take his little Daughter Lucie if he doesn't deliver Avery and Ursula before the next full moon,' Darion explained.

'He has a Daughter?' everyone asked in one voice and looked at each other in surprise.

'I didn't even know that he has a wife,' John said in wonder. Did any of you know that?'

'It's the first time that I hear about it,' said Adelaide

'When did he get married, and why did he keep it secret? Who is his wife?' Annette and Adelaide inquired.

'As far as Nissa can tell, he bought his bride from the Mac Neil's of Barra,' Darion replied.

'They are bloody pirates! Their chief is not even a Scotsman. Ruadhri is one of the last Vikings. They are known for their raiding trips from their island stronghold of Kisimul. He had been arrested and charged for piracy of an English ship last year. Where is the lassie from, Darion?' John asked in an angry voice.

'Nissa told me that she is from France.'

'Did you say France, Darion,' Adelaide asked, staring at him in disbelieve?

'Aye, Nissa told me her name is Anne and that she is the daughter of a Scottish nobleman in Touraine.'

Adelaide went pale and had to hold on to her chair.

'What's the matter, Adelaide? Are you okay?' shouted Avery jumping up to keep her from falling.

'I think Anne could be my niece,' she replied in a voice barely over a whisper. 'I expected her five years ago but was told that the ship sunk near Edinburgh and that there were no survivors. Who is this, Nissa, and can I talk to her?

'Well, she is a Brownie that lives in the household of the midwife that delivered Lucie and still looks after her and her mother at Kilchurn Castle,' Darion said. 'I will try to get her to talk to you.'

'Please, I need to know if this lassie is my brother's Daughter,' sighed Adelaide wiping her eyes.

'Speaking of Brownies, Ma has asked ours to help your Brownies remove all your valuables from the farm and bring them here to Adelaide. As far as we know, the Laird's men have the order to burn the farm down before sunrise,' said Hugh laying his hand on John's shoulder.

'Goodness, what will happen next? We have to stop those men!' cried Annette.

'Don't fret. We will build it back bigger and better than before. Let's give the bairns all the help we can to defeat this so-called Lord,' said John defiantly, taking his sobbing wife in his arms.

'Well then, let's make some room for all the things the Brownies are about to bring,' said Adelaide, taking Annette by the hand leading her into the pantry.

'Now, while ma is gone, Darion, tell us more about the Redcaps and the Boobird,' said Ursula.

'You mean the Boobrie,' answered Darion and could not suppress a smile.

'Well, the Boobrie is a giant savage bird which will devour anyone who Dares to cross his path.'

'If the bird is that big, how come that we have never seen it?' Hugh interjected. 'You can consider yourself lucky. That beast lives near water, so it could show up at the mill at any time. It can transform itself into a horse and canter across water and land.'

'Good crivens, so what about the Red Caps? I heard that they live in ruined castles and caves, but I don't know anything else about them,' said John.

'Well, they are even worse than that bloody bird,' Hugh replied. 'The villagers say that the Red Caps are murderous goblins that soak their caps in the blood of their victims and that no human, even if he is as strong as an ox, could overcome them.'

'Oh, come on, Hugh, if they are goblins, you just outrun them,' replied Ursula

'Sorry, Ursula, but there is no chance a human can outrun a Red Cap. They are extremely fast, even with the heavy pike staffs they carry and their iron-tipped boots.'

'So, if they are that strong and that fast, how are we supposed to fight them?' Avery asked, turning to Darion.

'They turn to yellow ashes when struck with an elven blade or injured by one of our arrows. That is why I will take you all to the Seelie Court, where you'll learn to use our weapons,' Darion replied.

'Brilliant. But we must make sure that our families are safe before we leave and find a way to communicate with them,' interjected Hugh.

'It would be best if your parents use the night of the Dark moon to move in with Adelaide. The cottage and the land around it is the gateway to the Seelie Court and, therefore, well-protected.

'Oh, that is why you can always appear out of nowhere! Good to know,' said Avery with a smirk.

'Aye, my dear and I must return now to prepare for your arrival. And ask Cait Sith to be our messenger for the time of our absence. We'll leave the night of the new moon. Only leave the cottage during the night while our warriors can protect you. I'll return for you as the moon is rising,' said Darion and disappeared.

12 The Seelie Court

Avery and her friends waited in great anticipation for the journey to the realm of the Seelie Court. Now that the time drew closer, the wait became almost unbearable. The friends knew that the acceptance of strangers to the realm of the Seelie Court was extremely rare, especially if they were not of pure fey or elven blood. Permission for mortals to enter was given to only a few over many centuries.

'Come on, lads, it is time to go. Darion is waiting for you at the bridge,' said Adelaide with an uneasy smile.

'I wish that I could go with you. The realm of the elves is so beautiful.'

'Aye Adelaide, believe me, we would love to have you by our side, but who would look after our parents while we are gone?' Glen replied as he stormed out of the cottage.

'You'll have to forgive him, Adelaide. My brother is not very good at saying goodbye. Take care, and please watch over our parents. Da has a very short temper, and ma always worries too much.'

'Crivens, are you talking about me, lad? I am as calm and controlled as anyone, and your ma worries so much because she loves you,' Bhaltair called from the kitchen.

'Never mind, I know your Da, my lad. Just look after yourself. Go now. The others are already down by the brook,' Adelaide sighed, pushing him out the door.

Hugh's knees felt as if they would buckle at any moment as he walked down the gentle slope to the bridge. Get yourself together unless you want to tumble down into the brook in front of the lassies, he thought.

'Well, well, it's about time you join us, dear brother.'

'Where are the lassies, Glen? They left before me and should have reached by now?'

'Aye, they are waiting under the bridge. Let's go.'

'Why are we hiding down here? I thought Darion was taking us to the Seelie Court. Where is he? 'Hugh asked suspiciously.

'I am right here, Hugh,' Darion replied as he appeared from under the bridge.

'Finally. Can we please get on our way? My boots are soaked, and I am freezing.'

'Certainly, Avery. Just follow me,' Darion responded as he walked into the brook and disappeared.

'What just happened? Where is he gone,' Ursula asked, with a startled look?

'Oh, come on, just step into the brook and pass under the bridge,' Avery called out as she stepped into the icy water, took two steps and disappeared.

'Jinks, that's a great trick! Well, don't just stand there, lads. Come on, let's go.' Ursula cheered and grabbed their hands. She took a deep breath and stepped into the brook, and pulled High and Glen along under the bridge.

The three friends did not believe their eyes as they left the shadow of the bridge and found themselves standing in a crystal-clear pond surrounded by islands of white and yellow water lilies and the brightest sunlight they had ever seen.

'Come on, don't just stand there. We still have a ways to go before we reach the great hall of the Seelie Court,' said Darion as he helped Ursula to climb out of the pond.

'My boots are dry! How is that possible?' exclaimed Ursula in surprise as she gazed at the staggering beauty of the landscape.

They wandered for hours through glens of soft grass and wildflowers, petals from blooming trees and butterflies danced in the gentle breeze. No one spoke a word until they noticed a majestic forest in the distance.

'Is that the home of the Seelie Court, Darion?' asked Avery.

'Aye. The throne hall is in the forest's centre and is guarded by Dryads and elven warriors. But don't fret. Asanopirh and Sorcha will escort us to the Queen.

'Who are Asanopirh and Sorcha?' Ursula asked.

'They are my brother and sister and the commanders of the royal guard.'

It did not take long until they found themselves standing at the edge of the forest and had to take the first step into the imperial grounds of the Seelie Court. They all felt this was a great moment, far greater than stepping into the Darkness earlier. This was the gateway to the ethereal world of the Queen of Lights. After a moment's hesitation and with a pounding heart, Avery stepped under the leafy canopies of the tree giants and felt a deep sensation of peace and happiness. She turned to her friends and waved them on before she continued her walk into the ancient forest.

'This is unbelievable. Pinch me, Glen, I must be dreaming,' whispered Ursula as she strolled through an ocean of bluebells.

'You are not. You are in the forest of Elfame. Welcome, Ursula,' said Asanopirh bowed and walked on.

'Oh, my goodness, was that Asanopirh?' Ursula asked Darion.

'Yes, and to your left, you see my sister Sorcha. She does not speak your language and therefore never makes contact with mortals,' Asanopirh replied with a chuckle.

'Glen, what are you looking at? Come on. We are going to lose the others.'

'I don't know. I could have sworn that I just saw a beautiful young lassie behind that big oak tree. Actually, it looked as if she was part of the oak tree,' answered Glen in a dreamy voice staring at his brother in disbelieve.

'You saw the Dryad Faerydae, one of the guards of the forest. She and her sister Laratbogh were the ones that removed your tracks in Eredine Forest. Come on, hurry, we are not far from the throne hall now,' Darion pushed them along.

'Aye, but why did you not tell me that Dryads are beautiful fairies?'

'I thought it best if you find out yourself,' laughed Darion.

After this encounter, Glen paid close attention to his surroundings as he followed Darion. His eyes scanned the trees, ferns, and patches of primroses and buttercups for any sign of the beautiful fairy. As they walked on, the trees became even more magnificent and looked like marble columns, their branches interlaced and forming a living canopy from which silken ribbons in the softest shades of lilac floated in the air. The path had changed from the mossy forest floor to ivory-coloured flagstones with embedded crystals that sparkled like diamonds in the glowing rays of the sun that filtered through leaves.

The friends were captivated by the beauty surrounding them and ambled on like in a trance until they stood at a luminous arbour and the Queen of Lights.

'Welcome to my court, Avery, Daughter of Murigen. I feel honoured by your visit and hope that I can help you free your mother from the Dark powers that bind her to the island.'

'Dear Queen of Elfame, I thank you for allowing my friends and me to come before you and for your generous offer to help my mother to regain her power and reunite my family.'

'Dear Avery, it is our tribute to your mother for all the wealth and security that she afforded us. I, therefore, pledge my incessant and unconditional support to you and your companions. Asanopirh and Sorcha, my commanders, will arm and prepare you for your quest, and my warriors will fight on your side until the end. Go now and rest. You must be exhausted. My servants will tend to your every need,' the Queen of Lights declared and left.

'Perfect, let's eat. I am famished. I wonder what sumptuous treats they have for us.'

'Oh Glen, how can you think of food in such a moment?' Avery asked.

'What, I am starving! What's wrong with eating? Aren't you hungry too?'

'I bet you all are. Keelin will escort you to your chambers. Eat and rest, my friends.'

'Thank you, Darion, but when will we see you again?' Avery asked.

'I'll come for you in the morning and take you all to our armoury to get your amours fitted and receive your weapons. Sleep well,' Darion said, walking away.

'Please follow me. Your meal is ready and fresh garments have been laid out for you in your bed-chambers,' Keelin said in a soft voice, leading the friends into the castle. Their chambers were bright, airy, and decorated with the most delicate carvings and gossamer veils.

'Oh, look at this, isn't it just wonderful,' said Ursula as she ran her fingers gently over the opalescent gossamer veil.

'Aye, it is. Look at all this food, roasted beef, chicken, lamb chops, bacon, tatties, peas, carrots, and gravy. I am in heaven!' shouted Glen pulling up his sleeve, ready to dig into the food.

'Och, stop it, Glen, you should at least wash your hands, you greedy scoundrel,' Ursula scolded him.

'Why the harsh words Ursula? I am hungry. What's wrong with liking the food, especially when it looks as good as this!'

'Glen is right, but let's freshen up a bit before we eat,' said Avery, pointing to a small waterfall and pond right outside. 'We have all night. There is no need to hurry.'

'We have our very own waterfall! Come on, you guys, let's check it out,' called Ursula. She hurried out into the garden, kneeled at the water's edge, and dipped her hands into the crystal-clear water. 'The water is warm. How wonderful is that?'

'Let's not fret about water when there is such sumptuous feast waiting for us,' laughed Glen while he hurriedly washed his hands.

Hugh and Glen loaded their plates with meats, veggies, and tatties and then smothered it all with gravy, like men who hadn't had a meal in Days.

‘Are you going to eat all that?’ asked Avery shaking her head in disbelieve.

‘Aye, we are hungry! We did a lot of walking today, remember.’

‘Right, and what did we do, fly? This is nasty. It's a good thing that we are alone! I would be so embarrassed if anyone would see you eating like that.’ Ursula countered and squinted her eyes in disgust.

‘Avery, let's take some fruits and eat in the garden. I can't look at this.’

‘I am a step ahead of you, Ursula. Come on. I took the fruit basket. The lads would not want any of this anyhow,’ Avery replied and pulled Ursula into the garden.

13 The Armoury

Ursula, Hugh, and Glen had gone to bed, and the chambers finally lay silent. Avery was grateful for the time alone and took a walk through the garden. The night air was warm and heavy with the scent of lilies. Avery enjoyed the moist grass under her feet and the gentle breeze playing with her hair and silken gown. She dreamily walked closer to the glimmering fairy pond and felt a strange pull. Avery kept on walking until she was completely immersed in the deep blue water and floated effortlessly on her back. She felt neither fear nor the need to breathe. It was as if she had become disembodied and one with the water. So, it is true that the magic of my mother also lives in me, Avery thought as she began to glide calmly through the water when she suddenly heard a gentle ambient voice.

'Welcome, Avery, to the realm of your mother, our divine Lady Murigen.' Avery spun around in surprise.

'Where are you? Please show yourself,'

'I am right here,' answered the water spirit appearing from the water. Avery was stunned by the beauty of the fairy that stood like a crystalline statue in front of her.

'My name is Ariana, and I am here to bring you a gift from your mother, Lady Murigen. She sends you this pearl as a token of her love and asks you to wear it at all times and to dip it into the water if you need help or protection,' said the fairy. She carefully placed the necklace around Avery's neck before she disappeared. Avery could not believe what just had happened. It seemed like a beautiful dream, but it was as real as the pearl on her neck. She did not feel the night slipping away until the rising sun began to replace the Dark starry sky with her golden shine. Avery realised that the time had come to leave the warmth and serenity of her mother's realm to return to her friends and left reluctantly. She felt her weight return with every step until she stood in the soft light of the new morning. Hoping that her friends would still be asleep, Avery rushed to her bedchamber, dressed, and dried her hair as Ursula stepped in.

'Goodness, where have you been?' Ursula exclaimed. 'I got scared when I saw your bed empty this morning.'

'Oh, Ursula, calm down. I got up early to go for a walk in the garden. Let's go and have some breakfast before Darion gets here,' she replied, walking over to the table and joining Hugh and Glen for breakfast.

'Guid mornin folks, I trust you had a good rest and feel as fresh as a fish in the water,' Darion said and smiled when he saw the pearl on Avery's neck.

What does he mean, feeling like a fish in the water? Did he see me in the pond last night? Avery wondered and tried to avoid his gaze.

'It is time to get on our way to the armoury. Bilobeal is waiting to fit your armours. I hope you did not overeat for breakfast so that your armour can get a nice snug fit.'

'How do you mean fitting the armour? Hugh asked, puzzled. Don't we just put it on?'

'The leather for your armour will be softened in hot water and then wrapped around you. It shapes itself to your body as it dries.'

'How can a leather armour protect us from blades and arrows,' Avery asked sceptically. Isn't it too soft to withstand such a force?'

'Bilobeal hardens it after it has reached its final shape. I am sure that he will be happy to explain it to you,' responded Darion as he led the group of friends out of the forest and into the mountains. It was a long, challenging climb up the snow-covered slopes of Ben Lomond. The sun stood high in the sky as they reached the icy peak and squeezed through a crevice into a cathedral-like cave in the rocks. After their eyes had adjusted to the dim light of the cave, the friends walked on through an extensive cave system deep into the mountain until they reached a brightly light chamber.

As usual, Glen could not tame his curiosity and was the first to enter, heading straight for one of the silver armours hanging from the ceiling. A very strong Drow with long flaming red hair stepped into the light and approached them.

'Aye, you made it! I am glad to see you, Darion. Are these bairns your brave warriors?'

'Aye Bilobeal, this is Avery, the Daughter of Lady Murigen, and these three are her friends.'

'What's your name, my bonnie lass,' asked Bilobeal as he walked up to Ursula and bowed politely.

'My name is Ursula. It is a pleasure to meet you, Sir Bilobeal.'

'There is no need to be so formal, Ursula,' he laughed. 'But tell me, what are the names of these two strong lads?'

'This is Glen, and this is his brother Hugh,' replied Ursula, pushing them forward to greet Bilobeal.

'Aye, right, let's get to work then now that we've all been formally introduced. Your armours are nearly ready. All that is left to do is to fit and harden them. Once they are done, they will feel like your second skin and protect you from any blade or arrow. So, let's get the armours wrapped around you while they are still soft so that they take their final shape on your body as they dry,' explained Bilobeal as he pulled four soft pieces of leather from a steaming cauldron.

'Hold on, I am not going to have my skin burned off for some boggin leather armour!' shouted Hugh, taking a decisive step back.

'It's not going to burn you, my brave young lad. It will be quite cool by the time it touches your skin.'

'Goodness, how embarrassing! Bilobeal, you can start with me so that my brave friend Hugh can see how it's done,' said Avery and stepped forward to be wrapped in the soft leather.

It did not take long before all of them stood wrapped in their soft leather armour and listened to Bilobeal's explanation of the hardening process.

'We are going to glaze your armours with pine resin and ground garnets, which will render them as hard as a stone itself. We will also add silver rivets for more resistance. Your arm and leg braces have been made the same way to protect and support you. Everything will be ready at the next full moon.'

'Bilobeal, my armour is getting pretty tight. Is that normal?' Ursula asked, fidgeting uncomfortably under the layer of leather.

'Aye right, my armour feels like a corset,' added Avery, as she tried to loosen the leather straps holding it together.

'Aye right, that is how it should be. It means the leather has dried. Let me help you to take it off,' Bilobeal replied.

'How come I don't hear anything from you lads,' inquired Darion with a broad grin.

'That is because we cannot breathe,' whispered Glen. 'Well, let's get them off you too, so that and that my apprentices can now take them all to be glazed and hardened,' said Bilobeal laughing as he placed the armours into a cart.

'Shall we go to our weapons arsenal now to arm your friends, Darion?'

'By all means, Bilobeal. We have to make sure that they have the right size and weight. Avery's wrists are very delicate, so she needs good braces. The same goes for Ursula.'

'No, bother, Darion. I thought of that and made special braces for the lassies. Follow me,' he replied and led the group of friends into a large chamber crammed with racks of gleaming blades, lances, bows and other Weapons. Hugh and Glen were speechless, staring in admiration at the sheer number of weapons on display and the magnificent craftsmanship of the Drows.

'Aye right, let's begin with Avery. I made two short blade swords for you. Their grips are dragon claws, and the single edge blades are of elven steel and can cut through even the heaviest armour. Your Scabbard was crafted to go onto your back so that your hands remain free when you are not in combat. Your arm and leg braces have silver shields,' said Bilobeal. He bowed deeply and laid the weapons at Avery's feet before he turned and looked at the lads.

'Well, let's continue with our bowman. Which one of you is it?'

'That would be me, Bilobeal. At least that's what Darion said,' Hugh answered in great anticipation and stepped closer.

'Aye right,' said Bilobeal as he lifted a beautifully shaped longbow from a rack near the wall. 'Your bow is made from the wood ancient white oak and strung with the hide from a stag. The arrows shafts are birch, fetched with falcon feathers and tipped with elven steel. We also made this special quiver for you that can hold up to thirty sixty arrows and a Dagger,' he said proudly, displaying the weapon in his hands.

Hugh was overwhelmed by this generous gift and bowed to Bilobeal before taking his splendidly crafted weapons.

'Now Glen, Darion told me that you are the master of the staff. I made your staff strong and reinforced its ends with elven silver rivets and black iron braces. I am a staff fighter myself and can assure you that a hit with your staff is deadly even for Red Caps.'

'That leaves only the bonnie lass,' he continued with a smile as he walked over to Ursula. 'Ursula, your slingshot is made from elder wood and strung with dragon sinew. It is mighty powerful and has a brace at the handle which straps on your wrist to strengthen and support it,' he said, showing her how to strap the slingshot to her wrist.

'So now you are all armed for your quest. It was a pleasure to work for you, and I am looking forward to seeing you all again in combat,' said Bilobeal. He seemed very proud and pleased with himself.

Avery picked up the Scabbard with her swords and pondered how to strap it to her back.

'Let me help you, Avery. It is hard in the beginning, but you will get the gist of it very soon,' said Darion as he helped her to strap the Scabbard onto her back so that she was able to draw the blades for the very first time.

'You have to cross your arms over your head. Grab the handles tightly and draw your swords upwards in an arch with outstretched arms.'

'Aye, I will give it a try,' replied Avery. She crossed her arms and pulled the blades without any effort from the Scabbard but shuddered when she heard the deadly hissing sound as she drew them.

'Perfect, I knew that you are a born swordfighter, just like your mother and all your ancestors. Tomorrow we will begin to strengthen your arms and wrists and work on your balance, rhythm, and speed to prepare you for the battle,' said Darion with a smile before he turned to Glen and Hugh.

'And you lads, let's not get carried away and risk getting injured. You still need to learn how to handle your weapons.'

The first excitement over the newly gained status of a fully armed warrior wore quickly as the friends descended from the mountain.

'Darion, please, let's rest for a moment. I can't breathe,' called Avery as she sat down on a boulder.

'We can't. We need to keep going,' answered Darion, turning around to look at the red faces of Avery and her friends.

'You have to adjust your breathing, or you will be helpless and dead before the battle even begins. You have to learn to breathe into your belly. Try it as we continue to walk, and we will practice it tomorrow at the start of your training,' Darion said and walked on.

The friends were relieved when they arrived back at the palace and into their chambers.

'Oh dear, I never thought that it would be this tough,' Glen sighed in exhaustion.

'Never mind, Glen, we will get the hang of it. For now, let's just eat and go to bed. I am dead tired,' Avery responded and placed her swords on her bed before joining her friends at the table.

14 Cait Sith

That night, the friends felt restless and could not sleep. The importance and urgency of their quest had become all too real and occupied their minds and conversations. Ursula, Hugh, and Glen were admiring each other's weapons and talking excitedly about the start of their training when Avery interrupted.

'Guys, you should stop talking and go to bed. We have to be up early in the morning and will need our strength and concentration if we want to make it work,' she said in a stern voice.

'What's wrong with you, Avery? Stop quarrelling. Where are you, anyhow?' Glen asked.

'I'm in the garden, trying to get some peace.'

'Aye right, your highness, no need to ruffle your feathers. Let's go, guys, before Avery loses her temper,' said Glen closing the door to the garden.

'At last, silence. I did not intend to be mean, but I hope they understand that I need time alone, she thought and sat down on the steps to the garden. She rested her head on her knees and listened to the calming sound of the wind when suddenly, a warm breath touched her neck. Avery jumped to her feet span around to see who was behind her but couldn't make out anything in the dark.

'Who's there? Show yourself,' she whispered in a trembling voice, trying to sound brave.

'Avery, you don't have to fear me. I am here to give you a message from Adelaide.'

'I don't have to fear you, very well, then why are you hiding in the shadows,' Avery responded, not entirely convinced?

'Aye, you are right, but I am not what you would expect. I think it would be best if you sit back down before I show myself.'

'Aye right, I am sitting, so come out now. I don't frighten that easy.'

'That's what Darion told me. I am Cait Sith.'

Avery turned her head toward the sound and did not believe her eyes when she saw a large black cat standing right behind her.

'Please, forgive me for staring, but Darion never told me that you were a cat. I expected a fairy or an Elf.'

'I am a fairy but can only show myself as such nine times during my life, and I have only four times left. So tonight, you see me like a cat.'

'You are an unbelievably beautiful cat, Cait Sith. Tell me what the message is.'

'Adelaide told me that she had spoken to a Brownie named Nissa and found out that the young Laird's wife is her long-lost niece, Anne. Nissa told Adelaide that the ship Anne sailed on from France was attacked by a Brilinn as they were approaching the harbour of Edinburgh. The crew was caught entirely off guard and could only offer little resistance as the Mac Neil's clan mob boarded the ship, stormed into the captain's quarters, and demanded his surrender. All the women and children on board were sold into slavery as they made port in Oban. That's when the young Laird Duane Campbell bought Anne and forced her to be his wife. Anne, her daughter Lucy, and the Laird's mother, Julia, now live locked up in the Castle.'

'Crivens, we must free them!' Avery exclaimed as soon as the cat had finished delivering her message. 'Especially since Lord MacNab' has vowed to take Lucy if Ursula and I don't show up at the Castle by the next full moon. Cait Sith, please tell Adelaide that we will return within the next three Days to free Anne, Lucy, and Julia. Forgive me, but I have to go now to wake my friends and devise a plan on how to liberate them,' Avery explained. She was about to run into the palace when Darion stepped out in front of her.

'Slow down, Avery, we have to talk. There is a way to free them without putting anyone in Danger.'

'Oh yea, is there such a way?' Avery responded, tapping her foot impatiently. 'Go on, let me hear it then.'

'Yes, Avery, you don't have to do it alone. All you have to do is to ask the Goddess Momu for help. She will be able to bring Anne, Lucy, and Julia safely to Adelaide without anyone noticing.'

'And how is she going to do this, may I ask?' she responded, her tone caught between sarcasm and hope.

'Momu is the Goddess of all wells and hillsides. She can take them to Adelaide unharmed. We have to convince them that it is safe to climb into the castles well. Cait Sith, go and inform Adelaide. She will know what to do, and Avery, you come with me,' Darion declared, took her hand and led her to the fairy pond.

'Dip your pearl into the water to call Ariana. She will deliver your call for help to Momu,' he instructed her calmly.

'How do you know about the pearl?' 'It's my job to know everything, and it was foreseeable that Lady Murigen would send you one of her pearls and ask an Ashray to watch over you. But let's not talk any longer. Call Ariana. Time is of the essence.'

'Aye, right,' Avery responded. She took the pearl from her neck and dipped it into the water. 'So, what now?'

'Now we wait. It will not be long before Ariana appears. Ashrays are faster than any current I know.' Darion had only just finished his sentence when Ariana appeared.

'How can I be of service to you, Avery?'

'Ariana, I need the help from the Goddess Momu to free three captives from Kilchurn Castle and bring them safely to Adelaide's house,' Avery instructed.

Before she had a chance to explain further, Ariana was gone. Avery shook her head and stared into the water in disbelief.

'Why did she leave? I didn't even tell her about Anne, Lucy, and Julia,' whispered Avery.

'There is no need. Ariana would have overheard our conversation. Ariana will stay close to you at all times but only show herself when you call,' Darion explained. 'Don't fret. Ariana will deliver your message. Adelaide and Momu know what to do to get Anne, Lucy, and Julia to safety. But it is time now for you to rest. I will return for you at sunrise,' Darion said and left.

15 The Training Begins

'Avery, wake up. It's late. Darion will be here any minute.'

'Oh dear, sorry, Ursula, but I went to bed late and didn't sleep well at all. Just after you went to sleep, Cait Sith brought me an important message from Adelaide. Can you wake Hugh and Glen? I'll tell you everything over breakfast.'

'The lads have been up for ages! Just get yourself ready I'll go and tell them that you have news for us,' Ursula replied and rushed out to alert Hugh and Glen.

'Goodness Glen, take it easy on the food. You won't be able to start the training if you keep stuffing yourself like a pig,' Ursula exclaimed as she walked into the hall.

'Oh, come on, Ursula, who knows when next we will get some food,' Glen replied, picking up another meat pie.

'Give it up, Ursula. You should know by now that he never listens to reason,' Hugh interjected and shook his head.

'He will listen to the news I am about to share with you,' Avery declared as she joined her friends. She sat down and began to recount last night's occurrences. After she had finished, Hugh spoke first.

'Oh wow, I would have loved to meet Cait Sith. I hope she will be back soon to let us know how the escape went.'

'Aye, Cait Sith will be our messenger whenever we are away from home.'

'Good morning, folks!' Darion's voice echoed from the garden. 'I hope you are ready to go. Keelin is waiting for us in the glen.'

The friends hurriedly left the palace and followed Darion through a small oak grove and onto a sun-drenched grassy glen, where Keelin awaited their arrival.

'Welcome, my friends. I hope you had a good rest so that we can start right away,' Keelin greeted them with a welcoming smile. 'In the beginning, I will work with you as a group and show you how to increase your strength and perseverance. Then I'll teach you to move with ease, grace, and sleek, help you to improve your breathing and finally enable you to control your anger to remain mindful in combat,' he explained.

'Laratbogh and Oren will show you how to calm your mind, use all your senses, disguise yourself and stalk your enemies safely. When you complete this basic training, you will learn to use your weapons efficiently. Lord Darion will teach you, Avery, how to fight with two swords and the use of a Dagger. Hugh, my sister Lady Sorcha will help you refine your skills to become a master bowman. Glen, my lad, Edana will teach you how to set and control fires, and I'll help you improve your techniques with the staff.'

'Aislinn is going to train you in the use of a slingshot, Ursula, and share her secrets to heal injuries through the use of herbs. But enough of that, let's start with our basic training by practising deep and controlled breathing. I want you to focus as you inhale and hold your breath while balancing on these small rocks.'

The group worked on their balance under Keelin's gaze for the following hours.

'Oh man, I can't take much more of this. My feet are hurting, and my head is spinning from all this funny breathing,' Glen complaint.

'It's not the breathing that is troubling you. It is the food you had before the training. You have to get used to eating smaller amounts of food,' Darion explained with a broad smile.

'Well done, you guys. I think it's time to work on your strength and stamina. Let's climb some trees,' Keelin shouted before he disappeared in a giant oak.

'Aye, fine with me. I climbed the wings of our mill before I could walk properly,' Glen chuckled. He grabbed one of the lower branches and followed Keelin like a squirrel.

'Well, that is easy for you to say. I don't have the strength to pull myself up and look at the size of these trees,' Avery sighed and looked defeated.

'Let's do it together. Come on, I help you up,' giggled Hugh, forming a step with his hands for Avery's foot and lifting her.

'Take hold of the trunk and then step onto my shoulders so that you can reach the first branch.'

Avery wrapped one arm tight around the tree trunk, swung the other over the nearest branch, and lifted her feet off Hugh's shoulders and onto a sizeable gnarl. She was genuinely grateful for her new soft leather boots, which allowed her to feel her way up the tree. Exhausted but proud of her achievement, Avery sat down on a branch and leaned onto the moss-covered tree trunk. She closed her eyes and took a deep breath to inhale the tree's spicy scent. The green essence gave her strength and the feeling of being one with the trees around her. She felt content and let her eyes wander up to the canopy of lush green leaves when she noticed a faint movement right next to her.

'Stay calm, Avery and sit tight. I mean you no harm. My name is Laratbogh, and I am one of the protectors of the forest.'

'Oh, Laratbogh, I've heard about you and your sister Faerydae from Adelaide. Where are you?'

'I am right by your side, holding your hand. Promise me you won't let go,' whispered Laratbogh.

You're holding my hand? Avery thought, looking bewildered at the large branch she had rested her hand on to steady herself when a beautiful woman with delicate features appeared from the wood. Her skin looked as if carved from softwood, and her long hair resembled the green foliage of the tree.

'Are you a part of this tree, Laratbogh,' Avery asked?

'Yes and no. My sisters and I are a part of all trees, but we favour the oak as our home. We never travel far from it unless we carry one of its acorns with us to remain in contact with it at all times,' Laratbogh explained.

'So that is how you were able to accompany us through Eredine Forest,' Avery exclaimed, slowly understanding. 'But how come I did not see you? Your green hair should have given you away between the snow-covered trees.'

'Our hair changes its colour as the seasons' change,' the Dryad replied. 'During the spring and summer months, our hair is lush and green, while during autumn, it turns red and eventually brown or white in the winter.'

'Well, that explains it,' Avery chuckled and nodded.

'I must leave you now. I just came to assure you of our help and protection on your quest. My sisters and I will see you all tomorrow morning,' Laratbogh whispered and vanished.

Avery remained in the tree for a little while before joining her friends again. The group practised moving from branch to branch until the sun was setting and it was time to return to the ground.

'That was great fun, but how do we get down without breaking our necks,' Ursula shouted, looking lost.

'That is not as hard as you think. Look for a mossy or sandy landing spot whenever you need to jump or drop from great heights. But never land straight-legged as the amount of impact would risk injuries to your knees and hips and therefore risk your life.'

'Thanks, Keelin, we'll try our best. Come on, Ursula, let's do it,' Avery said, letting herself drop to the ground.

'That was fun, but don't look at my hands now,' Ursula laughed, looking at her hands in disgust. My fingers are swollen, and my nails are black from the tree sap.'

'It's a good thing that you can't see your hair, Ursula. You look like a tree yourself with all the leaves and twigs in your locks,' Hugh teased, pulling some leaves from her fiery red hair.

'Hugh, Glen, come and join me for a moment. I would like to show you something before we return to the palace,' Keelin called out from the edge of the woods.

'We'll see you later then,' Avery and Ursula suggested hurrying out of the forest and straight into the fairy pond. When Ariana suddenly surfaced right next to Ursula.

'Oh, dear, you startled me!' Ursula jumped. 'You must be Ariana. I am Ursula.'

'Aye, I know who you are. You are Avery's best friend,' Ariana replied and swam across to Avery with a big smile.

'I didn't expect you back so soon, Ariana. Do you have news from Adelaide?' Avery asked as she climbed out of the water.

'No, I can't reach Adelaide's cottage. The brock is too shallow. But I bring you a message from Lady Momu. She will help Anne, Lucy, and Julia escape from Kilchurn Castle under cover of the Dark moon when no one can see them leave.'

'How she is going to do that without drowning them, 'Avery asked, a concerned look crossing her face?

'Lady Momu is creating a large air chamber for them once they are in the Castle's well, and I will move them through an underground river to Adelaide.'

'Oh, thank you, Ariana, that eases my mind. I hope Cait Sith was able to contact Adelaide so that she can prepare and get the message to Anne and Julia.'

'You can ask Cait Sith. She is awaiting you in your chamber,' Ariana replied before disappearing in the dark blue water.

'Well, let's go then, Avery! I want to meet her before the lads get here, hurry,' Ursula cheered excitedly and hurried into Avery's bed-chamber.

'My goodness, is that Cait Sith Avery? Let's not wake her. Who knows how she would react,' Ursula mouthed as she saw the large black cat curled up on Avery's bed?

'It's her, but you can relax. She is not Dangerous, at least not for us.'

'Are you sure about that? I think I'd rather keep my distance. You go and wake her,' whispered Ursula, hiding behind Avery.

'No need to whisper. I heard you come in,' Cait Sith murmured. She arched her back and stretched before walking up to the two girls.

'Ariana told me you have a message from Adelaide, Cait Sith,' Avery said.

'Aye, Adelaide is very excited and has begun to prepare for the arrival of Anne, Julia, and wee little Lucie. She sent Nissa to talk to them about the plan and asked her to stay at the castle to make sure everything goes well.'

'That is great news, Cait Sith, Avery sighed, relieved that everything is coming together smoothly.'

'Aye, but I also have bad news. The laird's men burned down John's stables and placed a group of Red Caps in his house to make sure that he and his family can never return.'

'Aye, which is bad news,' Avery replied, a tear escaping her eyes. 'But at least we were warned and able to move all his belongings to Adelaide. What about the mill? Wo is running it now since Bhaltair and Madge left?'

'Nobody, I am afraid. The laird's men plundered their stocks, blocked the wheel, and removed the sails from its wings.' Cait Sith explained. 'But you should not fret about that now. Just concentrate on your training.'

'Aye right, we will. But let's go and join Hugh and Glen. They are eager to meet you,' Avery said, waving Cait Sith to follow.

'Help ma boab, that's a big cat!' Hugh exclaimed, taking a step back.

'Lads, this is Cait Sith. She brought us a message from Adelaide. Everything is ready for Anne, Julia, and Lucie's escape,' Avery exclaimed and could not suppress a smile.

'Thank you, Cait Sith. Please forgive our reaction. Avery had told us about you but failed to mention your size,' stammered Hugh and bowed.

'That is alright, laddie. I am used to mortals staring when they see me, I would love to stay, but I am needed at the cottage to keep an eye on things for Lord Darion. Take care,' Cait Sith replied and gracefully pranced out of the palace.

'Dear me, did you see the size of her paws? They are as big as a platter, and her green eyes gleam like fire.' Hugh exclaimed in amazement.

'Aye, and she moves as silent as a ghost, and her black fur blends in with the trees perfectly, rendering her almost invisible,' Glen remarked.

'Right, my dear brother. She must be deadly when she prowls the forest at night.'

'Come on, you two, Cait Sith is our friend and protector,' Avery said. 'The only ones that should fear her razor-sharp teeth and powerful legs are our enemies. I am sure they'll know the meaning of fear and terror whence they hear her roar.'

'That's for bloody sure, but let's not fret about that now,' Ursula interjected. 'It's late, and I am sore from head to toe. Let's call it a day.'

'Ursula is right. We should go to bed. Tomorrow will be another hard day,' Avery agreed. 'Guit nuit, sleep tied.'

'Guit nuit Avery!'

16 Laratbogh and Oren

Exhausted and sore from the strenuous training, Avery dropped onto her soft bed. She closed her eyes and thought back to her encounter with Laratbogh high up in the majestic oak tree. Lost herself in a Daydream when she suddenly heard the muffled sound of steps in the garden.

Who could that be in the middle of the night? Avery wondered if Cait Sith was at the cottage, and Darion was indeed sleeping by now. She got up and tiptoed to the door leading to the garden for a closer look and was surprised to find it wide open.

Who opened the door? Ursula and the lads are in bed fast asleep...? She thought, went back to her room, dressed, and picked up a candlestick as a weapon, just to be safe.

She felt foolish holding the candlestick in her hand. Who on earth could harm me here, with all these guards around? She thought as she stepped out and noticed fresh footprints in the grass leading to the woods. She followed them until she noticed the glow of a small campfire and saw Hugh, Glen, and Keelin sitting at the fire talking to another man.

'What are you guys doing out here in the middle of the night?' she called as she approached.

'Crivens, Avery, I could ask you the same thing! Why are you out of bed at this late hour?' replied Glen. He stood up and blocked Avery's view.

'Well, I followed you! Who are you hiding there? I thought that we agreed to have no secrets,' she said, crossing her arms, vexed.

'That's right, we most certainly don't, but Ghilli Duh is very shy and wants to gather some courage before meeting you,' Keelin explained, bowing to Avery.

'Am I so terrible that a grown man needs to gather the courage to meet me?'

'Well, to be frank, yes. After all, you are the Daughter of a Goddess and can't be approached like an ordinary mortal,' Keelin explained.

'Where are you, Ghilli Duh? Please step forward so that I can see you.'

'As you wish, Avery, Daughter of Lady Murigen,' answered a voice coming from the shadows. As he stepped into the light of the fire, Avery could see that Ghilli Duh was a gigantic fairy with long black hair, tanned skin, and gentle eyes. His cloak had been made of leaves and moss, and he carried a massive staff.

'I am honoured to meet you, Avery and humbly offer you my help and protection in your quest to free your mother.'

'I am very pleased to meet you, Ghilli Duh and thank you for your generosity. But I can't stay and talk to you tonight, as I am exhausted and need to rest. I am sure Keelin told you that we all undergo rigorous training for our quest. Please forgive us for cutting our meeting short tonight. I hope we will meet again soon,' Avery stated. She bent her head and returned to the palace with Hugh and Glen.

The next Day began entirely different. Laratbogh, Faerydae and their younger sister Oren took the four friends on a relaxed walk through the woods. They learned to find and follow the tracks of all the creatures in the realm of Elfame. The friends were introduced to pixies and learned to walk through the woods without leaving the faintest mark before approaching the more difficult lessons of disguise and stalking.

'When stalking your enemies during an ambush, place a branch between your teeth to hide your face. And wear the light, soft leather shoes the elves gave you. So, your steps are soundless and leave little or no imprint,' Oren explained, showing them how to cut a branch without leaving a trace.

'We've got you some green suede jerkins to wear over your armour. They will hide you just as effectively as your plaids but won't hinder your movements,' Faerydae announced. She walked away from the group and gently parted the branches of a hazel bush, revealing a Dryad child with a basket filled with wild berries.

'This is our youngest sister, Hazel. Since Dawn, she has been up to pick berries and fetch cool water from the spring for you. Let's unwind for a while,' Oren whispered, kissing her little sister before she sat down on a large stone.

The friends were grateful for the break, spread their plaids on the mossy ground and enjoyed the treats while basking in the afternoon sun chatting with their gracious hosts.

'Let's listen to the forest. Hear the sound of the wind playing with the leaves and the hum of the bees and dragonflies. Listen to the sound of birds flapping their wings and their beautiful songs. Pay attention to the thud of the deer's huff as it ambles through the woods without fret or fear,' Oren was whispering and closing her eyes.

The friends followed her example and sat perfectly still, silent, and focused, listening to the beautiful songs of nature. Suddenly, they heard the trot of the deer quicken and turn into a gallop. The birds began to beat their wings in fright, and the sound of breaking branches echoed through the woods.

'What is happening, Oren?' Ursula shouted, scanning the surrounding nervously.

'Something is approaching, so the forest is sounding the alarm,' Oren replied as she jumped to her feet.

'Did you do that to show us the reaction to Danger, or is it real?' Avery asked, sounding tense.

'It's real, alright. Look at Cait Sith. No wonder every creature is trying to flee. No offence Cait Sith, but I am sure you know your effect on your prey,' Glen said.

'No offence was taken, Glen. After all, I am a predator. But I am not here to hunt. I have an urgent message for you all.'

'What's wrong? Is everything alright at the cottage,' Avery asked, looking alarmed?

'Nothing happened at the cottage, but we got word from Nissa that William and Maighread had been taken to Kilchurn Castle last night.'

'Why, what could they have possibly done to warrant an arrest?' Avery asked.

'Nothing, but after the disappearance of John, Annette and now Bhaltair and his entire family, the Laird grew suspicious. William and Maighread were the last ones to speak to all of them. We can only pray that he doesn't make the connection to Adelaide.'

'He can't possibly suspect Adelaide. We were so careful, and the cottage is protected by powerful magic.'

'Aye, Avery, they will be safe as long as they remain at the cottage. The Goddesses Momu and Coventina placed another enchantment on the cottage and its land. No malicious person can pass over the bridge or approach the cottage from the fields or the forest. So, you bairns need not fear for them.'

'But we should go to the fairy pond call all of our friends and allies to gather and assess the situation,' Faerydae suggested with determination. The Dryad walked up to a large rowan tree and drummed rhythmically on its trunk.

'What is she doing?' Ursula asked, looking wide-eyed at Laratbogh.

'She is calling the Dryads, Pixies and Ghilli Duh to assemble at the fairy pond. The tree will carry her message through the root system of the entire forest,' Laratbogh replied.

Glen, Hugh, and Ursula stood rooted. All colour had drained from their faces, and their eyes were wide in terror.

'Snap out of it,' Avery ordered. 'Come on. We must act. There is no time to hesitate. Let's get to the pond to make a plan of action.' With that, she ran into the forest.

17 The Gathering

Dark storm clouds soared like birds of prey across the blazing red sky while the sun melted in the glen, like iron ore in a black smith's forge.

It's a bad omen, Avery thought as she ran panting and with a stabbing pain in her side through the thickets of the woods.

'Avery, stop. There is no need for haste. Do not allow your feelings to blind you,' said Darion as he appeared right in front of her blocking her path.

'That is easy for you to say!' she replied angrily. 'William and Maighread mean nothing to you, but they are everything to me. They are my family, and I will not abandon them.'

'I would never ask that of you, but we have to be cautious and plan our actions well so we do not place William and Maighread at risk. Please, Avery, stop and breathe. We will find a way to free them. Let's talk it over with our friends. They are waiting at the fairy pond,' said Darion softly, taking her hand gently in his.

'Look at the sun, Ursula. It looks as if drenched in blood. I am sure that this is a warning and that the time has come for us to fight.'

'Oh Hugh, what's wrong with you? You used to like a red sunset! Why are you in such a dreadful mood?' asked Ursula, shaking her head and walking away.

'Since our homes and livelihoods have been destroyed and our families live in hiding,' shouted Hugh with an angry expression.

'Come on, laddie, chase the Dark clouds out of your mind,' said Ghilli Duh as he walked up to him. 'You are not alone in this. We will all be at your side until we have defeated this evil.'

'You are right,' Hugh said, gaining courage with his words. 'Let's join the others at the fairy pond to devise a plan of action.'

'That's better, Hugh. Lift your head and face whatever comes your way..., speaking of what comes your way. I must leave you for a while to greet a friend of mine who has just arrived,' Ghilli Duh remarked.

'Who? Where? I don't see anybody.' 'The Wulver. Look at him, right there at the edge of the woods. He doesn't like to show his face when mortals are around. Come on, let me introduce you,' said Ghilli Duh, leading Hugh to the edge of the forest.

'You can come out of hiding,' he called out, seemingly to no one. 'Hugh is an old friend and a good lad and doesn't frighten easily,' he chuckled to himself as he searched the surrounding shrubs for his friend.

'If you say so, Ghilli Duh,' a voice spoke from behind them.

Hugh turned around and expected a horrid looking old fairy or elf but was not ready for what faced him. He took a deep breath to calm himself and tried hard to keep his knees from buckling.

'Are you all right, laddie?' Ghilli Duh asked. 'You look awfully pale.'

'I am good, but I am starving. A handful of berries was not enough to keep me going, and that's all I had for the Day. Will you please excuse me while l get some food,' answered Hugh nervously and walked away?

'Aye right, I am hungry myself. Let's see what the Elves have for us at the palace. Come on, Wulver,' said Ghilli Duh, placing his hand on his friend's shoulder and steering him in the direction of the fairy pond.

'We should all calm down,' Asanopirh said. 'No harm was done to William and Maighread, as the Laird still sees him as a friend,'

'Oh, is that so?' Avery said with sarcasm. 'As a friend, would you throw your friend in a dungeon too?'

'They are not in the dungeon, Avery. Relax. They are in the tower house with Julia, Anne, and Lucie. That is how we found out about their arrest. Nissa saw them there and informed Adelaide,' replied Asanopirh.

'What will happen to them after Julia, Anne, and Lucie escape? Can we not get them out as well?' Avery asked.

'No, their chambers are locked and guarded. But Nissa will remain at the castle to look after them and contact us. She watched over William from the Day he was born and would never leave him in such a situation,' said Cait Sith.

'Thank your swift action, Cait Sith,' said Bilobeal. He got up and looked at the friends with a severe expression. You have to hasten your training as the situation is changing rapidly. We will do our part and work on your armours with increased speed to get them ready in time.'

'Dear friends, it's time to get some rest and clear our minds so that we can come up with a level-headed plan as to how to proceed. Sleep well. We'll meet in the glen at sunrise,' said Darion. He was about to leave when Avery grabbed his arm and asked.

'What about our training with Laratbogh and Oren? We haven't finished.'

'Don't fret about your training, Avery. My sisters and I will accompany you wherever you go to advise you and ensure that you are safe,' replied Oren, bowed and left.

'So, since that's settled, let's go and have something to eat before we hit the sack. I am starving,' said Glen ushering his friends into the palace.

'I can't eat now. My stomach is in a knot,' Ursula said, a troubled expression twisted on her face. 'I'll go to bed and think about what we can do to free William and his Ma.'

'We will have a bite or two and then put our heads together. We should be able to come up with something,' answered Hugh.

'Well, you guys do that. I go to the fairy pond to talk things over with Ariana. Let's discuss what we came up with on our way to the glen. Goodnight' Avery announced as she walked into the garden.

Why is it that something terrible happens every time things seem to be going well? She thought as she dipped her pearl in the crystal-clear water of the fairy pond.

'I am here, Avery. I overheard your conversation.'

'Thank you, Ariana. What do you think about the situation?'

'Well, Lord Darion is right. They are safe for now. But you should quicken your training so that you will be ready to free William and Maighread before the next full moon. Lord Darion, Lady Sorcha and Lord Asanopirh are already devising a plan of action.'

'What are they like, Ariana? Are they as fears as everybody seems to think they are?'

'Lord Asanopirh is the most fearless warrior I know. He is utterly ruthless when safeguarding his queen, realm, or family. He and his warriors will never hesitate to use every trick at their command. The Dark princess Lady Sorcha is known for her slight recklessness and evil temper. She most certainly will not hesitate to kill,' Ariana explained and rested her hand on Avery's knees.

'Normally, I would shudder at what you just told me, Ariana. But lately, I look at these vices as virtues. Have I gone bad?'

'No, Avery, you haven't. You and the ones you love are being threatened by something so venomous that you must retaliate even though it horrifies and sickens you. Unleash your power and let them feel your fury. Don't think twice, as they would not hesitate to kill you. But please, don't fret about that now. You need rest so you can focus on your training tomorrow morning. To fight with two double-bladed swords is very Dangerous and demands a high level of control and concentration. Go to bed, Avery. I will be here when you return,' Ariana said. She held her gaze for a moment, then disappeared in the deep blue water of the fairy pond.

Avery could not sleep and began to pace the garden. The thought of William and Maighread locked up at Kilchurn Castle made her restless, but what troubled her most was that she could do nothing to get them out of the Laird's grip.

'Why are you not resting, Avery? Don't you remember me telling you that you need all your strength and focus for our training,' Darion asked in a hushed whisper.

'Aye, I do, but I can't close my eyes and pretend nothing's happened. I feel so helpless.'

'I understand how you must feel, but you are not helpless. Very soon, you will be a fearless sword-yielding warrior, lightning-fast and just as bright once you start spinning,' he reassured her. 'We never told you the other name your mother gave you. It is Evelyn, which in our world means the light. You have the power to create clarity and warmth and erase everything Dark and ruled by dark magic. Asanopirh has the gift of light too. His name means Death Shine, but his light cannot create. He is the bringer of death to everything malevolent or treacherous.'

'Is that why he is the only one wearing a silver armour?' Avery asked.

'Aye, Avery, it is a gift from the Goddess Arianrhod. It magnifies his light and his power to blind and defeats his enemies.'

'This explains a lot but still leaves many questions unanswered. For instance, why are you here? I am sure that you did not come to me tonight to explain all of this,' she stated, raising her eyebrows.

'No, in fact, you are right. I came to ease your mind by bringing you news about a significant development,' Darion replied.

'After I left you tonight, I remembered that Nissa once told me about hidden passages in Kilchurn Castle. So, I inquired if these passages could be used to get William and Maighread out. Nissa confirmed my suspicions and told me that these passages led out of the castle but had been flooded by the waters of Loch Awe many years ago. But don't fret; it does not present a problem for us, as we can ask the Goddess Coventina for help. Nissa agreed to lead William and his Ma through the passage up to the flooded part and call Coventina to drain the waters. That will allow them to reach the shore of Loch Awe where Asanopirh, Sorcha and I wait to take them to Inistrynich and onwards to Adelaide's cottage.'

'When are you planning to do that? Can I come, please?' Avery urged. 'I must know that they are okay.'

'We knew you would ask,' Darion said, unable to hide his smile. 'So, we agreed to take you along, but please keep it secret this time. We are leaving during the night of the Dark moon to make sure all captives are free and safe at the same time. Lady Arianrhod is going to wrap the castle in darkness until we reach the cottage, after which it no longer matters.'

'Oh, that is fantastic news!' Avery exclaimed. 'I'll be so happy to see Adelaide and the others. Thank you, Darion.'

'Go and rest now so you can focus on your training. And please, encourage your friends to do the same. Sleep well, Avery. I see you at sunrise,' he said and left.

18 The Dark Moon

Avery leapt out of her bed, bursting with energy and ran to wake her friends. She felt as if a halo of joy had surrounded her since she had heard last night's good news.

'Good morning out of bed, you guys! The sun is about to rise, and a great adventure awaits us.'

'Oy, miss sunshine, what's up? Who scattered your thunderclouds? Not that I mind, but your change of mood is spooky, to say the least.'

'Nothing up, Glen, but I realised last night that it is not an option to lose control if we want to set things right. We must put all our energy into the training so we can face every challenge that comes our way.'

'Aye Avery, that's the spirit!' called Keelin from the garden.

'Good morning, folks,' Darion greeted the friends. 'I hope you are ready, come on, pick up your gears and meet us in the glen.'

'Aye, but first, I need some food. See you there in a wink,' Glen replied as he washed his face.

The friends rushed through their breakfast, grabbed their weapons, and raced each other on the way to the glen. Out of breath but with fire in their bellies, they reached the training ground where Darion, Keelin, Aislinn, and Sorcha awaited them.

'Well, finally you are here, and all warmed up, I see, so let's begin. Hugh, you go with Sorcha and remember she doesn't speak your tongue, so you will have to follow her gestures and movements closely,' said Darion with a big smile on his face.

'Glen, come on, follow me, replied eagerly, following Keelin down to the river.

'Ursula, we will climb up into the rocks to have a good view, plenty of targets, and enough ammunition,' giggled Aislinn and waved Ursula to follow.

Hugh waited patiently for his turn and bowed to Sorcha to show her he was ready to follow her wherever she chose to take him. She acknowledged his readiness with a coy smile and gestured him to follow her into the woods.

'So that leaves the glen to us, Avery. And we will need it. You have to have free reign while you practice handling your swords. Shall we begin?'

'Aye, Darion, I am ready. Tell me what I have to do.' 'Draw your weapons and look at me,' he instructed.

'To fight with two swords, your movements have to be circular, fluid, evasive, and deceptive.' He began to spin his arms like the wings of a mill in a storm.

'The spiralling deflections will enable you to move lightning-fast and lead your opponents to anticipate a different attack entirely, thus making its reactions uncoordinated and leaving him to stumble. You never have to use smashing blows or crushing strikes because of the momentum you create by spinning. This motion lets you use elegant manoeuvres to deflect your opponents' blades while you drift back to score hits yourself. Are you ready to give it a try?'

'Aye, but you better stand back,' Avery warned. 'I don't know where I land once I start spinning. I might get dizzy and lose direction.'

'That's okay. We have the entire heath to ourselves this morning, so go ahead. Just make sure to hold your arms away from your body,' Darion replied as he lifted his swords as a precaution.'

Avery drifted like a whirlwind over the grassland, fast and soundless, the blades of her swords reflecting the sun and flashing like lightning as she performed the Dance that would bring certain death to any assailant. Darion was stunned. He had expected her to discover her inborn gift of swordsmanship quickly but could not have dreamed of such a high level of mastery.

'What's wrong, Darion?' she said, seeing his expression. 'What did I do wrong? Did I hold the swords at the wrong angle? Was my spinning uncoordinated? Shall I try again?'

It took Darion a moment to respond. 'No, you were unbelievable, Avery.

Your speed, balance, and grace are unsurpassed. All that's left for me to do is to show you defensive moves and how to fight with one sword in case you should drop one during a fight or get injured.'

'Really?' Avery said, not sure how to take the compliment. 'I never held a sword in my life before, but I always enjoyed Dancing and spinning.'

'Well, I see that your coordination and stance are flawless. Let's begin to engage in actual combat training,' replied Darion. He bowed deeply, raised his swords and opened Avery's first-ever sword fight.

Avery spun around Darion with swinging swords blocking all his attacks and even landing a few strikes. She felt strong and fearless. Her breath was deep and even. Her strides and spins were fluid and without effort.

Meanwhile, Ursula and Aislinn stood perched at the top of the rocks, preparing their weapons.

'Ursula, come on, lass, pick a target. Start with something big if you like. I just want to see what you have to offer,' Aislinn said.

'As you wish, Aislinn. What about the tree stump right next to Darion?' giggled Ursula. Without waiting for approval, she lifted her slingshot and fired.

'Oy, what you think you are doing?' shouted Darion as the pebble hit his sword. He turned around, looking for the attacker.

'Sorry, I just wanted to get your attention, Darion! I promise not to aim for you again,' shouted Ursula and could not suppress loud laughter.

'Well, I guess you showed me,' Aislinn remarked, impressed. 'So, let's try something a bit more demanding, shall we?'

'Bring it on,' Ursula replied in confidence. 'What do you have in mind?'

'Try to knock an apple off that tree without bruising it,' answered Aislinn with a broad grin.

'Aye, no problem. Any apple or do you have a favourite?' replied Ursula and winked at Aislinn with a mischievous smile. She aimed and hit the stem of an apple, sending it to the ground. Aislinn looked at Ursula with a Dazzled smile and patted her shoulder in approval.

'Marvellous shot Ursula. I could not have done it any better myself. I believe the only thing I can still teach you is what ammunition to use, how to find it, and how to collect it. So, let's have a look around for the right ammunition to mark, and finally, take out our targets.'

'Certainly, Aislinn, I am sure that there is a lot that I can learn from you about the right ammunition. Up to now, I only used whatever I could lay my hands on.'

'Good, so let's go down to the river and pick up some smooth and round pebbles. They are perfect for long-range targets,' said Aislinn, signalling Ursula to follow.

'Wow, Glen, which was a good blow!' shouted Ursula as she stepped out from behind a large boulder onto the riverbank. But it is rude to take your teacher out on your first Day of training.'

'Oy, don't distract him. This could cost him dearly,' replied Keelin. In an instant, he swung his staff and struck the back of Glen's knees, sending him into the river with a big splash.

'Crivens Ursula, why did you do that?' Glen shouted. 'Well, you looked hot, so I thought you could do with a cold dip!'

'Don't fuss, Glen. This was a good practice. It showed you that you need to focus and not allow anything or anyone to distract you in combat. This time you only got wet, but the next time it could cost you your life.'

'Aye right, thanks Keelin, for setting him straight. I only meant well,' chuckled Ursula. She continued to collect river pebbles for her target practice when she suddenly heard the hissing sound of an arrow and felt it graze her boot.

'Who did that?' exclaimed Ursula, casting a startled look around her.

'I did. I had to stop you from bothering my brother!' Hugh laughed.

'Are you out of your mind, Hugh? You could have killed me!'

'Only if I had my eyes closed, Mo Lennan .'

'Oh, I'll get you for this. Just wait! Where are you hiding anyhow? I can't see you.'

'Look up. See me now? I am in the ash tree, right across the river from you.'

'No!'

'Perfect, this means our training with Oren and Faerydae helped to improve my disguise.'

'Aye right, can we all go back to our training now, 'said Keelin interrupting their conversation and raising his staff to continue the mock fight with Glen. 'We don't have forever to get you ready for your quest,' he reminded them.

When the light faded, the friends and trainers returned to the palace to enjoy a hearty meal and wine while assessing their achievements.

'I have to say. You guys did very well. I've been astonished by your skills. We are now confident that you will be victorious in any combat and complete your quest. Slàinte mhath'! Cheered Darion and lifted his chalice.

'Slàinte mhath!' responded the round of friends, raising their goblets to drink to each other's health.

The friends celebrated their success late into the night.

Until they couldn't manage to stay up any longer and finally dropped exhausted but happy into their beds. Only Avery stayed awake. She sat at the edge of the fairy pond gazing at the stars.

'Good evening, Avery,' Ariana's voice appeared beside her. 'Why are you not in your bed? You should be exhausted after such an eventful day.'

'I am far too excited to sleep,' Avery said, pleased to see her. 'It won't be long now before we travel to Kilchurn Castle to free William, Maighread, and the others and move them to safety in Adelaide's cottage. It will be a wonderful night for us all, we will be able to share our experiences and plans, and most of all, we can celebrate the first defeat of our enemies.'

'Aye, that is a wonderful thought indeed. Nevertheless, you need your sleep, Avery. Why don't you come and join me? The warm water, weightlessness, and silence will help you to relax.'

'You are right,' Avery conceded, walking into the fairy pond. After only a few steps, she felt weightless and ethereal and began to float gently to the ground.

19 The Escape

This time, Avery kept the promise not to tell her friends about the night's intervention, which was quite an achievement since she was not good at keeping secrets. Finally, the time had come to leave the realm of the Seelie Court and travel down the River Awe to Kilchurn Castle.

'Is everyone asleep, Avery?' Darion asked.

'Aye, they'll sleep till late in the afternoon tomorrow. Laratbogh prepared a herbal tea that knocked them out like a bear in winter,' whispered Avery and could not stop giggling.

'Did you bring a Dagger, Avery?' 'Aye, Asanopirh, I have one in each boot just in case.'

'Good. Oh, and there is one more thing. We have to stay perfectly silent and use only hand signs when we enter Loch Awe until we return to the shore of Inistrynich.'

'Aye,' Avery replied. Climbed into the boat and helped Darion push off from the shore and into the deeper waters of the River Awe. Soon, they drifted swiftly with the current downstream, as if guided by an invisible hand.

Lady Arianrhod most certainly kept her promise. The world looked cloaked in black shrouds, Avery thought and felt a cold shiver run down her spine. She had to shake off this eerie feeling and break her silence.

'What do you know about Kilchurn Castle, Darion?'

'Well, the castle was built on the small island of Kilchurn by the young laird's father, Sir Colin Campbell, the first Lord of Glen Orchy,' Darion explained. 'At first, it was only a five-storey tower house and courtyard with an outer wall which could only be reached by a low-lying causeway. The causeway and the passages leading into the tower house were claimed by the water of Loch Awe soon after.'

'So, the tower house is where the laird keeps William, Maighread, Lady Julia, Anne, and Lucy?'

'Aye. Luckily, William and Maighread are kept in the chamber with hidden access to the passages. No one at the castle knows about it. No one used the passages since before the birth of the young Laird. The Goddess Coventina flooded them to punish Sir Colin Campbell after abducting Lady Julia and forcing her to marry him.'

'Oh, I understand, so the Goddess is helping us because of Lady Julia.'

'She is helping us to let the Laird feel the pain and sorrow so many had to endure because of his and his father's cruelties,' Darion said with a stern voice.

'Shortly after the death of his first wife, Sarah Mac Dougal, Sir Collin Campbell attempted to gain control over the lands of the Mac Arthur clan. When the coup failed, he kidnapped Julia Mac Arthur and forced her to marry him. He locked her in the tower house and only allowed her to walk in the courtyard under heavy guard. Their only child Duane was raised by his father, who poisoned his heart with hatred and fed him with lies so that he too would despise Julia.'

'I see now why the Goddess will punish the young Laird,' Avery said. 'He is just as cruel as his father. But I can't understand how my Da, I mean William, could be his friend. People even called them brothers, and now look what the Laird has done to his brotherly friend! He locked him and his mother in the tower.'

'Aye, Avery, but we are about to change all that. But let's stop talking. We are almost there,' Darion replied in a hushed voice, putting his hand over Avery's mouth to feel her nodding in agreement. Moments later, the boat bumped onto the shore of Kilchurn Island and made a crunching, scraping noise as the Waves began to push it further up onto the gravel-covered beach.

'Hurry, Darion, push the boat back into the water. We can't afford that anyone sees us now,' Asanopirh urged in a whisper.

'Aye, hand me the rope to pull the boat back in before I go and check the passage. William and Maighread should be there already.'

'Right, here you go,' Asanopirh replied, handing Darion the rope before the boat slipped silently back into the black water.

Darion had taken a few steps towards the passage when he saw the faint flickering of a torch upon the parapet. He reacted swiftly, pressing himself against the wall close to the tunnel's exit.

'William, are you there?' Darion whispered?

'Aye, we are coming. Who are you?'

'Never mind who I am. Kill the light and don't talk. The guards are right on top of us. You're almost out.'

There was no answer, and moments later, the light disappeared too.

'We're out. Come on, mother, we're safe.'

'Not quite yet,' Darion answered.

'Keep low and make no noise,' he instructed while pulling the boat back onto the shore.

'Climb on board and lay down,' Asanopirh whispered, taking Maighread's hands and helping her into the boat. Not much later, when they reached the middle of the loch, Sorcha stood up, lifted her arms, and called Lady Coventina to the darkened sky. The Goddess responded instantaneously. High waves rolled across the loch, crashed against the walls of Kilchurn Castle, and reclaimed the causeway and all the passages. Darion and Asanopirh lowered the oars into the water and rowed the boat onto Inistrynich.

'You can get up now and make your way to the carriage so that we can get you to Adelaide's cottage,' Avery while helping Maighread across the beach and onto the carriage. Only after everyone was seated, and the horses had pulled the carriage away from the beach did she take off her hood.

'Oh, dear, Avery, it is you! I am so happy to see you well and unharmed,' Maighread sighed, overwhelmed with joy and could no longer hold back tears.

'Ma, why are you crying. That's a happy occasion. We are reunited, free, and on our way to safety. Thank you, thank you whoever you are,' William whispered excitedly.

'You can thank us when we are inside the cottage. Until then, do not talk and keep yourself covered with these blankets,' Asanopirh replied, handing William the blankets Adelaide made. No one spoke as the carriage travelled over rough roads and sandy trails until Avery heard the familiar sound of the small brock in front of Adelaide's cottage.

'We are almost there, 'Avery cheered, lifting her blanket to survey the surroundings. Just then, she saw the door of the cottage open, and John and Bhaltair came running out to welcome William and Maighread.

'Oy, Avery, what a great surprise! Come in, come in, hurry up,' John called out and excitedly ushered Avery and Maighread into the cottage, where they were received with warm hugs and loud laughter.

'Oh, what a glorious moment! I am so relieved that you are here, Maighread. You have to tell us everything,' Adelaide rejoiced. 'Oh, my goodness, Avery, I did not expect you! Oh, my sweet lass, come here, let me hug you.'

'I had to come, Adelaide. I couldn't remain in Elfame and let Darion, Asanopirh, and Sorcha do all the work. I am so happy to see you all. We have so much to talk about, but wait, where are Julia, Anne, and Lucy?'

'The three arrived just before you and were drenched since they travelled by water. All of them are in your old room to change and put wee Lucy to bed. Oh, I still cannot believe that you all are here! Let's go into the kitchen Annette and Madge cooked up a storm.'

'Aye, I can smell it,' William replied. 'It smells heavenly, like mutton stew and fresh bread.'

'Aye right, and we got some ale as well! Come on, let's celebrate,' John cheered and pushed them gently into the kitchen, where Annette and Madge were waiting with tears in their eyes. After a heartfelt welcome, and when everybody finally sat at the table near the hearth, Adelaide lifted her cup to make a toast of thanks to Darion, Sorcha, Asanopirh, and Avery.

'Slàinte mhòr agus a h-uile beannachd duibh!'

'Mòran taing, Adelaide,' Asanopirh replied lifted his tankard and was about to take a sip when he heard a noise outside. He made eye contact with Darion and Sorcha and rushed out.

'Oh dear, I hope we didn't cause that,' Lady Julia exclaimed as she and Anne entered the kitchen.

'I don't think so. Come on, sit with us,' Adelaide answered, clearing space on the bench.

'How is Lucy?' Madge asked.

'She is sleeping soundly. I guess the excitement was too much for my granddaughter,' Julia answered with a smile.

'Anne, why don't you take a seat near the hearth? You're still shivering, my love.'

'Merci beaucoup, Adelaide,' Anne replied.

'Please, tell me what you said as we entered.'

'I made a toast of thanks to Darion, Asanopirh, Sorcha, and Avery, wishing them good health and every good blessing!'

'Let's go and see what's going on, guys,' Avery whispered and rushed out through the back door, followed by Darion and Sorcha.

'Oh dear, it's Harris. No need to be alarmed,' Avery sighed, walking up to the carriage where Asanopirh and Harris stood talking in a hushed voice.

'Why aren't you coming inside? I am sure that it is not all that safe out here. How did you even get past that bridge Harris,' Avery asked?

'I am not malicious, nor do I practise Dark magic, so I have no problem coming here. But I was quite surprised when Asanopirh came out of nowhere and stopped my carriage. He just gave me a rundown of all the happenings while I was gone when you showed up.'

'Where have you been all this time, Harris,' Avery pressed on?

'I went to France to stock up on some wine and visit Adelaide's brother, my old friend, the Earl of Douglas. You can imagine my surprise when Asanopirh told me that Archibald's Daughter is not only alive but also has a child and is right here at Adelaide's cottage.'

'Aye, I can well imagine how you must have felt. Adelaide will be so happy to hear from her brother. What a great night!

Come on in, Harris, don't let her wait,' Avery said with a smile.

'Hold on. I need a moment to compose myself before I face Adelaide,' Harris replied.

'What do you mean? You are her best friend. Surely she will be overjoyed to see you.'

'Aye, but the joy will be short-lived. I'm afraid I have sad news for her. Her brother is very ill and may not live to see the summer.'

'Oh no, how terrible! We must get Anne to him right away so that he can die in peace, knowing his daughter is alive and well and that he has a granddaughter.'

'Aye, which is what Asanopirh and I were just talking about. Let's go and continue inside. There is no way around it. I must tell Adelaide and Anne,' Harris sighed, opened the door and stepped inside.

'Oh, good, you are back. What was it?' Adelaide called across the sitting room, looking anxiously at Darion and Avery.

'We brought you a visitor, Adelaide,' Avery said as she stepped aside, revealing Harris behind her.

'My goodness, Harris, how wonderful! Adelaide exclaimed joyfully and embraced him.

'We have good news. You will never believe what happened since you left.'

'I know Adelaide, Asanopirh filled me in. But I also bring news,' he said softly. 'Come, let's sit down and talk.'

'Aye, I can hardly wait! Tell me, how is my brother? Is he finally coming to visit this summer, or did he come up with another excuse?' Adelaide said with a laugh.

Harris kneeled in front of Adelaide, took her hands and said, 'Adelaide, I am afraid I have bad news for you. Archibald is very ill and does not have long to live. He asked me to bring you home to spend the remaining Days at his side.'

Adelaide's face dropped, her eyes were wide in terror, and tears ran down her cheeks.

'Adelaide, I am so sorry to bring you this dreadful news on a day that was supposed to be joyous and free of fret. Forgive me,

Mo Ghràdh,' Harris whispered, wiping away her tears.

'I am alright, Harris, don't fret about me,' she said, composing herself. 'The Day had to come. After all, Archibald is ten years older than I am, and he has not been in good health ever since Margaret passed. But it will be hard for Anne. We must get her back to Touraine as fast as we can. You must get her on a ship Harris. You know all the captains that sail to France.'

'Aye, Adelaide, but the Laird posted armed men at all ports. He is desperately looking for Avery and Ursula. You can be sure that all hell breaks loose once he finds out that his captives are gone.' Harris said solemnly. 'We must act quickly. Go and inform Anne. I will see what we can do with the help of the elves.' Harris got up, kissed Adelaide on the forehead and left for the barn.

20 The Revelation

Adelaide was devastated. The news of her brother's failing health had knocked the wind out of her leaving her unable to speak. Streams of tears ran down

her cheeks. She wished that she could stop the dismal mix of grief and frustration strangling her. But her anguish intensified when she thought about how to bring the news to Anne.

She dried her tears and told herself that the time to grieve would come but that she now needed to be strong for Anne. With that thought, she walked into the kitchen, where Anne was joyously celebrating her newfound freedom.

'Adelaide, there you are! We were wondering where you went. What's wrong, you look pale?' Annette asked. 'I am fine,' replied Adelaide. She cleared her throat to stop her voice from trembling. 'I need to talk to Anne alone. Would you all please excuse us? It will not take long.'

'Of course, come on, folks,' John replied, ushering everybody out of the kitchen and closing the door.

'What's the matter, Auntie? Did Harris bring bad news?'

'Aye Anne, he brought news from Touraine, and I am afraid it is not good. Your father is dying and wants me to return to be at his side when his time comes,' she said solemnly.

'I would love to fulfil his wish, I but don't know how to get past the Laird's men. The ports are under surveillance, and every ship is searched before departure. I am so sorry, Anne.'

'No, this can't be true,' Anne cried out, shaking her head in denial. 'I was hoping to return to Touraine with Lucy to live with him, and now you're telling me that he is dying and that I can't get to him?' her voice shook through her tears.

'Harris and the elves are in the barn discussing all the options and will do everything to get you home in time, so please don't despair. If there is any way to get you home, trust that they will find it.'

Anne was unable to speak and huddled in her chair. Her skin had turned pale, her eyes had glazed over like lifeless mirrors and reflected the despair and hopelessness she felt. Harris returned a moment later and called out to Adelaide.

'I need to speak to you and Anne. I believe we have found a way around the laird's men.'

'Aye Harris, we are coming,' Adelaide answered and rushed into the sitting room, followed by Anne.

'We decided that I'll ride to Inistrynich before sunrise and make sure that Asanopirh's boat is well hidden, then I make my way to Dallmally to see what the Laird is up to. Avery and the elves will return to Elfame and gather their friends to guard us on our journey.'

Anne wiped the tears violently off her cheeks and gathered the strength to speak.

'What exactly did you plan, Harris? And is it safe? Please remember that we have Lucy with us. We can't afford to lose her too.'

'Aye Anne, it will be safe,' Harris answered, leaning over, resting his hands on her shoulders.

'We thought that Lady Julia should come as well. She will not be safe here as long as her son rules over the land. She had been locked away for far too long to remain trapped in the cottage.'

'You should not decide on Julia's fate Harris. That is up to her, but, and as you know, there is another way to keep her safe,' Adelaide whispered, looking Harris straight in the eye and nodded.

'Aye, I know. I agree the time has come,' Harris replied. He got up and disappeared into Adelaide's workshop.

'Well, now you all heard the news Harris brought from my brother,' Adelaide announced to the room. 'We must get Anne, Lucy, and Lady Julia out of here.'

'Aye, Adelaide, and we want to help. But how? We can't very well leave the cottage when the Laird has placed a price on our heads,' John said in despair.

'Don't fret, John. I know you all have a heart of gold. We will be okay, and if things go well, Anne, Lucy and Lady Julia will be on their way to France by the next full moon.'

'Aye Adelaide, that's right,' Harris interjected as he re-entered the sitting room with a roll of parchment in his hand.

'You all know that I have many friends in the maritime business, so I will be able to find a small cargo ship to take us to France soon enough. I will arrange for the ship to anchor in Loch Etive to take the lassies and me board and to the port of Rochelle. If the winds are with us, we should be able to get to Archibald in time so he can go in peace with his Daughter and grandchild at his side,' he said, handing the parchment to Adelaide.

'Thank you, Harris. I know you will do your utmost best to reach him before his time has come,' Adelaide sighed. She began to unroll the parchment.

'You might be wondering what this is all about,' Adelaide addressed the group, holding up the parchment. 'Well, I think the time has come to reveal a long-held secret and to release Harris, Maighread and myself from an ode we swore to Lady Sarah Mac Dougal thirty-five years ago.' She took a breath, looked to Harris and Maighread firmly, and continued.

'Lady Sarah asked us on her deathbed to keep the existence of Lord Collin's firstborn son secret until he would be old enough to claim his land and title as the heir of the Dukedom of Glen Orchy.'

'But why? Bhaltair asked. Didn't the child die together with his mother that night?'

'No, the child did not die. Please hear me out. I'll tell you what happened on the winter solstice night in the year 1187. Lord Collin insisted he did not want a Dougal to inherit his land and commanded Marianne, the midwife, to kill the boy as soon as Lady Sarah was dead.

He ordered me to take care of the body. You may remember that this was a forced marriage after the Campbell clan had lost a land dispute with the MacDougal's. Anyhow, we could not bring ourselves to kill this child and vowed to Lady Sarah to hide and take care of him. She wrote a sworn testimony that the child was Lord Collin's rightful heir and sealed it with her ring before she died. This document cannot be challenged as Lord Collin had ordered the ring that bore her seal to be destroyed moments after she died,' Adelaide declared and rested the parchment on the table.

'So, whatever happened to the boy?' John inquired after a moment of silence.

'He sits right here,' Maighread said, pointing to William. 'The midwife, Harris, and Adelaide brought him to me on the night of the Winter Solstice, just after my new-born son had died. They asked me to raise him as my own and never to reveal who he truly is.'

'Ma, are you saying that I am not your son?'

'Aye, William,' Maighread replied with quivering lips. 'You are Lady Sarah's son, the Laird's heir and elder brother of Duane.'

'He is not,' Lady Julia interjected with gritted teeth. 'Duane is not Collin Campbell's son. He is the son of the one you all call The Stranger,' she whispered.

'Hold it, are you telling me that you knew all along that Duane is not the rightful Laird? John exclaimed angrily, studying her face with caution. 'And you did nothing, all this time?'

Julia shrugged her shoulders and spoke with a broken voice. 'I could not tell Collin the truth. He would have killed us both. I did not care for my life. I have lived locked up behind the tower's walls from the Day he abducted me, but I could not risk my son's life, so I kept silent.'

'How on earth could you have fallen in love with such an evil man like Lord MacNab and have a child for him?'

'He was the only one that Dared to visit me, John,' Julia replied weakly. 'He treated me kindly and with respect, took care of my injuries and bruises whenever Collin had beaten me for not giving him an heir. He brought me flowers and messages from my family. So, I fell in love with him. Then, one Day, Collin grew suspicious and sent him to the mines of Wemyss. I never saw him again, and when Duane was born eight months later, Collin told everyone that I had died in childbirth. Dougal's heart broke, and he swore to take revenge on all members of the Campbell clan until his last breath. He does not know that I am alive and that Duane is our son.'

'Oh dear, please forgive me, Julia, how painful for you to live locked up and without love for so many years,' apologised John.

'I am so glad that we could free you, Julia, and I promise to keep you safe from here on,' Adelaide said.

'Thank you, Adelaide, and thank you all, I never thought that the day would come when I could leave Kilchurn as a free woman.'

'Well, we better make sure that you will stay free and unharmed by removing Duane from Kilchurn castle and our lands,' Bhaltair said, rising defiantly.

'Slow down, Bhaltair, we have to get Anne, Lucy and Julia to France before we can reveal William as the rightful Laird,' Harris said.

'Aye, and we have to ask William if he wants to claim his title,' John said.

'Thank you, John,' William said softly, speaking for the first time since the truth had been revealed. He picked up the parchment delicately and began to examine it.

'You will see that your lineage and claim cannot be disputed. The document was registered and certified by the Third High Stewart of Lothian, Walter Fitz Alan, shortly after being instated in 1214. And here is your mother's ring,' said Adelaide as she handed

William Lady Sarah's ring that bore the seal of the MacDougall clan.

'How is that possible? You said the Laird ordered the ring to be destroyed?'

'Aye, just as he ordered to you kill you, but we saved you and your mother's ring.'

'So, with all that settled, my dear friends, let's focus on our task at hand to take our three lovelies to France,' Harris said, trying to lift the mood.

'Aye, Harris, and to do all this, we will need a clear head. Let's call it a day and go to bed,' Adelaide suggested.

'I agree. Let's go to bed. Guit nuit to you all,' Harris replied, kissing Adelaide before leaving the cottage.

'Where is he going, and where are the elves and Avery,' Anne asked, looking around nervously.

'Harris is sleeping in the barn, so not wake us when he is leaves in the morning. Avery and her friends have left already, so you go and get a good rest. Guit nuit,' Adelaide said and kissed Anne on the forehead.

21 Hope and Sorrow

Avery had not spoken a word since they left Adelaide's cottage. Too many thoughts tumbled through her mind. The guys will never believe half the things that happened tonight. It's just mind-boggling. But I am relieved we could get everybody out of the castle unnoticed, she thought as she stumbled sleepily through the forest of Elfame.

'It's been a long night, Avery. You better go and take a rest. You look as if you are sleepwalking. We'll be back later to discuss our journey,' Darion said as they reached the great hall of the palace,

'Aye, Darion, I am exhausted. I hope the tea has not lost its effect yet, so Ursula and the lads are still sleeping. See you later,' Avery replied, as she shuffled into her bed-chamber. With her last bit of strength, she managed to kick off her boots just before she dropped dead tired onto her bed. She slept like a log until Ursula shook her awake late in the afternoon.

'Wake up, Avery! I can't explain what happened, but we slept through most of the Day and missed our training.'

'Never mind about the training. We have more important things to take care of.'

'More important than our training? You must be kidding. What could be more important?'

'You're about to find out. Just get the lads out of bed and meet me in the garden. I'll explain everything to you there.'

'Aye, right if you say so,' answered Ursula and left to wake Hugh and Glen.

'Oh man, why do we have to get up this early? It's still Dark!' Glen grumbled as he stumbled drowsily out of the palace.

'Oh, dear Glen, it is not still Dark. It is getting Dark again,' replied Avery with a mischievous smile.

'Blimey, what's up with all the excitement? What could have happened while we were sleeping?' Hugh asked through a yawn.

'Well, not all of us were so lucky to sleep till now. Darion, Sorcha, Asanopirh, and I got William and Maighread out of Kilchurn Castle last night and brought them safely to Adelaide,' Avery explained.

'Why didn't you wake us? I thought we agreed to do everything together, especially as it involves our parents! And what about Anne, Lucy and Lady Julia?' Hugh asked angrily.

'Aye, Hugh, you are right. We did agree. But it was safer to go in a small group this time. And you can relax, it all went smoothly, everybody is safe and in good spirits. But we received some troubling news last night which makes it necessary for Anne, Lucy, and Lady Julia to sail to France as soon as possible.'

'I don't understand anything anymore. Wouldn't the three be just as safe at Adelaide's as our parents are?'

'Of course, they would, but that's not the reason Hugh. I am afraid Anne's Da is dying, so you will understand that we have to act quickly. Harris left for Dalmally this morning to get hold of the captain he sailed with from France. His ship is due to return to Rochelle soon. If he is willing to take them, we will have to guard them on their way to Loch Etive, where they will board the ship.'

'Good, finally some action, so when are we leaving?' Hugh said.

'As soon as Cait Sith comes to get us. I hope it will be soon since there is another issue we need to tackle once the three are safely on their way to France.'

'Aye, we know, we have to free your father and all the girls,' Glen said.

'Right, Glen, that's part of it,' Avery nodded. But we have to unseat the young Laird before we can do that.'

'Hang on, do what? How are we going to topple the Laird? Do you want the sheriff to come for us?'

'The sheriff might even help us! Duane is not the rightful Laird. William is. Let me tell you the whole story right from the beginning.' Avery said and began to tell her friends what she had learned during the night at Adelaide's cottage. Her friends were just as bewildered by what they heard as she had been. It certainly was hard to believe that everything they thought to be true turned out to be an elaborate deception. The friends were still busy discussing Lady Julia's revelation of the Lairds' true ancestry when Darion arrived, accompanied by Asanopirh. 'By the looks of your puzzled expressions, I gather that Avery told you about last night's events, I understand that it must have come as quite a shock to you, but you have to shake it off so we can focus on our journey to Loch Etive,' said Darion wasting no time.

'Aye, right, Darion, what's the plan?' Hugh asked, looking at him in great anticipation.

'You guys must secure the riverbanks to make sure that the Laird's men wouldn't launch an ambush on us on the way to Loch Etive,' Darion explained.

'Aye, no problem at all. So how soon will we be leaving? And have you considered the sea change?' Glen inquired.

'Aye, Glen, we are hoping to make the journey during the night of the next full moon so that we can catch the high tide,' Asanopirh nodded.

'This sounds good, but won't the bright moonlight make you an easy target once you row out to the ship?' Hugh asked with a look of concern.

'We thought of that. That's why we asked the Selkies to pull the dinghy through the Loch and to Oban's outer harbour, where the ship will be waiting for them with set sails. So even if the Laird's men see them, there is no way that anyone could catch up with them.'

'So, if all goes well, they should be on their way to France before sunrise,' Hugh said, satisfied with the plan. 'Now then, let's hear what exactly you want us to do?'

'We need you to guard the rugged riverbank on our right, together with Sorcha, Ursula, and Aislinn, while Avery, Glen, Ghilli Duh, and the Dryads protect the wooded shore on our left,' Asanopirh explained. 'We have to be extremely vigilant since we have no idea what to expect. Always keep in mind that Lord MacNab' commands not only the Laird's men but also a group of Red Caps, and I am sure that you know what to expect of them,' he warned.

'Aye, we do, but tell me how you expect us to keep up with the boat? The river runs faster than we possibly can, especially on the stony riverbanks and through the thickets.'

'Aye, right, Hugh, but you don't need to fret, the boat will be pulled and controlled by a group of Ashrays, and they will make sure to keep in line with you.'

'Brilliant, then let's not waste time with discussions. Let's go to get more combat practice. It would be good to learn how to move and fight in total Darkness,' suggested Glen.

'Aye, nothing wrong with that, but keep in mind that we will be out there during the full moon. I asked Oren and Bilobeal to show you how to disguise yourself. Oh, and Bilobeal is going to bring your armours so that you can train fully fitted by tomorrow.'

'Oh, wow, so he kept his promise, that's brilliant. I can't wait to try it on,' Hugh exclaimed excitedly over the news.

'Aye, neither can I, my dear brother. But before we get too excited, let's look for some food. I am starving. I haven't had any food all day,' replied Glen, rushing inside. 'Do you ever think of anything other than food, goodness gracious!' shouted Ursula as she followed Glen into the palace.

'Oh dear, Glen loves food far too much. I better go and help Ursula stop him from stuffing himself again,' said Avery with a sigh and left.

'Hugh, can I have a word with you, please?' Darion said, signing him to stop before he could join the others.

'Sure, Darion, what is it?'

'I would like Ursula and you to meet Bilobeal at Ben Lomond so that he can show you how to move fast and safe over rugged terrain and how to signal the others if it becomes necessary.

You will have a better perspective to see the wooded bank. Our beloved Goddess, Arianrhod, will watch your group. She will circle above you in the shape of a large owl, and trust me when I say that she doesn't miss a thing. She can even see the Darkness of the mortal soul.'

'Crivens, I did not know that she could become visible for a mortal's eye,' Hugh said in wonder.

'Oh, you saw her before, at the lake when she guided us as the Northern Light.'

'Wow, which was Lady Arianrhod? Well, she is truly magnificent. Alright, I am ready to get Ursula. What about Aislinn and Sorcha?'

'They'll join you later,' said Darion. He walked into the palace to talk to Avery and Glen while Hugh and Ursula picked up their weapons and left to meet Bilobeal.

'Goodnight, Hugh and Ursula, my bonnie lass, it is nice to see you again,' Bilobeal greeted them as they arrived. 'I heard that the time for some action has come, at last, so let me begin by giving you some important information about the art of disguise.'

'Aye, Bilobeal. That be great. Ursula replied that we hadn't had the chance to practice between rocks yet.

'But I am sure Laratbogh and Oren would have told you that you mortals have a distinct shape by which your enemies can easily recognise you. I'll show you how to obscure your form by tucking grass and bramble in your hair and clothes and how to cover your hands and face with charcoal, ash, or mud so that you blend in with your surroundings.'

'Yikes, must we do that? My hands are okay, but I really don't like mud or charcoal in my face and hair.'

'Oh, come on, Ursula, it will look good on you! In fact, why don't we test it out?' said Hugh and picked up a hand full of stone dust.

'Don't you Dare Hugh, or I kick your behind up and down the rocks,' she threatened.

'Well, in case she does, it most certainly would be good to know what you have to do when you meet an obstacle,' said Bilobeal, laughing as he slapped Hugh on the shoulder.

'Well, let me tell you what to do in such a situation. Always try to avoid climbing over obstacles by all means. But if you have no choice, then you must keep your body in line with its top to prevent showing yourself against the sky,' said Bilobeal and turned around to face Ursula. 'And as for you, Ursula, my bonnie lass, I'm afraid you will have to cover your face. But you can use wood ash instead of mud. It's almost as if you were powdering your face. Here you go,' Bilobeal explained, reaching her a small satchel filled with ash. Ursula looked at the satchel with disgust and reluctantly covered her hair, face, and hands.

'I like that look on you, Ursula. You should do that all the time from now on,' Hugh said, cracking up with laughter.

'Oh, that did it,' Ursula yelled. Dropped the satchel and chased him up and down the hillside until she suddenly tripped and fell.

'Are you okay, Ursula?' Hugh called out in shock and rushed over to help her.

'Aye, I am okay, but what did I trip over? I placed my steps so carefully,' wondered Ursula and began to search for what had caused her fall.

'I found it!' she exclaimed, picking up a shiny object. 'But what the heck is a water flask doing here between the rocks?'

'A flask? Let me see lass,' Bilobeal inquired and hurried over to where she stood.

'Aye, which is a flask carried by the Laird's man. So, they were here and might even still be around. Let's be careful and only communicate by hand signs,' Bilobeal whispered, signalling Ursula and Hugh to crouch low and follow him.

The three advanced slowly, hidden by the shadows of passing clouds and behind large boulders, when Ursula suddenly noticed smoke rising from a campfire close to the shoreline of the loch. She tapped Hugh and Bilobeal on the shoulder and pointed to what she discovered. Bilobeal nodded and signalled for her, hiding behind a boulder, while he and Hugh moved closer to the shore. Ursula's heart was pounding like a blacksmith's hammer, and her hands began to shake. Crivens, we could have stumbled right into them, she thought and began to collect small pebbles for her slingshot while glancing over the top of the boulder now and then, making sure that Bilobeal and Hugh were safe. But she could not see them and was about to leave her hiding place to take a closer look when she suddenly heard stones rolling down on the slope behind her. She loaded her slingshot and positioned herself to fire when Sorcha appeared silently in front of her, followed by Aislinn.

Ursula placed a finger on her lips, signalling them not to speak, and pointed to where Bilobeal and Hugh had disappeared. Sorcha nodded, readied her bow, and rushed with lightning speed down to the shore without making the faintest sound. Aislinn loaded her slingshot and signalled Ursula to follow. The two moved cat-like, gracefully down the slope until they could see seven men sitting around a fire at the shore of Loch Lomond.

'What are you doing here? Didn't Bilobeal tell you to stay hidden and wait?' whispered Hugh behind a nearby boulder.

'Oh, hush Hugh, why should you have all the action?' mouthed Ursula and began to walk further when a firm hand gripped her wrist and pulled her back.

'Ursula, my bonnie lass, didn't I ask you to wait?' Bilobeal said in a hushed tone. You hear that this is not the time to get reckless and take unnecessary risks, you hear? We have to get back to the palace now and change our plan. Come on.'

'Aye Bilobeal, alright. But don't we have to wait for Sorcha? She went down to the shore to look for you.'

'I know I saw her and asked her to return to the palace and alert everyone, so let's go. Hugh, come on, lad, let's hurry. We need to act swiftly now.'

'Hugh, what happened? What did you see?' asked Ursula nervously.

'It's not what we saw. It's what we heard, Ursula. It makes me extremely sad and furious at the same time. Let's not talk about it now. We have to hurry back and tell the others, come on,' Hugh declared. He took Ursula's hand and started to run.

When Hugh and Ursula reached the palace, they were surprised to see that everybody had already assembled and awaited their arrival with heightened anxiety. Ursula could not imagine what Hugh and Bilobeal could have overheard down at the loch to merit all this excitement. She shook it off as an overreaction and walked across the hall to get some water. That's when she noticed that everybody was fully armed and ready to storm out at a moment's notice.

'What did you hear, Hugh? I am getting anxious now. Did anything happen to our parents? Come on, tell me, tell me now,' she urged.

'Sit down, Ursula. Bilobeal is about to share what we heard with all of you,' Hugh said, trying to calm his voice.

'Where is he? I don't see him anywhere. Where did he go, Hugh?' Ursula asked, looking around the hall nervously. Moments later, Bilobeal entered the Great Hall accompanied by four other Drows carrying large, heavy bags.

'Dear friends, you might be wondering why I sent Sorcha to call you to arms. But as it seems, the Day to fight has come earlier than we expected. Sorcha surely told you that we discovered a group of the Laird's men at the shore of Loch Lomond and were able to overhear their conversation. And I am afraid what we heard is very troubling indeed.'

'Oh, for goodness sake, what did you hear? Please, Bilobeal, spit it out.'

'Aye, Avery, I will, but please brace yourself for some truly terrible news. The same goes for you, Ursula, me bonnie lass,' he said before continuing.

'At first, we thought these lads were boasting about their romances, but we soon recognised the names and realised that they were talking about Marianne the midwife and her Brownie Nissa.'

'What did they say, and how could they have known about Nissa?' ask Laratbogh.

'Well, according to one of the men, Nissa was discovered at the castle shortly after a chambermaid alerted the Laird to the disappearance of Anne, Lucy, Lady Julia and the other two captives. All guards were called to search the castle grounds at once, but all they found was a strangely coloured rooster in the courtyard.'

'Oh no, please tell me that they were unable to catch her,' Laratbogh said, a look of despair washing over her face.

'I am so sorry, Laratbogh, they were. One of the maids knew that Brownies shapeshift into a rooster if they are in danger of being seen by mortals, and she knew that this rooster was Marianne's Brownie. They killed her and brought the beheaded rooster to Marianne, who collapsed at the sight of Nissa.'

'So, what happened to Marianne?' Avery asked.

'They took her to the castle and tortured her until she told them that they were at Adelaide's cottage. The Laird sentenced her to hang in the market square by the next full moon and readied himself and a group of soldiers to raid the cottage by nightfall,' Bilobeal explained solemnly. So, you understand the urgency for action.'

'Aye, Bilobeal, you are right. We have to act swiftly even though the cottage is impregnable, but it is high time to show the Laird that he is not all-powerful. Avery, Hugh, Glen, Ursula, put on your amours and let us pick up our weapons. We will show the Laird his boundaries.' Asanopirh exclaimed.

22 The First Encounter

Usually, Avery hid her emotions well by keeping her face blank. But today was different. The anger and fear that welled up inside her began to show. Her eyes were narrowed and cold, and her lips had tightened. A chill of apprehension washed over her as she stepped out from under the small bridge to make her way to Adelaide's Cottage to deliver the heart-breaking news.

'Are you all right, Avery?'

'I am fine, Darion. It's only the lack of sleep. You don't have to fret about me.'

'I'm worried. You're pale, and you are trembling. When this is over, you must rest.'

'Asanopirh, Oren just saw a group of soldiers rushing through the glade. We have to act swiftly now. We can't afford to hesitate,' shouted Bilobeal.

'Aye, we're coming. You best stay at the bridge. I'll send you Hugh and Glen to observe the situation,' replied Asanopirh.

'Are you ready, Avery, or would you rather secure the cottage?' whispered Sorcha in a soft and measured voice.

'No, Sorcha, I am ready to face the Laird and his men. After all, this is what we trained for,' said Avery with cold determination, signalling her friends to follow.

We have chosen the right time to return to the Cottage. Avery thought as she watched the evening mist spreading over the Cottage. The woods supplied perfect cover as Elves took position around the Cottage and on top of the barn. Ghilli Duh, Oren, and Laratbogh lined up at the edge of the forest, ready to take on any intruder who Dared to approach the Cottage.

'Avery and Ursula, please go inside and brief everybody about the latest development. And please make certain that they sit tight. Tell them to keep up their routine, so our visitors remain unaware of our presence,' Asanopirh instructed.

'Aye, what about Hugh and Glen? Shouldn't they accompany us?' Avery asked.

'No, the lads are securing the brook and the bridge with Bilobeal and his men. Go, go now,' said Asanopirh and sank back into the mist.

Avery and Ursula heard Adelaide talking to Annette as they approached the Cottage.

'This is the strangest weather. How can we have such dense fog after all the sunshine we had today?'

'You are right, Adelaide, it is very unusual, and it appeared out of nowhere. I've never seen anything like it before,' Annette remarked.

'Shush, hold it,' Adelaide stopped her. 'Did you hear this?'

'Hear what?'

'It sounded as if the back door opened. Is that you, Madge?'

'I am right here,' Madge replied. I just put the kettle on the fire for some tea. What's the matter?'

'Where are John and Bhaltair?' 'They went to the barn to check on

the animals.'

'Well, then we have a problem. I could swear that I heard the back door open. Let's hope the enchantments haven't been compromised,' whispered Adelaide.

She walked up to the fireplace, picked up the poker, and lifted it over her head, ready to strike.

'You can put the poker down. It's just us,' said Avery as she walked into the sitting room.

'Goodness, you gave us quite a scare, Avery. How come that you are back so soon, and who is that with you?' Adelaide asked.

'We are all here, Adelaide, Ursula is at the back door, and the lads are at the brook. The Drows, the Elves, Ghilli Duh, and the Dryads came as well.'

'What happened? I thought we took care of everything and covered all of our tracks?' Annette said worriedly.

'Unfortunately, we didn't. It looks as though our worst fears have come true. The Laird and his man are on their way to storm the Cottage and capture anyone they find,' answered Avery trying to avoid Annette's frightened stare.

'Why? What has caused him to do that?' asked Anne in a trembling voice.

'Nissa was recognised by one chambermaid as she was trying to leave the castle. They killed her and then went to Marianne's home and arrested and tortured her until she gave you all away. The Laird accused her of treason and condemned her to hang on the eve of the next full moon,' said Avery biting her lip to stop herself from crying.

The women were paralysed and stared at Avery with wide eyes as they heard the news about Nissa and Marianne.

'Say it isn't so, please. Nissa can't be dead,' pleaded Anne, reaching out to Avery for support.

'I am so very sorry, Anne,' said Avery. She embraced Anne, who was shaking violently with grief.

'This is terrible news, yes, but we cannot allow ourselves to fall apart now. The Laird and his men are on their way to get us too, but we will not let them succeed. Annette, you go and call the men in from the barn. Best tell them to bring more firewood not to look suspicious. Madge, continue making the tea. We all could do with some calming lavender,' said Adelaide in a surprisingly calm and collected voice.

'Don't fret about us, Avery. We have prepared ourselves for all eventualities. Annette and Madge have braced themselves for a moment like this and should be able to stop John and Bhaltair from flaring up. Focus on what you have to do, and don't forget that many enchantments protect the Cottage.'

'Aye, Adelaide, I hope that they are as strong as we all think they are since we will be under attack soon,' Avery said.

'I think we got a message from the elves. The smoke from the kitchen fire just turned red!' called Madge from the hearth.

'Aye, that's a sign from Sorcha. It means that the Laird and his men have arrived. Goodness, where are John and Bhaltair? They should be in here now,' shouted Avery and ran to the back door, through which Annette and the two men appeared.

'Crivens, Avery, you came back quickly. Oh Ursula, my bonnie lass, you are here too. How wonderful! Come here, hug your old Da,' laughed John and embraced his Daughter.

'Bhaltair asked Avery and Ursula about their heavy amours but stopped mid-sentence when he saw flaming arrows soaring towards the cottage.'

'We'll explain later,' Ursula said in a rushed voice. 'You all better go into the kitchen now. Stay there and lock the doors until we come back to get you.'

'But Ursula!'

'Da, please, we know what we are doing, and we are not alone. Ma come hold Da,' said Ursula as soon as they had safely entered the Cottage. She slammed the door closed and leaned against it with all her weight. The Day they had feared had finally come. Please, Lady Coventina, protect this house, Ursula thought while looking with Avery. Both girls nodded and took position behind the windows.

Hugh climbed onto the parapet wall of the small bridge. He stood upright, with his bow drawn, ready to fire while Glen had poised himself in the middle of the bridge's arch prepared to charge, but nothing had happened after the first flaming arrows did not reach across the brook.

'Why are they just standing there staring at us?' Hugh asked cautiously. 'Are they afraid?'

'No, they can't see you. Powerful enchantments protect the Cottage and the land surrounding it.' Bilobeal reminded them. 'Did you think that I would have you two standing there if they could see you?'

'Oh, I hadn't thought of that. But if that is so, then why did we even come? I thought we were needed for protection.'

'To teach the Laird not to attack anyone under the protection of the Queen of Elfame,' chuckled Bilobeal.

'You can lower your weapons, lads. You are up here to see and to listen to their conversation. It would be good to get a little closer, but under no circumstances step off the bridge. Do you understand?'

'Aye Asanopirh, alright. Let's go and listen to their bramble, my dear brother,' whispered Hugh. He jumped down from the parapet wall and relaxed his arms.

'What is wrong with your men?' they heard an angry voice say. 'They are useless drunkards, all of them.'

Even though they had never seen him, the brothers recognised at once that this was the Laird.

'But my Lord, it wasn't their fault. It's magic. Remember that the people in the village say that the weaver is using magic,' another man pleaded, trembling with fear.

'I'll show you magic. Hand me my bow, Sean,' shouted the Laird. He pulled an arrow from the fire and aimed it at the Cottage. Everybody's eyes followed the arrows high arch expecting it to land on the Cottage's roof and set it on fire. Instead, it disappeared into thin air just as all the others before.

'That's impossible. Hand me another arrow,' the Laird said in denial. Hurry, don't just stand there,' he screamed! His face was red hot as he kept trying to set fire to Adelaide's home. Yet he couldn't manage even to get one of the arrows to cross the brook.

'Blood bas! He screamed, throwing the bow into the fire. He mounted his horse in raging fury and galloped right through a crowd of his men, injuring everyone who couldn't get out of his way fast enough.

'What a brut! Oh, I would love to pull him off his horse and give him a few gentle touches with my staff,' said Glen bursting with anger.

'Glen, look, one of the soldiers stopped his horse,' Hugh interrupted his brother, 'He is either extremely brave or damn stupid.'

'Aye, but it seems he has a message for the Laird. Can you hear anything?'

'No, let's watch them close. Maybe we'll be able to figure out what he had to say.'

Glen and Hugh didn't have to wait long. Moments later, one of the Laird's men broke out of the brushwood, pushing and shoving an older man in front of him.

'Crivens, that's Harris!' Hugh exclaimed. 'Why did he come. He should have known better! Damn, what was he thinking?'

'Maybe he didn't know. I am sure the Laird did not announce what he was up to. It doesn't matter either way. We have to get him out of there,' Glen said. He was about to step off the bridge when Hugh grabbed his tunic and dragged him frantically back across the bridge.

'Glen, are you blooming mad! Have you forgotten what Asanopirh said? We can't leave the bridge!' shouted Hugh. 'Let's tell the others. There must be a way to free Harris.'

'For a moment, I thought you had gone mad. What on earth's name were you thinking, lad?' shouted Bilobeal.

'That's just it, Bilobeal. He wasn't thinking,' Glen said. 'He saw Harris being pushed around by the Lairds men and lost it.'

'Aye, but one more step, and you would have been pushed around too. You have to keep calm and controlled and not allow your rage to control you, Glen. Let's go up to the elves and see what we can do,' said Bilobeal signalling his men to surround Hugh and Glen to make sure they wouldn't do anything reckless.

'What's up? Why did you leave your posts?' Asanopirh asked when he saw Hugh, Glen, and the Drows approaching the Cottage.

'The Laird just took Harris hostage and will surely use him to pressure Adelaide. We can't let that happen,' Bilobeal said resoundingly.

'Aye, and we won't. Let's go inside and talk things over. I'll be back to join you. I just have a quick talk with Ghilli Duh,' said Asanopirh and was gone in a blink of an eye.

'Ghilli Duh, I need your help. Where are you, my friend?' Asanopirh said after the others had gone inside.

'I'm here, Asanopirh. I saw what happened. There is no need for an explanation. I informed the Dryads and asked them to block all escape routes. Now you can drive them away from the Cottage and into our arms. We will teach them a lesson they'll never forget, that is if they survive,' said Ghilli Duh. In an instant, he swung his cloak around him and disappeared.

'Hugh, Glen, what happened? What is all the commotion about?' asked Avery as they entered the Cottage.

'I'll tell you, but first tell me, where are the others?' 'They are all in the kitchen. What is it, Glen? Tell us,' whispered Ursula, bending over to peer out of the window.

'You won't see anything from here, Ursula. The Laird and his men have backed up into the woods,' said Glen as he opened the door to the kitchen.

'Brilliant, so they have given up,' hailed John as he entered the sitting room.

'No, they haven't, John. They've captured Harris. It will not take long before they use his life as leverage against everybody inside the Cottage,' replied Glen in a hoarse whisper.

'Well, what are we waiting for. We have to get Harris out of there!' replied Avery as she headed for the door.

'Where you think you're going, Avery?' Darion jumped up to stop her.' What are you planning to do? Walk up and shake the Laird's hand?'

'Oh, come on, we have no time to talk. Harris needs our help.'

'Ah, and it would do what for him when you get caught? No, we have to devise a new plan of action to give them a surprise they will not easily forget,' said Darion with a big smile.

Soon everybody was in deep discussions about what approach to take— everyone except Adelaide, who stood trembling and clenched fists at the window. After a heated deliberation, Asanopirh gave his orders.

'Bhaltair, Hugh, and John, I would like you to remain and defend the Cottage should it come to that. I am going to leave Keelin and Sorcha with you. Ursula, you take a position on the roof with Aislinn. Cover our backs and signal us when it is safe to leave cover. Darion, Avery, Glen, and Hugh, you come with me. Bilobeal, you and your men must guard the brook and bridge.'

'Aye, Asanopirh will do. No one is going to get past us,' said Bilobeal and left to position his men.

'Well, all that's left to do is to check our weapons and keep an eye on our enemies. Has there been any movement, Adelaide?' Asked Asanopirh stepping closer to the window.

'Aye, the soldiers are busy collecting wood; I assume they are planning to hold their post throughout the night.'

'I am not so sure that that is what they have in mind, but I will ask Faerydae to take a closer look,' said Asanopirh. He was about to turn to leave through the back door when he heard Adelaide scream in terror.

'What happened, Adelaide?' John asked, running to the window. He barely managed to catch her as she collapsed.

'The Laird is going to burn him! The soldiers have piled wood and straw on top of the carriage and tied Harris to a stake. Darion, Asanopirh, you have to save him!'

There was no answer from the elves, only a whirl of wind as they flew past John and out of the door.

'That bastard will not succeed,' hissed Asanopirh through his clenched teeth. 'Darion, you go to the brook and ask Lady Coventina for help. Meet me with Avery on the other side,' whispered Asanopirh and vanished.

Darion rushed to the edge of the brook, dipped his hands into the water and called out to the River Goddess, 'Lady Coventina, please come to me. Show your fury and aid us to set this innocent free.'

He barely had time to step back from the shore before the water of the brook began to rise and flood the land where the Laird and his men stood. The Laird started to shout at his men in the commotion.

'No one moves! Stand your ground. We are not afraid of a bit of water,' he screamed at the top of his lungs as he mounted his horse and picked up a torch to light the pile of wood. As he closed in on Harris, the water began to rise, forming a towering wave that crashed and ripped away everything in its path. The soldiers struggled desperately to stay afloat and reach dry land but were washed away by a second wave. The stake Harris had been tied to broke in the surge. He was freed and swam across to Adelaide's land in an instant.

Adelaide stood waist-deep in the ice-cold water, frantically searching for the man she loved. She desperately fought against the raging current and the cold that was slowly making it harder for her to breathe. Her hands were turning blue, and her legs felt as if they would give in at any moment. Please, Lady Coventina, don't let him die. Return him to me, she thought. That's when she saw him bobbing in the current. He was struggling to hold on to the same stake he had been tied to. She launched herself into the raging water, caught his tunic and pulled him onto the shore before she fell to her knees, clenching him in her arms.

'Mo ghràdh, I was so afraid!' Adelaide said with heaving breath. 'Why did you come? Surely you must have known what the Laird was about to do.'

'Aye mo chridhe, I did, but I had to come and make sure that you were safe. I would not be able to live on if anything should happen to you,' answered Harris and kissed her hands.

'Crivens, you two, you really know how to get an old man's heart beating,' Bhaltair said.

'Aye, there is never a dull moment with these two. Come on, let's get the two lovebirds up to the Cottage,' said John with a heavy sigh. Julia and Annette came running towards them with large towels in their hands, ready to wrap Adelaide and Harris in warmth.

'Let's get you into the house and out of these wet clothes Madge and Anne have some hot broth waiting for you,' said Annette as she wrapped her arm around Adelaide to support her on the way up.

‘Did you see that, guys? Harris is safe, and half of the Lairds men were washed away by the brook!’

‘Aye, Glen, but that is not good enough. He has to pay for his malice. Let's go and make sure that he is not about to try again,’ said Darion. He hurried to the Rowan tree, followed by Glen and Avery.

‘I can't wait to pay him back for all the suffering he has caused,’ Avery said through gritted teeth. ‘Let's teach him the meaning of fear.’

‘Aye, let's chase him back into his castle. Lock the door and throw away the key! Are you ready?’ Shouted Glen, raising his staff and looking expectantly at Darion.

‘Aye, let's go. Be fast, strong, and safe!’ shouted Darion and took off running.

Avery and Glen followed him into the woods, ready to fight anything or anyone that crossed their path. In no time at all, they had reached the edge of the forest where Laratbogh and Oren stood guard and gave them a headcount of the men at arms.

‘There are around fifty men out there, twenty of them lined up at the brook, a dozen surrounding the Laird, and about eighteen in the forest,’ Oren informed them with military precision.

‘Why would they split up? Does this make any sense to you?’ asked Glen, looking puzzled.

‘Makes perfect sense. The men at the brook serve as a distraction so that the second group can approach the Cottage unnoticed. At least that is what they have planned,’ mocked Laratbogh and giggled quietly.

‘Blimey, it will be hard to fight with the staff in the underbrush,’ Glen remarked, looking down at the cumbersome weapon in his hands.

'Don't bother yourself with the group in the forest, Glen. Ghilli Duh is looking forward to giving them a good thrashing. You will be fighting alongside Asanopirh,' Darion explained. 'He is waiting for you behind the blackberry bush, which, by the way, is Faerydae in disguise. She is making sure that you don't get ambushed. Her thorns will rip everyone to shreds before they can get close.'

'Brilliant, see you on the other side, Darion. And please, look after Avery,' called Glen before he disappeared into the thickets.

Meanwhile, Ursula and Aislinn sat on the cottage roof, keeping a close eye on the Laird and his men so that they could alert their friends to any Danger and give the signal when it was safe to leave their cover to attack.

'Aislinn, I think it is safe now. The Laird is addressing his men, and not one of them is checking on the surrounding.'

'Aye, these fools feel safe. I think it is time to give Avery and Darion the go-ahead.'

'Yup, let's do it. Ursula nodded in agreement. She loaded her slingshot with a ball of red candle wax, aimed at Avery's shoulder and released the sinew.

'Are you sure she'll get your message?' asked Aislinn, concerned.

'Oh yes, most certainly. This is Avery's favourite way to send signals,' Ursula replied with a big smile.

Avery and Darion stood silently hidden behind a large oak tree awaiting the signal to attack when something struck Avery's shoulder.

'Damn, what was that?' she exclaimed. She passed her hand over her back and smiled as she wiped the red wax from her shoulder.

'What's wrong, Avery?' Darion asked. 'Did you get hit?'

'No, I just got the message from Ursula. It is time to attack,' Avery giggled, pointing to the red wax on her jerkin.

'Aye, Avery, let's lash out against injustice and black magic,' he said firmly. Avery nodded and felt a rush of strength and courage as she drew her swords. She began to run alongside Darion Through the thick green forest before they finally broke free of the brush and into the enemy lines. They at once spiralled through the surprised armed men, cutting them down like weeds. Glen had also reached the Laird's guards and began swirling his staff masterfully through the air, sending the Laird's men flying. Asanopirh mounted his horse to pursue the Laird, who had fled the scene and raced back to the castle.

The screams of the terrified men alerted their comrades at the water's edge and in the forest, sending them into a frantic run towards the Cottage. Arrows hissed through the air and struck the Laird's men without a warning just as Bilobeal and his men came running across the bridge with raised staffs and axes, lashing out at anyone still trying to get to the Cottage. The band of soldiers in the forest flung their weapons into the bushes and scattered in all directions in terror, making them easy targets for Ghilli Duh. Laratbogh and Oren sat in their trees and watched as Ghilli Duh tripped and bush-whacked the terror-stricken soldiers as they stormed through the woods.

It was over as quickly as it had begun. Dead soldiers covered the blood-soaked ground. The few survivors that had the strength to stand ran for their lives.

Avery felt exhausted and nauseous as she looked around. Throughout the fight, she had been able to keep a cold detachment from her opponents by keeping her mind numb and empty. But the sight of the dead men made her feel distressed. She lowered her eyes and saw that her boots and jerkin were drenched in blood. It was not hers but the men's she had slain and wounded.

'Avery, are you alright? You look like a ghost,' Darion uttered, walking up to her.

'Aye, I am alright,' she said in a dead voice. 'But I have to get away from here. I can't breathe. The smell of blood sickens me. Let's go to the brook and wash off.'

'Right, Glen and Bilobeal's men are already there. But stop a moment, where did you get this?' asked Darion and pointed to her breeks, which was covered in yellow ashes.

'I have no idea…' she said, looking down and noticing the ashes for the first time. 'Wouldn't that mean that there were Red Caps among the soldiers?'

'Aye, and that you killed some of them. But I am certain that there will be more around, so we have to return to the Cottage as fast as possible. The Red Caps surely tried to get to the Cottage,' Darion said, lifting his arm to signal Bilobeal and his men to follow him. Avery and Glen had difficulty keeping up with the charging elf and only caught up with him after crossing the bridge and stopping to speak with Bilobeal.

'Bilobeal, we have to search the forest and the fields for Red Caps. I am sure that they tried to break through to the Cottage.'

'They didn't. Nothing got past us. Relax Darion. But if they were here, that means that Lord MacNab' is not far,' Bilobeal said.

'You are right. We have to set off as soon as Asanopirh returns and get William to his family and Anne, Julia, and Lucy on a ship to France. The MacDougal clan owns a huge fleet of galleys. – Surely, they are willing to take care of them,' Darion said.

'Aye, and Clyde MacDougal will be fuming when he finds out what Colin Campbell had planned for his grandson while his daughter lay dying. You guys better return to the Cottage to get our travellers ready. My men and I will take the fallen soldiers back to Dalmally,' said Bilobeal.

'Let me come with you and talk to the members of the Guild. I am certain they will help us free Marianne,' said Bhaltair as he approached Darion and Bilobeal.

'We'll use any help we can get,' Bilobeal conceded. 'But you must remain in the Guildhall. You cannot be seen in the streets of Dalmally.'

'Agreed. Let's go and load the bodies onto Harris's carriage,' replied Bhaltair.

23 The Guild

Morning broke over the small village of Dallmally. Its streets began to fill with people, rich and poor, young and old, all headed to the market square to make their purchases. At first glance, it appeared to be a typical market Day. But instead of the usual hustle and bustle with merchants excitedly shouting to sell their wares, the air was pierced with palpable grief.

The wooden stalls, where the villages would meet to exchange news and listen to the latest gossip, were eerily silent. Even the pickpockets and beggars stared petrified at the grim sight in the middle of the market square.

The Guild's Lord Dean was called to read out the writing on the carriage the fallen soldiers lay. It was a sombre moment for the community. The slain men were the husbands, fathers, brothers and sons of many villagers. Angus McNell walked around the carriage for the fifth time, trying to gather the strength to read the inscription aloud. Finally, he spoke.

'Here lay the men that had been led astray as all they learned was obey. Blindly accepting injustice and cruelty.' Angus's voice began to falter as he read the second paragraph.

'Cailleach Mother of the mountains, withered, aged and older than time, embrace these men forgive their crime. Guide them back to your womb, beloved mother and crone.'

After a long silence, Gavin, the baker, said. 'Let us lay these men to rest and then meet at the guildhall to mourn their death.'

'Aye, Gavin, let us bury them and notify their families,' said Angus. He led the procession out of the village.

Late in the afternoon, after the fallen soldiers had been laid to rest, the guild members of Dalmally and the surrounding villages had assembled in the dimly lit Guildhall to pay their final respect with solemn prayer. Their voices rang solemnly through the hall.

'If ever there is a tomorrow, we'll meet again without pain or sorrow. When it will be we dinna ken. May you sleep well in the arms of the Morrigan.'

The hall, which usually echoed with laughter and heated discussions, lay silent. Only the fire's soft crackling sounded through the room, and the reflections of its flickering flames Danced on the walls.

'I've enough of this slaughter!' shouted Gavin, breaking the painful silence. Too many have died for the Laird's crimes. We can't sit by any longer and allow this to continue.'

'Aye, I agree, enough is enough!' shouted the butcher Ross, slamming his fist on the table. His eyes blazed with rage, and his chest heaved ominously.

'You are right, Ross, but there is little we can do. We owe the Laird our allegiance as we had sworn when he was instated,' Angus said, shaking his head in defeat.

'You're wrong. Angus,' Bhaltair announced as he entered the Guild Hall, Duane is an impostor. The rightful Laird is William. It is to him we owe our allegiance.'

'Crivens Bhaltair, we thought you and your family were dead.'

'We would have remained in our homes. But because of my wife's foresight, we were able to flee and find refuge before the Laird's murderous gangs came for us.'

'I am so glad that you are safe,' Ross said. 'But tell me, how can the innkeeper be the rightful Laird? He is merely a commoner like us.'

'No, he is not, Ross. He is the son of Lady Sahara and Lord Collin Campbell.' Bhaltair said, raising his voice for all in the hall to hear.

'Nonsense, how can he be?' Angus protested. 'We all know that their only child died soon after its birth.'

'That is what we were led to believe, Angus, but the truth is quite different indeed. Lord Campbell ordered the midwife to kill the child at once after Lady Sahara had passed on and demanded Adelaide bury his body in the courtyard. But the woman did not obey his cruel order but swore an ode to Lady Sarah on her deathbed to keep her son safe until he was ready to reclaim his birth right. The midwife knew that Maighread's son had died the same night shortly after his birth and asked Adelaide to take him to the castle grounds to bury him instead. Maighread took William and raised him as if he was her own. Now the time has finally come for him to claim his inheritance,' he concluded.

'Is there any proof of what you say, Bhaltair? And either way, how could we if we ever depose Duane? We are no soldiers, and our sons are in the Laird's service, which means they would have to fight us! How could you expect us to take up arms against our flesh and blood?'

'No, Gavin, no one expects you to fight. William is on the way to his grandfather Clyde MacDougal as we speak to ask for support and protection. All we have to do is provide food and shelter for him and his men when he returns.'

'He has my support,' shouted Peter the cobbler and looked encouraging at his fellow guild members.

'Aye, I will give him my support and feed his men!' 'Thank you, Ross,' said Bhaltair. He turned expectantly at Angus.

'Aye, I think that the Guild gives William its support and protection. What say you?'

'Aye,' hailed the guild members raising their tankards.

'Well then, it's settled. Let's hope William returns before the next full moon,' Bhaltair sighed and sat his tankard down.

'What is so special about the full moon?' asked Peter.

'The Laird sentenced Marianne to hang on the eve of the next full moon,' answered Bhaltair in a low and sullen tone.

'Blood bas, what could she possibly have done to deserve that? Is he trying to silence her so he can remain in power?'

'No, Angus, Duane is not aware that he is not the rightful Laird. Neither does he know that his father is the one we all call the Stranger.'

'What! So, he is responsible for the disappearance of our Daughters? Let's go for him now. We cannot allow him to kill Marianne.'

'We certainly won't!' Bhaltair said. 'We will be able to free Marianne the moment they walk her out of the castle and over the bridge. I think the best place for an ambush is right outside your forge, Douglas.'

'Aye, right, I will create some billowing smoke and have a boat ready to move her out one time,' Douglas agreed. But what about the Laird's men? They are not going to give her up without a fight.'

'Oh, don't you fret. We will get help from the Queen of Elfame and the Drows. No one would be able to stop us.'

'Brilliant! So, let's make haste and prepare for the return of William and his men,' Angus proclaimed to the hall.

'Aye, Angus,' the guild members cheered in a chorus, clinking their tankards once again.

'Let's go, Bhaltair. We don't want the lamplighter to see you. He will give you away in a heartbeat, that spineless bastard,' whispered Bilobeal from behind the Guild's flags. 'Aye, you are right. Let's hit the road. I am dead tired.

'Madge will be worried by now. The sun is setting again. Where did you hide the carriage Bilobeal?'

'Behind the blacksmith forge. I wanted to check the planned escape route.'

'And are you satisfied?'

'Aye, it's perfect. The elves will block the bridge by pretending to be a group of quarrelling drunkards, distracting the guards while my men get Marianne into the boat. She will be gone before they even have time to look around,' laughed Bilobeal and slapped Bhaltair on the shoulder.

'Oh, I can hardly wait to see their faces,' replied Bhaltair with a broad grin.

'I'm sorry, my friend, but I am afraid you won't be seeing that. That was your last visit to Dalmally until William has been officially instated and accepted by all the clans.'

Bhaltair looked at Bilobeal with raised eyebrows and was about to flare up but stopped himself when he thought about the Danger that his presence in Dalmally brought and how fortunate he had been today.

'Aye right, Bilobeal, I should not push my luck,' he conceded. Let's head back.'

'We can't wait for Bhaltair and Bilobeal to return,' John decided. 'William must reach his clan before morning. And we have to get the lassies on their way to France.'

'Aye, I agree. Madge and Annette are already helping me to get them ready. The elves want to leave shortly,' replied Adelaide as she walked into the kitchen. Anne sat curled up near the hearth and glared lifelessly into the fire. Her beautiful blue eyes were red and swollen from crying all night.

'Anne, my love, you have to ready yourself for the journey. I'll take care of Lucy. Come on, Mo Lennan,' said Adelaide gently as she ran her hand over Anne's golden blond hair.

'What's wrong with Anne, Julia? Do you think she has the strength to make this journey?' asked Annette.

'Aye, she will be fine. She is a strong young lass. But the news of Nissa's death and Marianne's capture has hurt her deeply.'

'Indeed, it shocked us all. But Marianne will be fine. The elves and the Drows will free her, don't you fret. Let's get the food ready for Lucy. She should eat something before you head out. With any luck, she will fall asleep as soon as the boat starts rocking,' said Adelaide placing some bannocks, cheese, and a flask of ale in a travelling bag.

'Very well, but where is she?'

'She is outside with Glen. He is showing her how to fight with a staff. She loves it so much that she already broke three of my new broomsticks,' chuckled Adelaide. 'I'm not surprised. She is a feisty wee lass. I'll go and fetch her,' answered Julia and left the cottage.

'Can I have a word with you, Adelaide?' Harris asked after Julia had left. 'It is rather important.'

'Aye Harris, I hope it's not more bad news.'

'Not at all, Mo ghràdh, it's good news.

I tried to tell you the night I arrived, but with all the dreadful events. I could not find the right time.'

'Oh, what is it? I most certainly could do with some good news for a change.'

'It has to do with the Count of Anjou. You see, he died last winter. Your brother persuaded the King to dismiss all charges of witchcraft laid against you. Adelaide, you are no longer in Danger. You can return to Touraine with me, Adelaide,' he said, his eyes open wide with hope.

She stared at him for what felt like forever before speaking.

'This is wonderful news, indeed. Harris,' she said with a soft smile. 'I would love to come with you. But I am needed here, at least until Lord MacNab' is defeated and Avery will be reunited with her parents. I hope you understand.'

'Aye,' he replied in a hoarse whisper. Adelaide's answer had taken the sparkle from his eyes and wiped away all happiness he had felt moments ago. It is not the answer I hoped for, but I understand,' he turned his head and looked out the window, trying to hide his pain and fight back the tears that began to well up in his eyes.

'It's time to get ready. The sun is about to set, and the elves are waiting for us at the shore of Inistrynich. I better get to the barn and span in the horses,' he said after a moment.

Adelaide watched Harris with tears in her eyes as he entered the barn to get the carriage ready. She thought her heart would burst into a thousand pieces and felt a searing pain spreading through her chest that made it hard for her to breathe. It was the same dreadful feeling of loss she had felt all those years ago when she had to leave her home in Touraine and flee to Scotland to avoid being burned alive.

Why is it that people fear what they can't explain? Why aren't they willing to open their minds and welcome the great mysteries that nature has to offer? She thought. It is disheartening that they choose to stay ignorant and destroy everything differently. Many years ago, they ruined my life, and now once again, I have to bid farewell to the man I love. I would have wished for nothing more than to return home to Touraine, to see Arthur one last time and spend my remaining years with the man I love. She squeezed her eyes shut, trying to stop her tears from falling.

'Adelaide, where are you? We are ready to leave,' called Avery as she entered the cottage.

'I'm here, Mo Lennan,' answered Adelaide wiping away her tears and forcing herself to smile.

'We are ready to move, but Anne doesn't want to leave without saying goodbye.'

'I am coming to talk to her, Avery,' answered Adelaide and followed her to the carriage.

'I cannot leave without saying goodbye, Adelaide, and thank you for everything you have done for us. I will carry you in my heart forever and hope to see you again one day.'

'Have a safe journey, Anne. Give my love to your father, tell him how desperately I wished to be with him and that I try my utmost best to come soon,' whispered Adelaide and kissed Anne goodbye.

'Lady Julia, please get in the carriage. It is time to leave,' called Glen reaching out his hand to help Julia into the carriage.

'I am not coming,' Julia said firmly. 'Scotland is my home, and I must help William to set things right. After all, I am the Lady of Kilchurn Castle,' she said and stepped away from the carriage. Her face was ashen, and tears streamed down her face.

Everyone looked at Julia in bewilderment. Their eyes filled with sadness, but they also knew that they had no time to argue over her decision. They had no choice but to leave now if they wanted to use the Laird's shock over his defeat for their getaway. Harris turned around and looked at Adelaide one last time before he cracked the whip in the air. The two brown horsed broke into a trot and pulled the carriage away from Adelaide's cottage.

24 Dunollie Castle

Dark clouds loomed above Loch Awe, blocking the sun and turning its water jet black. The silhouette of Kilchurn Castle appeared from the mist like a menacing spirit.

After his failed attempt to override Adelaide's cottage, the young Laird had taken refuge in his bedchamber. Unable to eat or sleep, he began to drown his desperation and fear in wine, hoping that Lord MacNab' would remain unaware of what happened. He had forbidden his servants and guards to speak about it under the threat of death to prevent Lord MacNab's spies from learning of his defeat.

An eerie silence filled the Castle. The Castle's servant spoke only in hushed voices now and then when orders needed to be passed and hustled through the halls and passages barefooted. No one dared to provoke the Laird's anger. He was well known for his violent temper and brutal outbursts, which had only gotten worse after his dreadful defeat last night. Even the kitchen lay silent since the cook had ordered the maids only to use wooden bowls and keep the chopping to a minimal.

'Blood bas, how many men had to die last night because of the Laird's ignorance? Didn't he know that no one with ill intent can cross that bridge?'

'Too many and many more will die because of his insatiable lust for power. He should have known better than to anger the Seelie Fae. Mark my words, Alan. This is only the beginning. Dark times lay before us,' whispered Kenneth the Laird's stable hand wiping the sweat from his bald head. He was a frail older man. His face hardened from lifelong servitude. His eyes were pale and lifeless, and his once strong hands were now stiff and deformed from arthritis.

'Lust for power, nay Kenneth, that's not it. He is desperate to get Lucy back and hand the two lassies over to his wicked master. You know of whom I speak,' hissed Alan and tightened the grip on his clay tankard so hard that it shattered in his hand. He had once been a soldier himself but resigned to working as a servant since he had lost a hand, fighting for the young Laird. He knew how wicked and bloodthirsty his master was and how much he feared Lord MacNab'.

'Aye, you're right, Alan. The grief over losing Lucy and the fear of Lord MacNab's wrath have made him wild. But you are going to join him soon. Look at what you have done!' said Rhona, the kitchen maid, as she picked the tankard's broken pieces off the ground.

'I hope you get a grip of yourself, me lad, when you bring the Laird his wine. I would not like to have to wipe it off the floor. My knees are not what they used to be', said Rhona and looked sternly at Alan. She was a lovely, motherly woman with greying hair and a warm smile for everyone. Rhona had worked at the Castle all her life and often spoke about the good old Days when Lady Sarah was still alive.

Every morning before she started the kitchen fires, she would go to the small graveyard behind the Castle to place fresh flowers on her Lady's grave and the one of her son.

'You know Rhona. The wine looks like the blood of the men he sacrificed last night. I hope that I will see the Day when he will be punished for all his wickedness.'

'Be careful what you say, Alan, the walls of the castle have ears,' Kenneth warned. 'You don't want to end up in the dungeons like the ten guardsmen that failed him.'

'Failed him? It wasn't their fault that the captives got away. They had help from the Seelie Fae! There was absolutely nothing they could have done,' Alan insisted.

'Stop tempting your faith, you two, and keep quiet. Come on, Alan, go and bring the Laird his wine before he loses his temper again and breaks more furniture. Just leave it by the door and knock,' whispered Rhona and pushed the men out of the kitchen.

The rain had started to fall, gently at first, then torrential and unforgiving on Kilchurn Castle and the loch, drenching the guards on the Castle's walls to the skin and obscuring their view of the loch and its shores. The men felt cold and weary. It had been two days and nights since they'd slept. The Laird had not given them a chance to rest ever since the escape of the captives and had forbidden them to light any fires, meaning the men had to find shelter in turrets.

'I hope that the rain continues for a while so that the guards don't see us,' whispered Avery.

'Let's hope so. We could do with some blessings from the clouds. But you better check that our travellers are comfortable. They are so quiet, I can't even hear little Lucy,' said Harris in a hushed voice as the carriage rolled down to the shore.

'Aye, Harris, they are snuggled up under Adelaide's blankets and look very sleepy. I am sure they will fall asleep as soon as the boat starts rocking.'

'Fall asleep? It's just past midday. How can anyone sleep at this hour?'

'With a little help from Laratbogh! We added a handful of herbs to their broth. Trust me, it is better for them and easier for us. Oh, look, Harris! Asanopirh and Sorcha got the boat ready! Could you get the horses to walk a little faster? I don't want to have to carry these guys to the boat!' giggled Avery and blushed.

'Aye, giddy up, my sweets!' shouted Harris. He made a kissing sound and slackened the reins. It worked like a charm, and a short while later, everyone was safely seated in the boat.

'Well, let's get the boat into the water,' Darion said, satisfied. Come on, Harris, help me push.'

'Hang on a moment. I don't see the oars anywhere. I know they were here when I checked the boat yesterday,' Harris stated, looking around nervously as the boat began to float.

'We don't need them. Come on, Harris, you should know that by now! Jump in so that we can get on our way,' Darion replied and pointed to the water, from which three Ashrays appeared, picked up the rope, and pulled the boat away from the land and out to the middle of the loch. Soon, the shore disappeared behind shifting sheets of steel-grey rain that floated over the loch.

'We will find shelter here behind the islands until Ioroth gives us the all-clear,' whispered Darion and dipped his hand into the water to signal Ariana. The boat slowed at once and drifted gently through the calm waters between the wooded islands. The rain had slowed by now, and the sun began to break through the branches in long, slanting silver rays.

'You should take the opportunity to rest a bit and have some water. It should not take very long till we hear Ioroth's call to leave the shelter and continue on our way across the loch,' murmured Asanopirh, scanning the sky for the golden eagle. Avery began to feel nauseous from the bobbing of the boat. She turned her head to the breeze to try to calm her churning stomach with long deep breaths until she heard Ioroth's high-pitched sound, the eagle's call was like no other and could be heard miles away.

I can hear you, Ioroth. Thanks for being our eyes in the sky, Avery thought as she climbed over William, Anne, and Lucy, who lay curled up in the back of the boat fast asleep. She took the pearl from her neck and dipped it into the water to tell Ariana that it was time to move out of their green shelter, cross the loch, and get on to the river. The rain had stopped, and the Dark clouds were gone, making the boats visible to the Castle's guards. The Ashrays knew the Danger they were in as they left the islands and soared across the loch and up the river until the boat disappeared under the green cover of the wooded riverbanks. Soon the river's current had gotten so strong that the Ashrays were able to release the rope and allow the boat to float freely like a swan, past the grassy riverbanks and through patches of tall reeds that swayed gently in the afternoon sun before coming to a stop in an ancient forest.

'Pick up your weapons, guys. It's time to step on land. Watch your steps on the smooth rocks and take cover between the reeds whenever you can,' Darion instructed.

'Aye, don't fret. We know what to do. I just wish we had time to fish! Did you see the size of the silver carps and river trout?' uttered Glen excitedly, pointing to the fish that rushed out from under large river stones and shot through the crystal-clear water like arrows.

'We'll come back for them as soon as we are done with all of this, I promise. Let's go, my dear brother, grab your staff and head for the bushes,' chuckled Hugh as he waded through the shallows of the river to the opposite bank where Ursula and Aislinn were waiting.

'Come on, Avery, let's go,' Glen urged. 'Oren and Ghilli Duh are waiting for us.'

'Just give me a moment. Ariana is calling me. Go on, I'll catch up with you,' replied Avery as she bent down to listen to Ariana.

'Avery, I have disturbing news. I saw Lord MacNab's banner being hoisted over the turrets as we left the islands, signalling his presence at the Castle.'

'Thank you, Ariana. That is truly troubling news indeed. Did you tell the others what you saw?'

'Aye, Harris and the elves know, so you just have to inform your friends about the new situation. I have to go now and get the boat with your charges out of here. We don't know if we are watched. It would be wise not to waste time,' whispered Ariana and disappeared.

Avery bent down and picked up a small river pebble, aimed carefully, and threw it at Hugh's back, who instantly spun around and looked Avery irritated.

'I have some important news for you,' she mouthed and waved excitedly.

‘Bullocks, Avery! Since when do you throw rocks at me? Why are you so agitated,’ Hugh inquired as he returned to the shore?

‘Never mind, it most certainly did not hurt you, and I had to get your attention before you reached the other side,’ she brushed his complaint aside. ‘Ariana just told me that Lord MacNab’ is at Kilchurn Castle. You know what that means.’

‘Aye, I do,’ Hugh replied, a look of seriousness washing over his face. So, we can expect that things will get pretty ugly soon. We can only hope that we weren't seen by his spies. Thanks for the warning, Avery,’ he said, hurrying back to Ursula and Aislinn.

Terrible visions swirled through Avery's mind as she ran into the woods to meet Glen, Oren and Ghilli Duh to tell them about the latest development.

‘Damn, we should have foreseen this. We only have three nights till full moon, so let's speed things up a bit,’ murmured Ghilli Duh. He walked up to a large oak tree and began to drum on his massive stem.

‘Who are you calling,’ asked Avery. She was scanning the surrounding shrubs and trees for any sign of movement when suddenly, a group of tall highland stags broke through the underbrush. They trotted up to Ghilli Duh and lowered their heads in respect and reverence.

‘Thank you for coming to our aid so quickly, my royal friends,’ said Ghilli Duh. He bowed to the group of stags before he turned to Avery, Glen, and Oren. ‘Make haste, my friends and mount the stags so that you can keep up with the boat and protect it. The river has swollen from the heavy rain and runs very quickly now,’ instructed Ghilli Duh as he helped Glen, Avery, and Oren climb onto the backs of the mighty creatures. He then whispered enchantments and stepped back. The stags reared high in the air and took off with giddying speed. The three friends had to hold on to their antlers with all their might not to fall off. As soon as they left the forest and galloped along the riverbank, they noticed the boat far ahead of them and began to fret that Bilobeal, Hugh, Aislinn, and Ursula would be able to catch up with them.

'Oy, what are you trying to do? Break your legs running like this over the rocks?' Bilobeal shouted from the top of the stony riverbank. Out of breath and soaked with sweat, Ursula stopped and leaned onto a large boulder to take a breath.

'We have no choice if we don't want to lose the boat! Don't you see the speed it is going? The river is so strong that not even the Ashrays can slow it down.'

'Well, yes, I can see that, but there is still no need to risk injuries,' answered Bilobeal rummaging through his sporran. He withdrew a silver whistle, blew it, and released a high-pitched whiz that echoed through the glen.

'Blimey Bilobeal, have you gone mad! They can hear you twenty miles away,' shouted Hugh and looked at Bilobeal quite perturbed.

'I bloody well hope so! After all, we require some transport,' said Bilobeal pointing to a herd of large mountain goats coming over the hilltop. 'Welcome, my lovely furry friends. I greatly appreciate your coming,' cheered Bilobeal and patted the heads of the large black and white mountain goats.

'Climb on, you, guys. We have no time to lose if we want to catch up with our friends.'

'Crivens, you can't be serious! They stink, Bilobeal. How should I ever get the stench out of my clothes?' exclaimed Ursula as the goats came closer.

'Hm, so tell me what you would like to do instead? Break your legs and bruise your pretty face, or catch up with the boat comfortably on the back of a goat?'

'Well, if you put it that way, I'll take the stench,' Ursula conceded.

'I knew you were a bright lass. Are you ready, Hugh?'

'Aye, Bilobeal, I am. This will be quite an experience. I have never ridden a goat before,' giggled Hugh. He jumped onto the back of one of the goats, holding on to its horns for dear life as it began to run and jump from rock to rock.

Meanwhile, across the river, Darion paced up and down the riverbank.

'I can't see Avery anywhere. It was a mistake to leave her,' Darion muttered, scanning the riverbank nervously. 'And the lads, they are not ready to fight upon their own.'

'Calm down. They are not alone,' Sorcha reassured him. 'They have Ghilli Duh at their side. What could happen as long as they are under the protection of the most powerful spirit of the forest? I am more worried about our friends on the rugged riverbank. I hope that Bilobeal will be able to keep them safe.'

'He is doing just that,' Asanopirh said. 'Didn't you hear his whistle a while ago? I am certain that he called his herd of mountain goats to carry them over the rough terrain. Knowing him, they are well on their way and might even show at any moment.'

'I can't hear a thing over the rushing waters, but I certainly hope that you are right, Asanopirh.'

'Aye, I am, just look! There they all are,' chuckled Asanopirh pointing at the two groups of friends riding along the riverbanks.

'Now that is a sight to behold!' Harris exclaimed in wonder. 'Who knew that you could travel on the backs of stags and goats.'

'You can if they are your friends,' replied Sorcha with a broad smile on her face.

The following hours went by without a sign of Danger. The rushing river had slowed and meandered along fallen trees and swamp-like pools filled with green water that sparkled like stars in the afternoon sun. I wish that we could stop and stay here for a while, forget about all the horrors, and make time stand still, Avery thought as she watched Oren following the boat through an archway of branches and soft green leaves high above the river.

Ursula was relieved and extremely grateful when she finally got off that goat. Seemingly unable to get rid of the creature's horrible smell, she kept sniffing her tunic while stumbling along the rugged riverbank. Ursula tripped and had grabbed a branch above her head to stop herself from plunging into the river.

'Yuck, what is this?' she screamed and looked at her hand in disgust.

'What, what did you do this time? I swear you cannot walk alone for more than five steps,' teased Hugh.

'Ha, ha, how amusing,' she sneered sarcastically. 'Just take a look at this mess! My right hand is covered in some smelly green gunk.'

'Oh, come on, Ursula, let me see. It can't be that bad. I am sure that you are overreacting again,' he replied and turned around with a cheeky smile on his face.

'Yikes, I take that back! It stinks worse than the bock I sat on. Come on, let me hold your other hand so that you can wash that green stuff off without falling into the river.'

'Hugh, you are such a good friend. Let me shake your hand,' said Ursula, lurching forward and reaching for Hugh.

'Don't you, dear!' shouted Hugh, barely escaping her grip by running into the river.

'What are you guys up to this time? You will give us all away with your silly games!'

'Sorry Bilobeal, but Ursula was trying to smear my face with the nasty smelling green slime she picked up from one of the branches over there.' Bilobeal stopped in his tracks.

'Green slime?' he said. 'Hold it, that's not a laughing matter. Ursula, my bonnie lass, don't wash it off before I've had a look at it.'

'Oh, but Bilobeal, it stinks and burns terribly! Hurry up. I can't stand it much longer.' He rushed over to examine her hand.

'Blood bas, which is what I feared it would be,' he said in a sombre voice. Go quickly wash it off thoroughly and cut off that sleeve! We cannot afford to take any chances,' he said, signalling Darion to bring the boat ashore.

'What's the matter, Bilobeal?' Asanopirh asked. Why did you stop us when we were so close to Taynuit? Couldn't you wait until we'd arrived?'

'We could all be dead by then. Ursula, my sweet lass, let me have the sleeve. Then take out your medallion and signal to Avery to stop. Do you recognise this, Asanopirh?'

'Aye, of course, I do. It's saliva from a Boobrie. That beast must have been flying above us for quite some time,' said Asanopirh while scanning the treetops for any sign of the bloodthirsty beast.

'And it's drooling looking down at you guys,' hissed Ghilli Duh as he appeared from the bushes.

'We can't risk continuing our journey on the river,' Darion declared. 'Let's wake William and Anne. I hope they'll be able to walk.'

'They will be. Let me handle this. It would not take long,' said Ghilli Duh. He bent over William and Anne, placed his hands on their eyes, and murmured an enchantment.'

'I heard everything, Lord Darion, and thought it best to ask my sisters Laratbogh and Faraday to join us. They should be with us in no time,' said Oren before she disappeared in a weeping willow on the edge of the forest.

'The sun is going to set soon, and if you are right about the Boobrie, then there is no doubt that the Red Caps will be on your trail as well. So, I think that it would be best if the Ashrays and I take the boat back to Loch Awe to give them a false lead.'

'Aye right, Ghilli Duh. It may not fool them for long, but hopefully just long enough for us to get to the forge,' Asanopirh said. He pushed the boat back into the river before turning to the willow and shouting up to Oren. 'Oren, tell me, what do you see? We should be close to Taynuit.'

'Aye, I can see the forge! It's about two miles ahead of us,' replied Oren.

'What's going on? Where are we? Please don't tell me that I slept the whole way!' asked William as he found himself lying next to Anne and Lucy.

'Never mind William, there is no time for long explanations,' Harris said. 'It would be best if you could pick up Lucy and head into the forest. I will fill you in on the way. Glen, come on me lad, go help me get Anne on her feet. You heard Asanopirh. We have to get away from the river as fast as we can,' he whispered and splashed some water on Anne's face before he and Glen pulled her up and helped her to keep her balance as she walked her first few steps.

It took Anne a while to shake off the sleepiness and open her eyes. Laratboghs herbs were very potent and meant to be active throughout the entire journey. But when Avery and Glen told her about the Boobrie circling above them, she lit up like a candle and began to run behind William. Soon, all of them had reached deep into the forest and were walking over the moss-covered ground past large patches of ferns and clumps of hazelnut trees. Laratbogh, Faraday, and Oren rushed through the treetops, dropping branches and pinecones to mark a safe trail until the forest opened up to a glen. It looked like a sea of tall waving grasses, deep purple thistles, and brilliant gold wildflowers.

'From now on, we have to continue without the Dryad's protection, so I think it would be best if we wait until the sky has Darkened before we leave the tree cover,' Darion asserted.

'I don't think it will be necessary to wait that long. We should be able to make a run for it. I go out to take a look before I give you all the go-ahead, but to stay on the safe side, you and Avery should take a position in the middle of the glen. I would feel a lot better knowing that I have your blades at a ready in case any Red Caps are around and willing to take the chance to attack us,' Asanopirh said. 'Hugh, you and Sorcha should position yourselves at the opposite edge of the glen. Have your arrows ready, and your bows were drawn if the Boobrie tries to attack. Ursula, you, Glen and Aislinn should remain at the edge of the forest and cover our backs. We cannot be sure that we aren't followed. Go, go, and be safe, my friends,' he said in a hushed voice before leaving the tree cover to search the glen and the surrounding shrubs.

Avery and Darion stepped out of the forest, crouched low, and Dashed through the high grass to a group of flowering elder shrubs in the centre of the glen. They pulled the swords from their scabbards and scanned the sky for the Boobrie. Hugh and Sorcha made their way to the other side of the glen and readied themselves to secure the sky.

'I hope he shows. I love to plug that bastard like a chicken.'

'Be careful what you wish for, Hugh. Many men and even elves have lost their lives to this beast. He is swift and powerful and doesn't forget that he can shapeshift into a horse. So do not take any chances. I would not like to lose you,' replied Sorcha and looked straight into his eyes with an intense expression of concern.

Ursula, Glen, and Aislinn took their position at the glen's edge and stood staring into the darkening forest.

'How are we supposed to see anything in this Darkness?' exclaimed Glen shaking his head in frustration as he leaned on his staff.

'You will be able to just close your eyes and stand still for a moment while Laratbogh and I give you the sight,' replied Aislinn before she and Laratbogh pulled Bella Donna stems from their hair and blew the flower dust towards Glen and Ursula.

'Open your eyes now and tell us what you see.'

'Wow, yes, yes, Laratbogh, I can see clearly! As if the sun was shining through the treetops,' replied Glen, rubbing his eyes in disbelieve.

'I have no idea how you did it, but thanks! Now they can come. I am ready,' replied Ursula and loaded her slingshot.

Suddenly, they heard Asanopirh's voice echo from across the glen.

'Run, Run! Don't look up, and you will be okay!' he shouted.

Anne held on to Harris', picked up her skirts, and took off running as fast as she could, stumbling over the rutted ground. She staggered through the waist-high grass and weeds while keeping an eye on William, who was carrying wee Lucy wrapped in one of Adelaide's blankets. The three were just a few steps from the elder shrubs in the middle of the glen, where Darion and Avery waited with outstretched arms, ready to pull them into the cover when they heard Oren's voice.

'Drop to the ground and don't move.'

Harris, William, and Anne dropped like stones to the ground and looked terrified up to Avery and Darion as the Boobrie circled above them and Darkened the sky with his broad black wings. The fading light of the sun caught his head and his black piercing eyes as he whizzed over the heads of Harris, William, and Anne, ready to attack.

At that moment, Hugh and Sorcha broke through the thickets with their bows drawn and aimed at the Boobrie's head. The arrows soared through the air and pierced the beast's neck but did not slow it down. The Boobrie shook his head and threw the arrows off like dewdrops before he returned for another attack. The enormous creature sailed through the air, then tipped his wings and went into a steep dive with his sharp talons fully extended to grab his prey.

Avery let out a scream that could freeze blood as she rushed out from the elder shrubs and charged the attacking beast. Her first shock had given way to burning fury and raged inside her like a blazing fire. She Darted across the glen with raised swords that flashed like flames as she leapt up in the air and slashed one of the Boobrie's wings, sending black feathers flying and spraying the grass with his blood. He turned around wildly, flapping his massive wings in pain, knocking Avery to the ground before he disappeared into the clouds.

'Avery, Mo Ghràdh, are you okay? Did he hurt you?' William whispered with tears in his eyes.

'I think I am okay, Da, but my shoulders are killing me,' Avery replied with a forced smile and flinched.

'Stay down, Avery. He's coming back,' said Darion. He swung his cloak over her and placed his hand on her chest to stop her from getting up.

'William, you all have to take cover under the blankets so that the beast will not be able to see you. We can't make another attempt to cross the glen until the sky has completely Darkened.'

'Aye Darion, I would like to agree with you, but I am afraid that it is too late for that, look up,' replied William and pointed to a gathering of shadows that swept over the sky like a flock of starling

'The Sluaghs are here, blessed be! They are the only thing this beast fears more than death. He will not return tonight - you are safe,' Darion breathed a sigh of relief. Darion lifted Avery off the ground as if she was weightless.

He closed his cloak over her and carried her into the forest to recover from the battle. Avery was trembling and felt as if all energy had drained from her body. She desperately clung to Darion with her last remaining strength and could hear his heart pounding under the heavy armour. Avery felt his warm breath on her skin as he lowered his head and gazed into her eyes.

'Don't ever frighten me like that again, mo ghradh. I would not be able to bear it if anything should happen to you,' he whispered. Darion pulled her close and kissed her, lowering himself to the ground holding her in his arms.

'William, my dear friend, I think the time has come to ask for your grandfather's help. I suggest you write him a short message and send your ring along with it. Ioroth is going to take it to the Castle before nightfall. Tell him to meet you at the stone circle of Strontoiller by sunrise,' said Asanopirh and handed William his Dagger. 'This will be your quill, William. The Boobrie's blood should make a fine ink.'

'Aye Asanopirh, let's hope he will recognise the ring and is curious enough to meet his dead grandson,' replied William. He took off his necktie, wrote a short message, knotted it around the ring, and tied it to one of Ioroth's talons.

25 Lord MacDougall

The Laird stood on the high stone wall of the Castle's tower and watched as the sun's golden orb slowly disappeared behind the hills and valleys in a haze of copper and purple, making way for the fast-approaching night sky. He was a man of extraordinary stature and strength despite his age. His eyes were as blue as the summer sky, gentle and bright. His thick wavy hair had lost its golden hue and shimmered like spun silver in the evening sun. The Laird had seen and fought many battles and had lost the two women that had meant everything to him. His young wife had died of a high fever many years ago, and his beloved Daughter lost her life in childbirth. He was still mourning their deaths and despised the silence surrounding him. He knew he would die alone and without an heir, leaving his land and people without protection.

'My Lord, you have to take a look at this eagle. Isn't he just magnificent?' whispered his servant Dunbar in admiration as the bird passed through the rays of the evening sun and revealed a flash of gold on its neck that gave him his name.

'Aye, I see him, Dunbar. You are right. He is breathtakingly beautiful. It has been a long time since last I have seen such a majestic golden eagle,' replied the Laird in a husky drawl.

'If I didn't know any better, my Lord, I would say that he is heading straight for the castle.'

'You are right, Dunbar, it most certainly looks that way,' replied Lord MacDougall, following the flight of the bird with great interest.

'Oh dear, my Lord, I don't want to be a spoil joy, but it looks as if he is going to attack! We better return to the tower.'

'Calm down, Dunbar, don't get your knickers in a knot! He has no cause to attack us, but it looks as if he is carrying a message. Look, there is something tied to one of his talons.'

'Well, I am not comfortable with this. Since when do eagles deliver messages?

Please, my Lord, let's take cover,' replied Dunbar in a high-pitched voice and ducking behind a rampart to get out of the way of the approaching bird.

'Would you look at this? I was right. He is carrying something!' exclaimed the Laird, trembling with excitement. The closeness to this majestic bird of prey made his heartbeat so loudly that it echoed in his ears.

'Is the message for me, my friend? May I take it off you, or would you attack me if I do?' Asked the Laird as he walked closer to Ioroth, who had perched himself on one of the ramparts with his enormous wings fully spread.

'Thank you, my noble friend. I am sure that this is an important message, and the way you look at me tell me you expect an answer for your master,' said the Laird in a soft, soothing voice as he untied the bundle from Ioroth talon.

'Dunbar, go to the kitchen and fetch a juicy piece of meat for my friend so that he can refresh himself before he returns to his master.'

'But my Lord, I can't just leave you. What if he attacks you?'

'He will do no such thing, don't be silly! If that were his intent, he would have done it already. Now go and do as I say, or would you like to offer him a piece of your flesh?' chuckled the Laird as he began to unfold the piece of cloth.

How strange, who would send me a ring? He thought. He froze as he recognised the ring's seal as the one of his deceased Daughter Sarah. His hands began to tremble, and his breath quickened as he went ahead to flatten the linen on which a message was written in blood.

Dear Grandfather,

This message must be bewildering for you, as you were led to believe that my mother and I had died during the night of the winter solstice thirty years ago. The truth is that my father, Lord Collin Campbell, ordered the midwife to have me killed at once after my mother's passing. She did not obey his order but pledged to my dying mother to keep me safe and hold the ring as proof of my identity. Again, a member of the Campbell clan is trying to take my life, so I must reach out to you, asking for your help and protection. My companions and I will await your response by sunrise at the stone circle of Strontoiller.

Sincerely yours William MacDougall

The Laird stared at the message in shock and disbelieve! Could it be true, had the boy survived? He felt torn between hope and doubt and sat down on the tower's steps to contemplate his next move.

'My Lord, what happened? Did the bloody bird attack you?'

'No, Dunbar, he did not. The message he brought was from my grandson William. Help me up, will you? We have to get our men armed and ready to make our way to the stone circle at Strontoiller. My grandson needs my help!' shouted the Laird, grabbing hold of his servant's hand pulling himself up.

The thought of his grandson being alive and asking for his help gave him a rush and made him feel energised, fearless, and purposeful.

'Come on, Dunbar, tell the commander to assemble the men and then go and get my armour. It's time to we have to bring my grandson home,' shouted the Laird joyously, crossing the oak-cladded Great Hall with long, fast strides. 'But my Lord, your grandson is dead, remember? He died the night he was born,' said Dunbar in a trembling voice running behind the Laird with his green Damask cloak flapping behind him like a pair of limp wings.

'Well, we now know that he is not. The boy survived and is on his way here. Hand me my sword and take my Dagger up to the eagle so that he can take it to my grandson. Go and do as I say. I can't wait to bring him home,' shouted the Laird in jubilation.

'You want me to go near that bird?' Dunbar said with hesitation. 'But my lord, what if he attacks me?'

'Don't be such a coward. He is not going to attack you! Just rest the Dagger on the rampart so that he can take it to my grandson, go on,' said the Laird and burst into laughter.

I used to love the full moon's magical silver light, but now it seems like an omen of death. William thought, sitting on a large boulder listening to the rustling grass and the sounds of the forest. The ground was still damp from the rain, and the evening mists had begun to rise and spread the rich fragrance of the wildflowers, leaves, and loam across the glen and the surrounding forest. The group of friends rested on the moss-covered ground under a large old fir tree and stared silently into the fire, trying to calm the anxiety that had built once they began to understand how close they came to losing William, Anne, and Lucy. Anne had withdrawn from the group and sat huddled under the tree's low branches clinging to Lucy.

'You are trembling, Anne. You must be cold, my love. Why don't you come closer to the fire and take a blanket?' asked Harris in a hushed voice. He picked up a blanket and placed it around Anne and Lucy.

'Thank you, Harris, that is very kind of you, but I think it's my nerves that are making me tremble. That was a close call today. I truly thought that the Boobrie would kill us all.'

'Aye Anne, it was truly terrifying, and I am sure that everyone is now painfully aware of the Dangers we will have to face. We can only survive if we stay close and act like one,' muttered Harris. He got up and added a large log to the fire. The fire hissed softly as the wood shifted and sent a shower of sparks high up in the air.

'Oh, Ma, look, fireflies!' shouted Lucy excitedly, throwing off the blanket and jumping up down in delight.

'No, my love, they are not, fireflies. Fireflies would not come so close to the fire they would burn. But come on, let's look for some in the bushes. They love to hide there,' said Anne as she took her Daughter's hand and walked away from the fire to some nearby hazelnut shrubs.

'I don't think that's a wise move,' Glen whispered. He looked across to Ursula, picked up his staff, and followed Anne and Lucy.

'Wait for me, Glen. I am not going to let you go alone,' said Ursula, strapping her slingshot onto her wrist. She ran into Hugh as she followed Glen into the forest.

'Where the heck you're coming from? I've been looking for you everywhere,' hissed Ursula and pushed him out of her way.

'Well, I was standing right behind you for quite a while, which you would have noticed if you weren't so busy with your slingshot.'

'So, and where were you before?'

'I had a talk with Sorcha, Asanopirh, and Bilobeal near the rowan tree, over there.'

'Oh yes, is that so? Why couldn't they come over to the fire and talk to all of us?'

'Oh, come on, Ursula, what does that matter?'

'Oh, quite a lot, my dear brother,' Glen interrupted, overhearing the conversation as he returned with Anne and Lucy.

'You were with Sorcha, which is enough to drive our bonnie lass Ursula crazy with jealousy,' whispered Glen teasingly and took cover behind Hugh when he saw Ursula picking up a large branch.

'Ah, what, what are you talking about, Glen? Anyhow they told me that Cait Sith brought a message from Ghilli Duh that makes it necessary for them to return to the cottage tonight.'

'Oh well, and what was the message,' asked Ursula impatiently?

'Well, she told them Lord MacNab' had ordered the Laird to sentence ten of his guardsmen to death by drowning, and the spineless coward obeyed and had them thrown from the tower.'

'Crivens, how could he do that! And why?' Ursula asked, staring at Hugh in shock.

'Because he is a gutless bastard that will do anything the so-called Lord tells him to do. But don't fret. They were saved by the Ashrays and taken to the cottage by John and Bhaltair. You can imagine how indebted they felt for their rescue and how stunned they were to see Lady Julia at the cottage. They now know the whole story and have sworn their allegiance to her and the rightful Laird.'

'That's bloody brilliant, but how do they all fit into the cottage? Isn't it getting crowded in there by now?

'Oh, Glen, have you still not realised that Adelaide's cottage is a place of magic? It will always have enough room no matter how many people Adelaide takes in,' Darion explained as he and Avery appeared right next to them.

'Blimey, I feel like a fool now,' Avery Glen and blushed.

'Never mind, we still love you,' giggled Ursula and ruffled his blond locks.

'Well, that's nice, but you don't have to mess up my hair, me bonnie lass,' Glen replied mockingly and reached for Ursula's hair.

'Oh, stop it, you two!' Hugh said. 'Let's go back to the others and tell them before Williams's grandfather arrives with his men.'

'If he arrives, that is,' Darion clarified. 'We can't be sure of that. Remember that he believed up to today that his grandson died some thirty years ago. Let's all go back to the fire and wait for Ioroth's return,' he said as he walked back to the campfire.

'Come on over, you guys, hurry, hurry! Ioroth has returned and brought me my grandfather's Dagger, which means he is coming,' exclaimed William jubilantly and held up a richly decorated Dagger that bore the MacDougall's coat of arms.

'That's fantastic news, William! We should leave right away. We can rest once we reach the stone circle.'

'Aye, Darion, I agree. I would feel much better knowing that we are all safe,' replied William. He lifted Lucy onto his shoulders and placed one arm around Anne to support her.

'Hugh, Glen, Ursula, you better join the Dryads and secure our flanks. I am not yet certain that we are out of Danger, so please keep your eyes open and your weapons ready.'

'Will do Darion,' answered Hugh and signalled Glen and Ursula to spread out and join Laratbogh, Oren and Faerydae.

The walk through the forest was tranquil, except for the chirping crickets and the whisper of small leaves dancing in the breeze.

'We should be close, don't you think, Darion?' inquired Glen as the trees thinned and the first fragments of the rising sun began to filter through the treetops.

'Aye, Glen, look at the glen right in front of us,' answered Darion and pointed to an opening in the underbrush. With their last remaining strength, the friends rushed out of the forest and reached the glen just in time to watch as the rising sun's Dazzling gold and orange hues spread over the mountains and the stone circle of Strontoiller that stood in the centre of the glen.

'Are we safe here, Darion?' Glen asked as he rested his staff on the ground.

'Aye Glen, the stone circle is a place of pure white magic. It will not allow anything Dark near it, so you can rest.'

Exhausted but relieved that they had made it to the stone circle, the friends sunk onto their blankets and enjoyed the spectacular display of the radiant colours, which had replaced the Dark blue and purple of the twilight sky and bathed the valley in a golden glow.

'Don't fall asleep now, you guys. Look up to the hillcrest. Do you see the riders? I am sure it is my grandfather with his men,' William shouted excitedly.

It was a spectacular sight as the group of armed men came closer. Each soldier was clad in the bright red and green MacDougall tartans. Right in front on a white stallion rode Clyde MacDougall, proudly holding the banner with his coat of arms.

'Fàilte mah, my dear brave men and noble ladies. Tell me, which one of you is my grandson, William?' shouted the Laird as he approached.

'It's me, my Lord,' William replied, stepped forward and bowed to the Laird.

'Stand up, William, a MacDougall bows to no one. Grab your things and mount your horses. I can't wait to hear your story over a good hearty breakfast.'

'As you command,' answered William and helped Anne and Lucy onto the back of the massive warhorse before he swung himself effortlessly up behind them.

'Oh, am I relieved that we have horses. I'll be glad if I don't have to see any more goats for the next ten years.'

'There is nothing wrong with goats, Ursula! I love them roasted on a spit over an open fire basted with red wine, herbs, and garlic,' Glen replied with closed eyes and an expression of delight as if he could taste the roast already.

'Well said, my dear brother. Let's hope the Laird means it when he says a hearty breakfast, I am starving,' Hugh shouted and broke into loud laughter.

'I hope you all are comfortable and ready to leave!' the Laird shouted as he gave the signal to move away from the standing stones towards Dunollie Castle.

Avery enjoyed the ride on the broad back of the warhorse. They rode along a small brook that meandered through pastures with grassing cows and sheep and through acres of pale green wheat that moved gently in the warm breeze like waves in the ocean. Everyone had remained silent and savoured the beauty that surrounded them and the feeling of safety between the Laird's armed men. They were pretty startled when Dunollie Castle appeared before them high above the busy harbour of Oban. The horses broke into a gallop as they came closer to the Castle as if they could smell their stables and the fresh hay. It did not take long before they passed through the castle's massive gates.

'Welcome back, my Lord,' Dunbar called out as he came running out of the Castle to take hold of the stallion's bridle. He tried to address

William, but the clatter of hooves on cobblestones muddled his words so that William looked at him with a puzzled expression.

'Speak up when you address my grandson, Dunbar,' the Laird commanded, incensed as he dismounted his horse. The Castle's servants must have heard their master's voice since they all came running out of the stables, kitchen, and pantries to see the Laird's grandson William MacDougall.

'Ah, I see curiosity got the better of you. Well, come closer and welcome your young Lord and Master. Sir William MacDougall,' the Laird shouted and pointed proudly at William.

The servants bowed deeply and only chanced a quick glance at William's face before they began to whisper excitedly.

'Aye, he looks like his mother, my beloved Daughter Lady Sarah,' the Laird said, a trace of nostalgia in his eyes. 'But enough with the talking. We are hungry! Hurry and bring us food and wine. We must celebrate William's homecoming,' he cheered, ushering William and his companions into the Great Hall. The Hall was an impressive sight, with its high loft ceiling, whitewashed walls with oak wainscoting and elaborate tapestries. Many torches spread their flickering light over a massive oak table covered from end to end with the most delicious foods and massive jugs filled with ale and red wine. On the flagstone floor lay large red and green coloured rugs, and the long wooden benches had been covered with sheepskins.

'Don't just stand there, my friends! Sit down, eat and drink with me to celebrate my grandson's return.'

'Aye, my Lord, let's celebrate the homecoming of Lord William!' shouted the commander and lifted his beaker in a toast to William. The feast lasted long past sunset with music and Dance before the servants showed everybody to their respective chambers. William, Darion, and Avery remained in the Great Hall to tell the Laird about everything that had happened ever since the so-called Lord MacNab' had appeared at Kilchurn Castle and in the surrounding villages.

'Wait a moment,' the Laird paused after hearing their story. 'The man that you refer to as Lord MacNab' sounds like an orphan I had taken in more than forty years ago. He had gone with your mother to Kilchurn Castle after her wedding, and he was the one who brought me the message of her death and the death of her son William. He used to be a very quiet and humble servant. I wonder what happened to him to turn him into such a wicked man. But that is nothing we should concern ourselves with right now. We have to get Harris, Anne, and Lucy out of here before we can make our way to Kilchurn Castle to unseat Lord Campbell's bastard son.'

'Aye, Grandfather, how soon would you be able to put them on a ship to France?' asked William. He walked up to a large window and looked down to the harbour where five galleons lay on their anchor.

'The high tide will come in tomorrow around sunset, so we should aim to get them out of here before midnight. But do you think that Lady Anne will be strong enough to make that journey after all that she has gone through in the last few Days?'

'I'm certain she will be. She wants to be with her father when he dies, and there is not much time left. And besides, little Lucy will enjoy this great adventure. I'll go to their chamber to bring them the message, if it is alright with you, my Lord,' said Avery as she got up from the table and looked expectantly at the Laird.'

'Very well, Avery, go and tell her. The earlier she knows, the better. I'll get Dunbar to deliver the message to the captain at sunrise tomorrow so that he can get the ship and crew ready to lift anchor around sunset.'

'Thank you, my Lord,' Avery replied excitedly and ran out of the Great Hall to bring Anne the excellent news.

'Well, William, me lad, I think it is time for us to retire. We have lots to do before we visit Lord Campbell. Guit nuit, my dear grandson. My servants will show you to your bedchamber. See you tomorrow morning bright and early,' said Lord MacDougal in a hushed voice. He smiled and left the Great Hall. My grandson. That sounds wonderful. He thought as he walked through the long corridors to his chamber.

26 The Farewell

The Castle's halls felt as bleak and cold as during the Darkest Days of winter. All candles and torches had been snuffed out on Lord MacNab's orders, and fires were limited to the kitchen and the Laird's private quarters.

'Wickedness can only dwell in Darkness,' Allan said under his breath as he left the kitchen with a basket of bannocks and a pot of tea for the Laird. He had contemplated many times leaving the Castle as many other servants had done since the arrival of Lord MacNab'. But he had nowhere to go, so he made his way through the dark corridors to the Laird's bedchamber, as he had done for many years, knocked twice, and announced himself.

'Come in, you fool, or do you expect me to open the door for you?' shouted the Laird in a hoarse voice. out

'Aye, my Lord,' replied Allan. He rested the tea on the ground, opened the door and entered. The Laird's chamber looked like a battlefield. Broken furniture and shards of glass lay scattered around the fireplace. And the neck of a broken jug stuck out of the ashes.

'Place it on the table near the fireplace. I will help myself to it when I am ready. Now get your crippled arse out of here.'

It's crippled because of you, you noble vermin, thought Alan as he left the chamber fuming with rage. The Laird enjoyed it immensely to make fun of the men that had been disfigured or maimed in the countless battles they fought for him. Instead of honouring the soldiers, they made them work as serfs for no more than a daily crust of bread and a place in the stables to sleep. Alan tried to control his anger with the thought of the bacon and eggs that Rhona had prepared for him as he hurried back to the kitchen.

'Bring me to the wounded so that I can find out who or what thwarted the attack on the weaver's cottage. And get this blasted inbreed out of his bed. My patience is running low,' shouted Lord MacNab' so loudly that his voice echoed through the corridors and halls of the Castle.

'As you wish, my Lord, please follow me. I'll show you to the place where we keep the wounded,' replied the commander of the guards in a trembling voice and bowing so low that he almost lost balance.

'Please, my Lord, place this silken handkerchief over your nose when we enter the stables. The stench of the decaying flesh is horrific,' whispered one of the Lord's servants, handing him a scented handkerchief.

Alan could not believe what he had just seen. The proud commander of the guards trembling in fear, and the Laird hiding in his chamber. He ran straight back to the kitchen and told Rhona what he had overheard.

'Goodness gracious, what does he want with the wounded men? Haven't they suffered enough? You better eat quickly so you can follow them. We must know what they are up to,' said Rhona in a hushed voice. She filled

Alan's tankard with ale before she returned to the heart.

Alan gobbled his breakfast down as fast as he could, swung his old cloak over his shoulders as he snugged into the barn, and hid in the straw just as Lord MacNab' and his servants made their entrance.

'Shame on you. Commander, for letting these brave men lie in their faeces. And what is this, is this supposed to help the men to gain back their health? This is appalling!' shouted the Lord, kicking over a bowl with watered-down broth before he bent over one of the wounded soldiers.

'Now tell me, my good man, how you sustained these injuries. You don't have to fear me. I am on your side.'

Yea, right you are. You are the one who brought all the grief and loss on us, Lucas thought as he stared into the Lord's dead grey eyes.

'Forgive him, my Lord. He lost his voice during the fight in Eredine Forest. We hope he will recover to return to his father,' Avery, the commander.

'Who is his father?'

'It is Ross MacDuff, the butcher, my Lord.'

'Very well then, who can tell me what happened in the forest?'

'I can,' whispered a severely wounded soldier as he tried to sit up. 'Stay down, my son and tell me what you witnessed.'

'Well, my Lord, it was no army that defeated us. It was magic. The trees came alive and battered us with their heavy branches, and the thorn bushes ripped the flesh from our bones. Only when we could do no more than crawl did it stop,'

'Commander, I demand that you move the men into the Great Hall without delay and light the fire so they can rest in comfort while my servants attend to their injuries,' Lord MacNab' demanded. He turned and made his way to the Castle's gallery, where Duane awaited him red-faced and fuming with rage.

'Get out of my way, you preposterous shadow of a man,' hissed Lord MacNab' and pushed Duane out of his way before he sat down in front of a large painting picturing Lady Julia on her wedding day. Her long copper coloured hair was held together with a glittering net of gold and pearls and on her shoulder rested a tartan sash in the colours of the Campbell Clan.

'My Lord, all men are now in the Great Hall. What would you like us to do with the old, stained bedding?'

'Burn them and get the men bread and wine so that they can gain some strength and recover. We need every man if we want to free this land of magic,' Lord MacNab' ordered.

Alan made it back to the kitchen without raising anyone's suspicion over his long absence. He was in the middle of telling Rhona and the cook what he had seen when Lord MacNab's servants bolted into the kitchen demanding bread and wine for the wounded.

'Very well, my good men. You can return to your duties while we take care of everything.'

'Damn you woman, who do you think you are, giving me and my men orders? Get the wine and the bread and crawl back into your hole,' sneered the lead servant and pushed Rhona so hard that she fell to the ground. The cook's eyes flashed with anger as he tightened his grip on the cleaver in his hand. He was about to teach the men some manners when

Alan stepped in front of him with a large wicker basket of freshly baked bread and blocked his way.

'Would you like me to take the bread to the Great Hall for you, sir?' Alan asked Lord MacNab's commander.

'Very well, you go and do that, but we'll take the wine. Go on then, move it, don't stand in our way!' the commander replied, pushing Alan out of the kitchen.

'There is something fishy going on, I swear,' said Rhona as she dusted herself off.

The Great Hall was cramped with bedsteads made of straw, and the maids of the Castle lovingly cared for the men.

'My brave soldiers, I am deeply troubled to see how little the Laird values the sacrifices you made and promise that I will change, starting right now. From now on, every one of you will receive double rations, and my servants will attend to your injuries while the women that cared for you thus far will return to Dalmally and spend two days with their families,' Lord MacNab' declared. He then turned and bowed to the maids before signalling his servants to lead them out of the Castle. He raised his chalice and made a to toast the men.

'Let us share this special wine as I solemnly swear that your suffering will come to an end today.'

'My Lord, we must talk,' hissed Duane from the entrance of the Great Hall, 'I will not tolerate these filthy men in my Great Hall. Nor will I tolerate them drinking my best wine and your servants turning my courtyard into a cabbage field.'

Lord MacNab' walked out of the hall and stared at Duane with an expression of disgust as he ordered his servants to close and lock the doors.

'Make sure that these doors stay locked and that the women are on their way to Dalmally to spread the good news. The villagers will be happy to know how well we look after our injured men,' he instructed his men.

'And now to you, my dear Laird Campbell. Don't fret. You do not have to trouble yourself about any of this much longer. My men are preparing graves, not a cabbage field. Did you honestly think that I would waste time with these worthless men, did you? The wine they are enjoying right now will be the last that passes their lips as their wretched lives will end with the setting of the sun,' Lord MacNab' replied with an ice-cold sneer as he left the Castle accompanied by his armed men.

'Where are you going, my Lord?'

'I have a forest to burn, Duane. Go back to your chamber and enjoy the spectacle.'

'Do you have everything, Anne? Adelaide's letter to your father, your blankets, and Lucy's staff?'

'Aye, Harris took care of everything when he and Lucy boarded. All that's left is to say goodbye,' whispered Anne, with tears in her eyes. She hugged Avery and Ursula one last time and boarded the ship. The dockworkers removed the gangway, untied the ropes, and gave the boatswain the all-clear as soon as Anne had reached the ship's bridge.

'Raise the anchor and set the sails,' ordered the captain welcoming his three passengers aboard. The anchor winch creaked as the heavy rope tightened and began to pull the anchor from the muddy harbour bed. The breeze caught the sails, and the ship moved slowly away from the harbour out to the open sea.

'Come on, you, guys. It is high time to get back to the Castle. I am sure that my grandfather and his men are ready to ride out,' said William

'You're right, William. Let's not waste time standing here and mourning. After all, we have things to do and places to go,' cheered Hugh as he mounted his horse.

'Race you to the castle!' shouted Avery. She picked up the reins, squeezed her horse gently, and galloped out of the harbour with thundering huffs.

'Oh, do you truly believe that you will get their first Avery? Well, let me show you how to do it.'

'Aye, Hugh, keep on dreaming,' chuckled Avery as she reached the ramparts just as Lord MacDougal and his armed men crossed the drawbridge.

'Oh good, you are back,' he greeted them. 'I gather you are all ready to leave.'

'Aye, my lord,' answered Avery. She turned her horse around and took one last look across the sea as the sails of the ship slowly disappeared behind the island of Jura.

'Now that's how I like to travel,' Glen remarked. 'Let's hope we will be able to do that for all our journeys from now.'

'You are right, and it's a lot faster too,' Hugh agreed. 'We should be able to reach Adelaide's cottage before sunrise. That is, of course, if you don't get too comfortable. We are falling behind. Look at Darion, Avery, and Ursula. They've almost reached the forest.'

'Well, you go, keep up with them if you like, Hugh. I'll stay with the Lord and his men.'

'Aye, see you later,' laughed Hugh as he pulled away from Glen and galloped after Ursula, Avery, and Darion. The four friends enjoyed the silence of the woods, the smell of the trees and the Damp forest floor as their horses ambled past moss-covered rocks and trees, through patches of tall ferns and blueberry fields, below the lush green canopy of the trees and the star-studded night sky.

'It is nice to see you back in the forest,' called Oren from a nearby tree.

'It is great to be back in the woods! I'd choose the glens and the forest over a castle's Great Hall any time,' Avery laughed. 'Are you alone, Oren?'

'No, Laratbogh and Faerydae are way upfront to make sure we don't meet any unpleasant surprises again. But I'll go and get them if you like so that we can continue the journey to Adelaide's together while you tell us about William's grandfather,' Oren answered and disappeared.

Shortly after, Laratbogh and Faerydae broke through the underbrush on the backs of the beautiful stags that had carried Avery and Glen earlier.

'Goodness, you startled me! I expected you in the treetops,' chuckled Avery.

'Well, Oren secures our path from the treetops while we check the underbrush. I am so happy to see you all back in the forest and that we have the chance to spend some time with you,' said Faerydae and smiled at Glen, who had just caught up with his friends.

'I am delighted to be back with you,' answered Glen with a warm smile. He could not take his eyes of Faerydae. Her waist-long green hair shimmered like emeralds in the moonlight as she leaned over to take his hand. The friends shared their adventures and plans with the Dryads when Hugh noticed an orange tinge in the night sky.

'Look up, guys. I wonder what is causing that glow. Could it be a Northern Light?' Exclaimed Hugh and pointed to the sky.

'Certainly not. It is flickering, so it must be a fire in the distance. Oren, can you see anything?' shouted Darion up to the treetops. He sped to a clearing nearby, closely followed by Avery and her friends.

'Eredine forest is on fire!' screamed Oren and looked at Laratbogh in terror. 'Where is Faerydae? Where is our sister?'

'She was right next to me not a moment ago,' Glen replied, turned his horse around and galloped back to where he had seen her last. He jumped off his horse and searched the thickets for a sign of Faerydae. His heart was racing, and his breath became quick and laboured as he fought his way through a field of tall ferns. All of a sudden, Faerydae's stag appeared in front of him.

'Where is she? Did you throw her off? Did you hurt her,' Glen shouted in desperation, grabbing the stag by his antlers?

'Leave him be. It's nothing that he has done. Faerydae is dying,' Laratbogh whispered as she parted the ferns next to Glen, revealing Faerydae as she lay motionless on the mossy ground. Her skin and beautiful hair had lost their colour and shine and looked ashen.

'Glen, mo ghradh, I have to leave you much too soon,' Faerydae said in a faint whisper. 'But I beg you to let me go and not mourn my passing, as I will return to you one day. So please, be happy and cherish every day of your life and the company of your friends. Take this acorn to the land of Elfame and plant it under the tree where I showed myself to you the first time. I loved you from the moment I saw you, and I always will,' she said with her last breath.

'No, no, don't leave me!' Glen screamed in agony, fell to his knees, and pulled Faerydae's lifeless body into his arms.

'Oh no, what has happened!' Avery and Ursula exclaimed in horror as they saw Faerydae in Glen's arms.

'Her tree died in the fire, and so did she. We must take her home to Elfame, bury her, and plant the acorn she carried so that she can be reborn,' Oren replied in a hushed voice.

Avery's heartbeat echoed in her ears, and a dreadful feeling of emptiness washed over her as she looked into Faerydae's lifeless eyes. Ghilli Duh passed his hand gently over her eyelids and closed them forever. He then took her out of Glen's arms and carried her to the river's edge to call his sisters Arianrhod, Coventina, and the Queen of Elfame.

Avery, Darion, Hugh, Lord MacDougal and all his men silently pulled their swords and raised them towards the sky in a salute to Faerydae. The river slowed to a gentle flow. Its soft curls gleamed like jewels in the moonlight as a silvery mist enveloped the forest like a mourning veil. Glen followed Ghilli Duh to the river's edge with his hands clenched in trembling fists, trying to battle the grief that tore him apart. Tears welled up in his deep blue eyes as he listened to the Dryad's beautiful mourning song.

Ghilli Duh walked into the river, raising Faerydae's body to the moon just as the Queen of Elfame broke through the mist on a raft that glowed as brightly as the full moon.

'Ghilli Duh, my dear brother, you called me to take your beloved Daughter Faerydae home. And so, I will. We will plant the acorn that holds her life's essence and wait for the day when she returns to us.'

Ghilli Duh bowed to his sister and lowered Faerydae gently onto the silver raft. He passed his hands over her body, covering her with a shroud of flowers before he returned to Glen to lead him to the float.

'You have to fulfil Faerydae's last wish and remain at her side during her last journey through the realm of the living.' Ghilli Duh gently whispered to Glen. The friends watched as Glen and the float disappeared in a cascade of brilliant shooting stars.

'We have to avenge Faerydae's death and bring Lord MacNab's reign to an end,' Darion hissed through clenched teeth. He embraced Avery and held her close to his chest as if he feared losing her too.

'Aye, let's make haste, my friends, to put an end to all this cruelty,' William said in a trembling voice before he turned to Oren and Laratbogh.

'I pray that you and your sisters will remain safe.'

'They will, William,' Ghilli Duh replied.

'Faerydae was the only one that had chosen a home tree in Eredine Forest, as she wanted to remain close to Glen. So, it is right that he will be the one to bring her home to Elfame and replant the acorn she carried. You mustn't dwell in Darkness and sorrows, my friends. Faerydae will return to us in time. Go now and continue your quest under the guidance and protection of our beloved Lady Coventina.'

Everyone had lost the energy to speak. The friends felt as if their hearts were bound and shackled as they rode through the ancient forest the remains. It had always supplied shelter to Avery and her friends and was home to many creatures. The once verdant forest had been reduced to smouldering ashes and blackened tree trunks. Lifeless sticks of charcoal that reached for the sky like lost souls. The voices of the wildlife that once dwelt here had been silenced. Many of them perished in the blaze.

After a seemingly endless ride, the lingering smoke lifted and reviled Adelaide's cottage as it stood untouched on the small knoll above the gurgling brook, like a promise of a better tomorrow.

Avery slid off her horse and ran to the cottage.

'We lost her, Adelaide. We lost Faerydae,' she cried, burying her face into Adelaide's shoulder and clinging onto her tightly as if she was drowning in the grief of the loss of her friend.

'I know, I know, mo chridhe,' Adelaide comforted her. 'Ghilli Duh told us what happened. I can't even begin to tell you how sad we all are over the senseless death of Faerydae, but I am so glad that you all have returned safely. You should rest, my love. You look exhausted. Come on. I'll get you some food that will help you to calm down.'

'That is a marvellous idea. Do you have enough food for all of our men, Adelaide?'

'Aye, William, I do, Ross brought enough meat to last for weeks, and Peter filled my pantry with enough bread and scones to feed two armies. I'll ask Madge and Julia to set up the food for you in the barn.'

'Thank you so much, Adelaide. Tell me, is that Marianne I saw as we came over the bridge?' William asked.

'Aye, the guild members freed her just after you all left. The Laird's guards brought her out of the Castle to hang her in the market square two Days earlier than planned. I guess Lord MacNab' was eager to get rid of her, but she'll tell you all about it herself, come along. Maighread can't wait to see you,' said Adelaide. She took William's hand and pulled him into the cottage to greet Maighread.

'Oh William, I was so worried about you! Where is Avery?'

'I am right here, Granny,' Avery shouted as she came running into the kitchen.

'Avery, my bonnie lass, I am so happy you are unhurt! But you look tired, come over here and rest while I get you a bowl of the stew you love so much.'

'Aye, alright, Ma,' William agreed. 'You do that, but then you and Adelaide must come with me so that I can introduce you to my grandfather, Lord Clyde MacDougal. He is waiting in the barn for you. So please give Avery the bowl and come along,' he said, placed his arms around Maighread and Adelaide and led them to the barn, where Lord MacDougal was engaged in a lively conversation with John and Bhaltair.

'Grandfather, please excuse the interruption, but I would like you to meet the two women that saved my life, raised me, and made me the man I am today,' William announced with trembling lips.

'I am honoured to meet you, Maighread and Adelaide. I will be forever grateful for your selfless devotion to my daughter and for raising my grandson with love and tender care. He has truly become a righteous young man,' Lord MacDougal declared, kneeling before Adelaide and Maighread bowing his head in gratitude.

'I thought a MacDougall bows to no one,' William whispered in his grandfather's ear and smiled.

'Oh no, my Lord, please get up. We feel honoured that your Daughter entrusted William's life and wellbeing to us. We love him dearly, and we are so grateful that you are finally united,' Maighread replied, taking the Lords' hand and pulling him up.

'What a glorious day, let us give thanks and celebrate! Lift our tankards in honour of the friends here with us today, the ones we lost and to a new beginning. Slainte mhath shouted Bhaltair as he lifted his tankard.

'Slainte mhath, my friends and companions! Let us all enjoy this special day and thank our generous hosts for their hospitality, good food, and wine. But let us not forget why we came and that our mission is not yet complete. So, eat, drink, and rest for a while!' Lord MacDougall cheered, pointing to the large table in the middle of the barn stacked with the most sumptuous food, wine and ale.

'Tomorrow, we ride on to Kilchurn Castle to put an end to the torment that was brought over these good people.'

Avery and Ursula had found a cosy place in a pile of straw, away from all the excited laughter and heated discussions. The girls were lost in thought.

'Avery, do you remember the cold morning when we first met Darion right here in the barn?'

'Aye, I do. Look how much has happened since,' answered Avery sleepily. She closed her eyes and tried to forget about all horrors they had met since that day in the barn. The loss of Nissa and Faerydae were fresh in her mind. As Avery lay in the hay, remembering her friend, she overheard a conversation between Hugh and Adelaide.

'I am so relieved to see that the fire did not reach the cottage and that you all remained unharmed,' sighed Hugh as he poured some red wine for Adelaide.

'Aye Hugh, the enchantments protected us from the blaze, but it consumed Eredine Forest and claimed the life of Faerydae, which is an act of unspeakable cruelty.'

'Do you know what happened, Adelaide?'

'Aye, we all do. We saw Lord MacNab' and his troops at the edge of the forest and overheard as he ordered a group of Red Caps to set fire to the forest. I believe he intended to flush us out of the cottage, but little did he know that the charms that protect the cottage are by far more powerful than anything that he could muster. He was furious when he realised that his plan had failed.'

27 The Caves of Wemyss

Avery was not in the mood to celebrate. The excited chatter and laughter were more than she could handle right now. The grief over Faerydae's death and the destruction of the Eredine forest still felt too raw. Instead, she had hidden in a large pile of straw, curled up in her blanket and fell into a deep sleep. In her dreams, she relived the escape from Kilchurn Castle, the Boobrie's attack, Nissa's and Faerydae's death, the happy moment when William embraced his grandfather and the happiness on Anne's face when the Galleon pulled out of Oban harbour.

'Avery, wake up. There is no time to sleep right now. We have to make our way to Wemyss,' whispered Darion and shook her gently. He deeply regretted having to wake her, her face was so relaxed, and a faint smile lingered on her lips. But he had no choice. They had to seize the opportunity to take possession of the Sapphire and free the captives while Lord MacNab' focused on Dalmally.

'What are you saying, Darion? We're riding to Wemyss now?'

‘Aye, that is precisely what Darion was saying, Avery,’ Ursula confirmed. ‘Come on, you sleepy head. You missed all the excitement.’

‘How long have I been asleep, and what have I missed? You are not referring to all ruckuses you guys made while I was trying to get some sleep, right?’ asked Avery as she sat up and rubbed her eyes open?

‘Oh, dear Avery, that's what I am talking about! Come on, stretch your legs. We have to go,’ Ursula cheered. She picked up Avery's scabbard and handed it to Hugh before she rushed out of the barn to help Darion with the horses.

‘Damn, what's the great hurry? Why are you all acting so crazy?’

‘Don't fret, Avery. I'll explain everything. Come on, grab my hand. I'll help you up,’ chuckled Hugh, pulling her to her feet.

‘Thanks, Hugh. Now that you mention it, I am feeling rather stiff. It's not very comfortable to sleep in the armour,’ Avery moaned, stretched and looked around. ‘Where is everybody?’

‘Well, William and his grandfather left for Dalmally, Lady Julia rounded up her guards and is on her way to Kilchurn Castle, and you already know where we are heading,’ Hugh explained.

‘Aye, that part I know, and trust me when I say that I can hardly wait to get there, but the rest of it needs some unravelling, which I hope you'll do once we are on our way.’

‘I will, Avery, but we have to get going. Ursula and Darion just left to check something out,’ urged Hugh and helped her in the saddle. Avery and Hugh took one last look at the cottage before forcing their horses into a quick trot. They Dashed through the woods, past

Dalmally, and caught up with Darion and Ursula in a small birch grove overlooking the River Lochy outside Tyndrum.

'What are you looking at, Darion? Are you contemplating passing through Tyndrum?' Avery inquired.

'No, we stopped so that I could take a closer look at the group of boats that seems to be heading for Dallmally,' Darion explained.

'Why, what is so special about them? Don't you think the men are just eager to get an early start in setting up their wares for the market tomorrow? After all, it's Beltane, and the market will be humming with vendors from all the surrounding villages.'

'Aye, right, and for the special celebration of Beltane, they are selling wood axes and swords made of scythes, right,' Darion replied with sarcastic laughter, pointing down to the passing boats.

'Goodness, I did not see that! What do you think they plan to do with these primitive weapons?' Avery asked, clearly disturbed by what she saw.

'I suspect they plan to join Lord MacNab' to fight side by side with his men and the Red Caps. He lures prisoners and peasants into his service with the promise of freedom and land, and these desperate fools fall for it, leave their families and run into their demise.'

'This is horrible. These lads won't have a chance against well-trained soldiers. All of them will be slaughtered like cattle!'

'Aye, Avery, it is high time to end this. But don't fool yourself. We must fight men like them in the caves of Wemyss' and the way to the Blue Glacier. You must promise me not to hesitate or show mercy to these men. They don't deserve your pity. They are driven by bloodlust and greed,' Darion insisted, looking sternly at Avery, Hugh, and Ursula.

After a moment of contemplating the grim fate of these men, the friends turned their backs on Tyndrum and continued their journey. They trudged determinedly through woods, across valleys covered with heather, and along with fields of barley and rye. A balmy breeze caressed their faces and ruffled their hair as the sun began to set over Ben Lomond.

After an arduous journey throughout the night over rugged terrain, the horses and riders were exhausted. The friends decided to rest and began to scan their surroundings for shelter. As soon as the first rays of the rising sun lit up the valley, the friends noticed a dreary old cottage behind a group of large oak trees.

They were exhausted and hungry. The friends slid off their horses and tied them to a group of trees on a small pasture behind the crumbling cottage. Hugh walked up to the weather-beaten door and knocked gingerly before opening it ever so slightly to peep inside. Judging by its neglected outer appearance, he expected to see broken furniture and rats rushing around. But to his great surprise, the cottage was clean and cosy. Bedding made of fresh hay had been placed along the walls, a steaming cauldron hung over glowing embers, and a basket with bannocks and bread stood on a table near the fireplace.

'Now that's a surprise. I could have sworn that the cottage was abandoned. The way it looks, its owner must be close by. Why else would there be a kettle on fire,' Avery exclaimed as she slipped past Hugh into the cottage?

'Oh dear, the mutton stew seems ready to eat. What do you think folks would they mind if we have some?'

'Aye, young Master Hugh, go on,' replied a soft voice. 'I prepared it for you all, have as much as you like. And make yourselves comfortable in the hay.'

The friends took a step back and scanned the cottage curiously to see who had spoken.

'Oh dear, come on and show yourself! My friends will not harm you,' Darion laughed. He lay down his weapons and stretched comfortably out on a pile of hay.

'Aye, very well, Lord Darion, as you wish,' stammered the delicate voice. A shy Brownie girl, dressed in a long brown and green dress, appeared from behind the door and lowered herself to a curtsey.

'My goodness! Please forgive me for staring, but you are the first Brownie I have met. My name is Avery, and I am delighted to meet you,' Avery said excitedly and stooped down to shake the Brownie's tiny hand.

'My name is Nala. I am honoured to meet you all,' the wee Brownie whispered and dropped another curtsey.

'Did you do all this by yourself?' Ursula asked in admiration.

'No, not really,' Nala replied. She turned around and pulled two other Brownies out of the shadows.

'These are my brothers, Ben and Fen. They cleaned the cottage and brought the hay, but I did all the cooking, just as Lord Asanopirh asked me to do. He and Lady Sorcha await you at the edge of the Dark forest, and Master Bilobeal will join you near the cave's entrance.'

'Thank you for the message, Nala. And thank you for all the hard work you and your brothers have done,' Avery said, took off her scabbard and sat down next to Darion.

'You three have done a marvellous job. The cottage is spotless, and the stew smells heavenly. My mouth is beginning to water. I can't wait to try it,' exclaimed Hugh and rubbed his palms together in high expectation.

'Blimey, you sound just like Glen,' giggled Ursula and patted his shoulder.

'What about a shot of ale before we serve the food?' suggested Fen as he handed each of them a tankard filled to the brim with ale.

'That's a brilliant idea, me wee lad, but you should drink with us!' replied Hugh and smacked his lips.

'Sorry, sir, we have to decline. We'll take care of the horses and then leave so that you can rest. We'll return by nightfall with provisions for your journey to Wemyss and make sure all traces of your presence be removed,' Ben explained as he filled four large wooden bowls with steaming hot stew.

The friends rolled up in their soft plaids, closed their eyes, and fell asleep well-fed and content. Their breaths slowed, and the expressions on their faces gave way from strain and stress to peace.

The Day passed, and its golden light began to make way for the deep blue night sky when the friends woke and started to stir.

'Oh, that felt good,' sighed Hugh, gave a big yawn and stretched like a cat. 'All I need now is a wee bit of stew before we head out. What about you folks?'

'Aye, I would love some. And while you go for the stew, fetch some water for me. I am terribly thirsty,' Ursula replied.

She got up and brushed the hay from her jerkin.

'No need to trouble yourself, Master Hugh. We placed food and water in the satchels.' Fen appeared. 'Your horses are fed and saddled so that you can continue your journey without delay,' the Brownie bowed and pointed to his brother Ben, who held the door open for the friends.

'That's very kind of you! Although I'll admit it somehow feels as if you were trying to get rid of us,' Hugh said with a cheeky smile.

'Oh no, not at all, Master Hugh!' replied Fen nervously and blushed. 'But we got word that about twenty armed men left Dalmally for the caves of Wemyss around midday, so we thought it would be wise to act swiftly.'

'You are right, Fen. Thanks for the warning, but tell me, where is Darion?' asked Avery as she left the cottage.

'He is waiting for you behind the cottage. Take good care and be safe. We will see you and your friends again soon,' Fen replied with a bow.

Hugh, Avery, and Ursula ran the last check on their weapons, leaving the cottage and stumbled into Darion. The Elf had once again appeared out of nowhere, despite his promise to Avery.

'Sorry, I did not intend to startle you, but we have to make haste. You heard Fen, we must cross Ben Lomond while the moon is high in the sky,' said Darion. He handed them their reins before he mounted his horse and sped away from the cottage.

It was almost midday when the friends finally reached the edge of the Dark forest. The journey across Ben Lomond had been highly challenging. The trail was steep and narrow, with straight rock walls on one side and an almost vertical drop. The friends had decided to dismount and lead the horses across by foot.

'Crivens, that was a grind. I hope we don't have to use the same trail on our way back,' remarked Hugh as he dismounted his horse.

'I don't think we will,' Avery said. 'It would be faster if we take one of Lord MacDougal's galleons to return the sapphire.'

'Aye right, I had completely forgotten that we have a fleet of ships at our service!' he replied with relief. But we have to get it first. Has anyone seen Sorcha or Asanopirh?' 'I haven't seen Sorcha yet, but Asanopirh is right behind you, turn around,' declared Avery as she pointed to a bright, blinding silhouette on a wooded bluff.

'Blimey! Now I truly understand the meaning of his name. I most certainly would not want to be his enemy. That gleaming armour will surely be the last thing you ever saw,' Hugh remarked through squinted eyes.

'Our horses will not enter the Dark forest, so we have to leave them with Ben, Fen, and Nala,' whispered Sorcha in Hugh's ear.

'Crivens, Sorcha, you startled me!' exclaimed Hugh with a shudder, placing his hand on his heart.

'You better calm your nerves before we enter the forest. It is not a place for the faint-hearted,' laughed Sorcha squeezing Hugh's shoulder.

'Come on, Sorcha, I am not faint-hearted, and you know that,' protested Hugh and handed his reins to Nala.

'Very well, Hugh, we all know that you're not. Don't fret. But before we enter the forest, I must caution you all not to touch anything. The forest has been poisoned and is dying,' Asanopirh instructed. His voice was stern as metal, and his eyes mirrored the anger roaring inside him.

The friends felt as if they stepped into icy waters when they entered the Dark forest. A dense and pungent mist rose from the ground, obstructing their vision and burning their throats and nostrils with every breath.

'Blood bas, I can't breathe,' mouthed Ursula, dropping to her knees in a violent cough.

'Oh, Ursula, I am very sorry! We forgot that you are mortals,' Sorcha whispered, ripping strips of cloth from her cloak and handing them to the three friends.

'Here, take these and place them over your mouth and nose. Our cloaks block Dark magic and poison, but I would still advise you to wear your gloves and to pull the blankets over your heads,' she added in a hushed voice as she made sure that the strips of cloth were tied appropriately.

'Let's use hand signals from here on. We don't want to alert the guards,' mouthed Darion after getting the all-clear from Sorcha. The friends rushed through the doomed forest like fleeting shadows without making a sound or leaving a trace. There was no sign of life anywhere, no bird's song or chirping crickets, not even the sound of rustling leaves. The forest floor was soggy and covered with decaying limbs, dead. Twisted vines hung from the trees like snakes. Noxious black and yellow lichens encrusted the trees and shrubs, draining them of their last drops of life's essence.

'Stop,' hissed Asanopirh. He pointed to the cave's entrance. It was framed by massive roots of a giant oak tree that towered on a gigantic rock before them.

'Majestic, isn't she? You should have seen her when she was healthy and strong. Now the ancient one is fading away,' whispered Ghilli Duh as he ran his hands gently over the tree's gnarled roots.

'We did not expect to see you here, Ghilli Duh. It must be tough for you to see what was done to these woods,' Asanopirh whispered as he greeted the mighty spirit of the forest.

'Aye, Asanopirh, it makes me shudder. But I had to come to see if there was anything the Dryads or I could do to set things right again. We have not given up hope yet.'

'Did you bring Laratbogh and Oren with you?' Avery asked, searching the trees for any sign of her friends.

'I'm afraid it would be too dangerous at this point. I wouldn't risk their well-being. But rest assured, the Dryads will nurture the forest back to life once you have driven the murderous scum out of here.'

'Oh, that we will Ghilli Duh, you can be sure of that,' insisted Bilobeal as he stepped out of the cave.

'How lovely to see you, Bilobeal. We were just about to enter,' whispered Avery and bowed to Bilobeal.

'Are you on your own, or did you bring your brothers?' Darion asked as he embraced his comrade.

'Aye, Sabaltalab and Phaervlon are inside scoping out the passages leading to the inner caves. They should return at any moment - that is, if they haven't been discovered....'

'Discovered? By whom? You are not talking about us, dear brother?' joked Sabaltalab in a hushed voice as he and Phaervlon appeared at the cave's entrance.

'Och, what happened to your beautiful amber coloured armour Sabaltalab? And your emerald, green jerkin Phaervlon? Why are you dressed in black today?' Sorcha giggled.

'We thought it would be wise not to stick out like a sore thumb. After all, we'll be dealing with some truly nasty vermin here.'

'Aye, you are right, Phaervlon. Your copper hair is bright enough. But tell me, what did you see?'

'About thirty Red Caps overseeing the mineworkers, and another fifteen men are guarding the Sapphire and Gregor's cell,' Phaervlon informed them. But to tell you the truth, Sorcha, they are easy targets.'

'What makes you think that?' asked Darion as he stepped closer to the three heavily armed Drows.

'Because they are all wasted, Darion! All these fools do is sit and drink while boasting what they will do with the riches they made guarding the caves.'

'Let's not waste precious time then! Bilobeal, since you and your brothers already know the tunnels, you should go ahead and clear the way for Darion, Hugh, and the lassies,' Asanopirh declared. 'Sorcha and I'll take care of the guards, get the Sapphire and free Gregor.'

'Aye, Asanopirh,' replied Bilobeal before rushing his brothers into the caves, closely followed by Hugh.

'Be safe, Hugh. Please don't do anything stupid,' whispered Ursula wiping tears from her eyes.

'I'll, I promise,' replied Hugh and threw Ursula a kiss as he ran after the three Drows.

It only took Hugh a few steps into the cave to realise how thankful he and his friends should be for their soft suede boots. The loud clatter of their old boots would have echoed through the caverns and given them away in a heartbeat.

'Stay close to the walls, Hugh. The guards could hear you when you walk through the puddles,' muttered Sabaltalab, pointing to the shallow water-filled holes in the cave's floor.

'Aye, but tell me, what's that sweet smell?'

'It's arsenic, in other words, the smell of death. No one would be able to survive in here for long, but Lord MacNab' doesn't care. He just roams the land and abducts strong, young men and women for the work in his mines,' replied Sabaltalab in a hushed voice, pointing to the shimmering veins in the cave's walls.

How many of the lassies will still be alive and able to make the journey back home? He wondered. What did Darion say about mercy for the Lord's servants? Well, they will not get any from me. That's for bloody sure they gave up the right to live when they agreed to guard these caves, he thought and bit his lip so hard that he broke through the skin. Tiny drops of blood trickled down his chin and were about to drop.

'Blimey, Hugh, are you bonkers!' hissed Bilobeal when he saw Hugh's bloodied chin.

'The Red Caps can smell blood from miles away! Here, take this. It will stop the bleeding. Let's just hope the Red Caps are not hungry today.'

Hugh looked ashamed at Bilobeal when he realised that his anger could have cost them their lives. Get it together, you eejit. Calm yourself and breathe just as Faerydae taught you, he thought, taking the leaves from Bilobeal and pressing them between his lips.

Avery followed close behind, suspiciously scanning the tunnel walls for holes or narrow crevices in which Red Caps or armed men could be lurking. She was surprised to see elaborate drawings and strange markings over the tunnel walls. She turned to Darion and whispered, 'Have you ever seen anything like that before?'

'Aye, these are drawings from my ancestors that used to live in these caves. But you should not allow yourself to be distracted. Keep your eyes fixed on the tunnels for any shadows,' mouthed Darion and walked ahead of Avery.

It is so quiet, too quiet for my taste, she thought, holding her breath and listening harder. Someone or something is close. It cannot be Ursula, as she is further behind. She could hear breathing close to her, steadied herself and pretended to be unaware of her pursuer. She stopped to bend forward as if she were fastening the laces on her boots. In a swift movement, she gripped the dragon tooth handles of her swords and drew them with a deadly whistling sound from her scabbards. She extended her arms and whirled through the narrow cave-like a deadly blizzard.

Avery was swirling so fast that it was hard to make out her form. Her blades flashed like lightning as she slashed everything near her. Sparks sprayed as the blades hit the cave's walls, while a blinding white light emanated from her and illuminated the tunnels. She had a deadly focus on anything that moved and remained ice-cold, but there were no more shadows, the air was stifling hot, and the smell of sulphur and blood filled her lungs. Yellow ashes had tinted the walls around her, confirming that her intuition had just saved their lives.

The eerie silence had returned. There was no other breathing than hers, so Avery decided to wait for Ursula, leaning against the wall to calm herself. *That's taking too long. What is she doing? Did she fall, or....,* Avery not dare to finish that thought and run back to look for Ursula? The most horrific images flashed before her eyes, and a singular, cold fear filled her chest.

'Ursula, where are you?' she whispered. She held her breath and listened into the deserted tunnel for a reply.

'I am here, Avery. I can't walk. You'll have to go on without me. I'll be okay.'

'Damn you, Ursula, how could I go on when I know that you are hurt? Where are you? I can't see you,' replied and hastened towards Ursula's voice. She nearly choked on her breath when she saw her best friend lying on the ground in a puddle of yellow-tinted water, her jerking wrapped around one of her legs.

'Damn, Damn, what happened, Ursula? How bad is it?'

'A bloody Red Cap came out from nowhere and slashed my leg! But I got the bastard. He must have thought he'd finished me and leaned right into my dirk. He looked stunned just before he dissolved into this,' whispered Ursula and tried to smile.

'We have to get you out of here. Can you walk?'

'I don't know. I'll try it. But we have to be careful that no blood will soak through. You heard what Bilobeal told Hugh.'

'Aye, I think we'll be okay. Your jerkin seems like it's holding up. Come, lean on me.' Avery and Ursula made it back to the cave's entrance, where Ghilli Duh met them.

'Hurry back in, Avery. I'll take good care of her, don't you fret,' Ghilli Duh said. He wrapped his cloak around Ursula and disappeared. Avery took a few deep breaths before running back into the cave to catch up with Darion. There were yellow ashes and pikestaffs everywhere. Blimey, we must have wiped out half of them already. I wonder how the lads are doing, Avery thought as she rounded one of the last corners and ran straight into Darion's arms.

'Crivens Avery, you had me worried. Are you all right? Where is Ursula? Come on. We must hurry back. Bilobeal is waiting on us.'

'Aye, Darion, I am sorry, it wasn't my intention to fret you, but Ursula got hurt, so I had to get her out. I'll tell you later what happened. Let's get back to the guys.'

'It's about bloody time,' Bilobeal exclaimed when the duo reappeared. 'Come on, you two. We have to make a move while half the group of Red Caps is gone. We should be done and out before they return.'

'They will not return, don't fret. Bilobeal, Avery, and Ursula took care of them. Let's finish the rest and then get everybody out of here,' replied Darion.

'Brilliant. But wait, where is my bonnie lass, Ursula?' Bilobeal inquired and walked three steps back into the tunnel,'

'She got hurt, so I had to bring her out. Ghilli Duh took her to safety. Come on, let's go and finish these bastards off,' hissed Avery as she pulled out her blades and walked over to Hugh, who stood in the middle of the cave-like a rock in human form, fearless and ready to kill. Hugh held two arrows between his fingers, pulled the bowstring and took a deep breath before he aimed at two Red Caps facing each other in a deep conversation. They won't even know what hit them. He thought as he released the sinew. The arrow's hissed through the air hitting the two Red Caps with such a force that the cloud of yellow ashes sprayed in all directions. He quickly placed another arrow between his fingers and scanned the cave for the next target. His rage over Ursula's injury had grown like a fire in a furnace. All he wanted was to make them pay.

'Blimey Hugh, now that was a nice shot! Leave some for us, will you,' laughed Sabaltalab. He ran towards a group of Red Caps, swinging his axes with a force that he severed their heads from the bodies with one strike.

'Darion, you go on and take Avery to her father. Phaervlon and I will get the other captives out of here Sabaltalab and Hugh are having so much fun cleaning up that I think we can leave the rest to them. See you outside,' Bilobeal smirked as he ran off towards the cavern where the captives were held.

'You heard him, Avery, let's go! According to Sabaltalab, your father's cell is next to the vault with the Sapphire. I am sure Asanopirh and Sorcha have taken care of the guards by now,' Darion stated calmly. He took Avery's hand and pulled her through the labyrinth of tunnels. They reached the cavern just as Asanopirh and Sorcha were about to unlock Gregor's cell door.

'Please let me,' Avery asked, breathing fast. She took a moment to steady herself and then removed the heavy cast iron bar from the door with trembling hands. It swung open gave way to total Darkness.

'Darion, hand me a torch. I can't see a thing,' Avery whispered, looking fearful.

'I'll come in with you, Avery. I am sure he is okay,' Darion said in a calming voice. He placed his arm around her shoulders and walked with her into the pitch-black cell. 'Father, it's me, Avery. Where are you? I have come to bring you home. Please, show yourself.' Avery called out, trying her best to keep her voice from trembling.

'Avery, Mo Ghràdh I am here. You came to free me. Everything will be fine.'

Avery listened hard and tried to follow the voice. She lowered the torch and saw a frail man with long matted hair leaning against the wall, trying to stand. Avery could not move or speak. Tears streamed from her eyes, and she began to shake violently.

'Sorcha, take Avery out of here while Asanopirh and I take care of Gregor. We don't know how many of these wretched men are left in the caves,' Darion instructed, releasing Avery into Sorcha's arms before he addressed Gregor.

'We have to place something over your eyes, Gregor, so that the light will not blind you. Give me your hand. We will get you out of here,' Darion whispered. He placed his cloak over Gregor's head and shoulders before he and Asanopirh carried him out of his cold and callous prison. The Elves made their way through the cave slowly and with great caution carrying the frail body of Avery's father.

'Well, it appears to me you got all the captives out. Let me make certain that no one followed you or spread the word of what happened here today. You better step back,' Ghilli Duh declared. He looked up to the mighty oak, raised his arms, and whispered an enchantment.

The tree began to moan and creak as she loosened her grip on the granite rocks beneath her towering stem. Soil and gravel began to trickle through her roots like grains of sand through an hourglass, counting down the last moments of her long life before she finally fell with a deafening roar taking the massive boulders with her and burying the cave's entrance.

Avery took a sigh of relief as the last rock came to a rest and the cloud of dust and debris finally settled. She appeared calm and composed, but her emotions of triumph and horror battled for dominance deep down. Her hands trembled, and her heart thumped so loudly Avery was sure everyone around her could hear it. After steadying herself, she walked over to the group of captives looking, hoping to find her friends. But their eyes were glassy and half-closed and appeared to look past her. Their hollow cheeks, bony forearms and hands showed Avery that they must have been starving for a long time. Their once rosy skin was red and covered with lesions and warts.

‘I can't make out any of my friends, Darion. I don't know these lassies, and my father might not have the strength to make the journey,’ Avery cried out in desperation and closed her eyes.

‘Give it time, Avery. Nala, Ben, and Fen take them back to the cottage, where Lady Brigid will help them regain their health and strength. You have to trust that everything will turn out well,’ whispered Darion pulling her into his arms.

28 The Change of Tides

William urged his horse into a gallop and Dashed through the forest with flying huffs, closely followed by his grandfather and his men. He was hoping to reach the Guildhall before things got out of hand. He knew the guild's members would not stand a chance against the Laird's heavily armed men and Lord MacNab's Dark powers. Shortly before they reached Dalmally, his grandfather caught up with him and signed for him to stop.

'William, me lad, let's rest for a moment to plan our approach. We can't afford to take chances if we want to avoid casualties. I think two of our men should ride to Dallmally and check the situation before we enter.'

'Aye, Grandfather, who would you like to send?'

'Seamus and my commander James are getting ready right now and could be in and out of Dallmally before nightfall. While they do what they must, we can get the horses' hooves wrapped with a cloth so that we can ride in without making a sound.'

'That's a bloody brilliant idea!' Well then, let's send James and Seamus in and get to work. We have quite a few huffs to wrap, but what are we going to use?' laughed William as he slid off his horse.

'Well, James thought of that and brought a bale of sackcloth. After all, this is not our first takeover, me lad,' chuckled Lord MacDougall, giving his commander the sign to leave.

'Perfect, I am ready to start wrapping when you are.' 'My men will take care of the horses. We have more important things to do. Let's walk up that knoll while we talk. I need to stretch my legs a bit. I am getting too old for long days in the saddle,' remarked the Lord resting a hand on William's shoulder for support.

They walked over a tree-covered mountain onto a flowery glen, where countless tiny fireflies glittered like a shower of sparks in clumps of blossoming hawthorn and rowan trees.

'Grandfather, I think we should split the men into two groups and enter Dalmally from both sides. That way, we can gain control of the two gates and the market square before the Laird's troops even know what hit them.'

'Aye, that is a bloody brilliant idea, William! That's precisely what we shall do. We must avoid any confrontation that could harm unarmed villagers,' replied the Lord. He was about to return to his men when the commander's servant ran towards him.

'My Lord, the commander has returned and would like to speak with you.'

'By all means, send him up, my good man. Tell me, is Seamus back too?'

'Aye, my Lord, both of them have returned and strapped back on their armours,' answered the servant as he bowed and backed away.

'Sir William, my Lord, I am happy to report that we should be able to unarm the Laird's men without a fight, as they are presently going from house to house pillaging and have their hands tied up carrying their plunder.'

'Bastards! Men get in the saddle and put an end to that,' He addresses his soldiers.

'Seamus, you enter through the North Gate and make sure that no one slips through your fingers. And James, you know what to do. I want the village cleaned out while William and I attend the gathering in the Guildhall. Meet us there with a handful of your men once you're done.'

'Aye, my Lord, it should not take long. See you at the Guildhall,' responded the commander bowing before he rounded up his men and hastened towards Dalmally. William and his grandfather mounted their horses and cantered slowly towards the village to give Seamus and his men time to take control of the north gate before they entered the village.

'This way, Grandfather. We best use the backroads and enter the Guildhall through the cellar. That way, we can remain hidden and observe what's going till the right moment presents itself.'

'Aye right, go on then and lead the way, me lad.'

William slowed his horse and guided his grandfather through the meandering narrow alleys to the back of the Guildhall.

'Here we are,' whispered William and gestured to his grandfather to dismount.

They tied their horses behind some heavy-laden carriages before he lifted the trapdoor to the cellar. The two men lowered themselves with the pulley and began to inch their way through the dimly lit cavernous basement past piles of barrels and unstable looking stacks of crates. The beaten earth floor was soggy and covered with broken glass forcing the two men to step gingerly so as not to make any noise or risk nasty cuts. Before they reached some narrow, unstable-looking steps leading up to the guild's Great Hall, it took them quite a while. William climbed up first and silently pushed two floorboards aside to listen to the conversation.

'William, me lad, be careful. Don't push them too far. We don't want to be discovered before the opportune moment has arrived,' whispered the Lord as he tried to find a secure footing on the narrow steps.

'Don't fret. We are behind the counter. The only one that might notice the planks being out of place is Marisell, and this will tell her to keep quiet about it,' replied William as he slipped a red scrap of cloth through the narrow opening.

'What did you do that for? Do you think she will understand the meaning of it?'

'Aye, she will, Grandfather. I learned that from Avery, this is how she messages her friends, and Marisell is one of them,' William replied with a broad smile and signalled his grandfather to listen.

'My dear Laird, we are deeply honoured by your visit today,' exclaimed

Angus as he raised his tankard. 'It has been a long time since last you shared a drink with us, so please allow us to toast to your wellbeing, Slainte mhath!'

'Thank you, Angus, my good man, and thank you all for being here tonight. But before we announce the reason for this gathering, I would like to present to you my counsellor and fatherly friend, Lord MacNab',' announced the Laird bowing to Lord MacNab'.

Angus bent his head ever so slightly to Lord MacNab in acknowledgement but did not address him nor raise his tankard to salute him. He noticed how the tension was building. The Guild members were shifting restlessly on their benches, so he decided to stop the pleasantries and ask straight why the Laird had come and why he thought it necessary to bring an advisor.

'Ah, I can see that you like straight talk and I respect that. So then let me tell you why we are here today, my honourable Guild Master,' replied Lord MacNab' with a nasty sneer. 'We are here to solicit your help. Aye, you heard me correctly. We need your help. As you most certainly know, your noble Laird had been attacked. His wife and Daughter were snatched from Kilchurn Castle and are held against their will. Many of our brave soldiers lost their lives in an attempt to free them. You will all agree that we can't remain idle and leave their death unavenged. With help from you and your sons, we can end this and reunite the Laird his Lady and Daughter.'

'William, we have to act. The room is ready to explode.'

'Aye, Grandfather, I believe I just saw Seamus and James enter the hall. Let's go.'

William pushed the two planks further apart, lifted himself up and hid under the counter before he gently tugged Marisell's skirt to alert her of their presence. She dropped her towel and stooped down, pretending to pick it back up.

'I saw your message, and I am glad that you are here to put an end to this,' she whispered. 'The members have heard more than enough and are ready to strike. Each and every one is armed and ready. Best stay behind me while I check out the six men that have just entered the hall.'

'Never mind them. These are my men. You best get out of the way. I would not like to see you getting injured me, bonnie lass,' Lord MacDougall whispered and helped Marisell climb down into the cellar. William slid the planks back into their place and stepped out from behind the counter, closely followed by his grandfather.

'You are a liar and impostor, Duane, and you, Sir, are no Lord. You are cold-blooded murderer and deceiver,' William shouted across the hall. He drew his sword and walked up to the dais where Lord MacNab and Duane were seated.

'How dear you threaten me, William!' the Laird screamed at the top of his voice, jumping up from his seat. 'You are an escaped prisoner, guards. take hold of the innkeeper and throw him back into the dungeons where he belongs.'

'You are the one who belongs in the dungeon,' roared Lord MacDougall, jumping onto the dais. 'You are a bastard and a fraud of a man. Look at your wretched father right beside you, the self-proclaimed Lord MacNab'. He was known as Douglas when he came to my castle, begging for food and shelter, which I granted him. He worked as a stable hand at my castle in Oban until my beloved Daughter Sarah wed Lord Colin Campbell of Glenorchy. I ordered him to accompany her as her envoy to Kilchurn Castle, and he deserted her.' He grabbed the false Lord by his tunic, picked him up and spit in his face before he threw him off the platform.

At that moment, all hell broke loose in the Guildhall. The Laird pulled his Dagger and tried to attack Lord MacDougall but was stopped by Seamus with a nasty blow to his face. Two of the castle's guards made a feeble attempt to fight the commander back but realised quickly that they would not survive that mistake and made a run for the door where Lord MacDougall's men met them. William and Angus had their hands full trying to stop the guild members from ripping Duane to shreds and did not notice that Lord MacNab' had used the turmoil for his escape. Only when the false Laird was tied to his chair and the Guild members had returned to their benches did they notice that Lord MacNab' had fled.

'Blood basm, where is that depraved creature! Did he get past you, Seamus? James, can you see him anywhere?'

'No, my Lord, he must have slipped out through the cellar,' shouted James. He flung himself over the counter and disappeared in pursuit of their target.

'Seamus, I need your help. That cowardice slime has stabbed the lassie, come and help me to bring her up.'

Seamus and James pulled Marisell from the cellar and rested her on a pile of cloaks the members had spread out to comfort her. She had a deep stab wound in her right shoulder, which bled profusely.

'Lukas, come me, lad, take our carriage and get Marianne and Adelaide. We have no time to lose if we want to save her life,' shouted Ross and pushed his son out the door.

'Angus, we leave the situation in your hands while we give chase to Lord MacNab'. I am sure he is on his way to Kilchurn to take over the castle, and if he succeeds, he will most certainly try to kill Lady Julia. Please look after Marisell, and don't let Duane escape!' William exclaimed before he and his grandfather stormed out of the Guildhall, followed by their men.

Lord MacNab' was fuming with rage when he left Dalmally. Did this stupid lass honestly believe she could stop me? Could it be true that that weasel of a man is, in fact, my son, he thought as he crossed the drawbridge of Kilchurn Castle.

'Up the bridge and take your positions on the wall-walk. I order you to kill anyone who dares to approach,' MacNab commanded.

The guards were not brave enough to ask for the whereabouts of the Laird nor question Lord MacNab's orders. They hurriedly lifted the massive bridge before they took positions on the castle's walls, wondering who would be bold enough to try an attack.

Lord MacNab' stormed across the bailey and into the Great Hall, with his cloak flying behind him like a raven's wings. He was determined to claim Lordship over Glenorchy when he saw Julia in the Lairds chair at the end of the Great Hall. He could not believe his eyes and had to draw a deep breath to suppress his fury over her sudden resurrection.

'Oh, blessed be, you are alive, mo chridhe!' he forced himself to say. 'Colin told me you had died in childbirth. I am thrilled to see you alive and well.'

'Do not insult me with your lies, sir,' Julia shouted back as she rose from her chair and stood towering over Lord MacNab'. 'You wished me dead so you could snatch the Lairds throne and land as you did with the caves of Wemyss. But mark my words, your reign has come to an end.'

'Who is to end it?' the Lord replied, dropping all pretences in an instant. 'Surely not you, you gullible wench! You clung to me like a wet cloak and were oh so willing to believe that my feelings for you were pure and sincere, while all I was looking for was Sarah's secret. But then I realised that Colin did not share it with you, and I decided it would be high time to search for it myself in the caves of Wemyss.'

'Colin never spoke of a secret. It's just another one of your lies. You just used me to gain control over the caves and their riches, you deceiving low life.'

'Oh, you ignorant female, you have no clue of what I speak, but let me enlighten you,' the Lord said with a hateful sneer. 'As a very young lad, I learned of King Somerled's sword and that the one who holds it would rule over Scotland and the kingdom of Elfame. So, I sought employment at the castle of Clyde MacDougall, who I knew to be a direct descendant of King Somerled. I soon learned that the secret of the sword's whereabouts was solely passed on to the eldest daughter of the Clan chief and realised that I had to go with Lady Sarah to Kilchurn. I read all her messages to her father as well as her diary. I even tried to squeeze it out of her as she lay dying after giving birth to her son. I told her that I would convince Lord Campbell to kill their son if she did not reveal the secret to me, but she chose to take it and her son to her grave.

After years of searching the caves for the sword, I found the enchanted Sapphire of the Goddess Cailleach and tried to lure the secret out of her in exchange for the stone, but she only laughed at me. So, I had no choice but to abduct Lady Murigen's mortal husband and banish her to the island. But still, she did not give up the secret. My last chance to get the sword is through their Daughter Avery, and trust me, I will. It's now only a matter of Days before I hold it in my hands.'

Julia had heard enough and screamed in his face.

'Don't you Dare speak about Avery, you heartless double-tongued miscreant! Your time to pay for all your cruelty has come at last. Avery and her companions are freeing her father and other captives from the caves. She will retrieve your precious Sapphire and return it to the Goddess Cailleach.'

Lord MacNab' stared at Julia in disbelief. His eyes were narrow, rigid, and cold. The blood drained from his already ashen face when he realised what Julia had said. In his rage, he pulled a dagger from his belt, lurched forward, and threw her on the ground. He was on the cusp of slitting her throat when the shouts of his commander stopped him.

'My Lord, a large group of armed men has assembled on the ramparts led by all the clan chiefs of Argyll. An escape from the castle will be impossible.'

'Not for me, follow me,' hissed Lord MacNab'! He let go of Julia and raced out of the Great Hall towards the submerged tunnels just as William and his grandfather arrived at the castle's ramparts, where Argyll's chiefs and their troops met them.

'My Lord, we have come to swear our alliance to your grandson, the rightful heir of King Somerled. We are ready to fight at your side against that swine. He terrorised the good people of our lands for far too long.'

'Well, well, I say, that is a welcome surprise. We can use every man we can get to end the reign of this murderous villain,' Lord MacDougall said. He led the men across the lowered drawbridge into Kilchurn Castle, where Julia and her guards awaited them.

'I am so glad you are here! Lord MacNab and his men must be hiding in the castle somewhere. There is no other way out than over the drawbridge.'

'There is Julia, you've forgotten. But he will not be able to get through without the help of the Goddess Coventina,' William replied. He rushed with a group of armed men to the submerged passage he and Maighread had used to escape from the castle. Once they arrived, he was stunned to see that the tunnel was dry and that there was no sign of Lord MacNab' or his men. He hurried down to the shore of Loch Awe and was horror-struck when he saw that Lord MacNab and his men had managed to escape. Five of the Ashray warriors that guarded the waters in front of the castle lay slain on the ground.

'William, he is gone,' Ariana said, appearing out of the mist. 'You have to get a message to Avery, we can't reach her in the dead forest, but Cait Sith can. You must hurry, he is going to kill her and her friends. He has large groups of Red Caps and armies of prisoners with him. I must leave you now and take my fallen brethren home,' she urged before she disappeared in the Darkened water of Loch Awe.

William returned to the castle's Great Hall with a heavy heart. How many of our friends must lose their lives at the hands of this ruthless murderer, he thought as he walked up to the large banquet table, where his grandfather sat with his face buried in his hands.

'What's wrong, Grandfather? What happened?'

'It's all my fault, William. I should have been more cautious when I told your mother about the sword.'

'What sword? What are you talking about?'

'Our ancestor King Somerled knew about the greed and thirst for power that poisons the hearts of even the noblest men. That is why he decreed that only our firstborn Daughters should receive knowledge of the sword's secret and its location through their mothers. My beloved Daughter Sarah was still a small bairn when her mother died, so the secret was passed on to me, and I revealed it to her shortly before she was leaving Oban. The bastard must have overheard part of our conversation.'

'I am lost. You will have to tell me all about this afterwards. Right now, I need your help getting a message to Avery.'

'Very well, me lad, but I don't know where she is.'

'Never mind, all you have to do is to get my message to Adelaide. She should already be at the Guildhall to take care of Marisell, and you can be sure that one or two elves accompany her.'

'Aye, so what's the message, William?'

'We must let her know that the so-called Lord knows about her quest and is on the way to stop and kill her.'

'Crivens, will this bastard never rest! James, you must hurry back to the Guild Hall and hand this to Adelaide,' Lord MacDougall declared, handing his commander a small roll of parchment.

29 Loch Ness

Darion's words were kind and heartfelt, but they couldn't ease Avery's mind. She needed time alone to come to terms with all that had happened since she had left the inn all these months ago. She yearned for the serenity of the fairy pond. Its warm crystalline waters and rainbow-coloured pebbles. It seemed like a lifetime had passed since she had been happy and free of fret or fear. She gazed at the pearl in the palm of her hand when she suddenly felt something moving behind her.

'Darion, is that you?' she exclaimed in surprise. 'No, Avery, my sweet, it is me. I am so glad to see you unharmed and well.' Cait Sith whispered as she appeared from the thickets and gracefully lay down in front of Avery. Her black fur shimmered like silk in the faint moonlight, and her green eyes glowed like emeralds. Avery was delighted to see her. She always felt safe and at ease in her presence.

'Oh, Cait Sith, it is wonderful to see you again. It has been such a long time. But what are you doing in this forsaken place?'

'I have a message from William for you.'

'Oh, how wonderful, is he all right?' 'Aye, he is. But he is very concerned about your safety. Lord MacNab' escaped from the guildhall, stabbed Marseilles, ruthlessly murdered five Ashray warriors, and is now coming for you.'

'How? He has no clue where I am,' Avery replied.

'He does! Lady Julia, unfortunately, let it slip, and now he is heading to Ben Nevis. You must arrive there before him to return the Sapphire and break his power,' Cait Sith urged.

'There is no way that we can make it there before him. Avery said with nervous laughter, 'he can make that journey in less than a day.

'Oh no, he won't, Avery! He must go to Black Mount first to make up for his losses at Kilchurn and Dalmally. It will need him at least two days to round up more Red Caps and arm his troops. And

another two to make it to Ben Nevis. You, on the other hand, have three Days to get to the Blue Glacier.' Cait Sith explained calmly.

'You make it sound so easy, Cait Sith. But tell me how we should make that distance in three days. There is no way Lord MacDougall's ships can sail to Wemyss and back in that time. And to make the journey by land is out of the question. Lord MacNab' has his murdering squads spread throughout the land and can summon them with his Dark magic.' Avery uttered, trembling with frustration.

'There is a way, Avery! We will catch us some Kelpies and ride to Moray Firth,' interjected Darion, who overheard the conversation.

'Cait Sith, you must haste back to Kilchurn now. Tell Ariana to meet us with a group of warriors at Moray Firth as soon as the sun sets tomorrow. And ask William to join us with his troops at Achterawe by midnight.'

'Aye, Darion will do! Good luck with the kelpies, and keep in mind that they are very cunning,' Cait Sith replied. She spun around and disappeared into the Dark of the forest.

'Darion, what did you mean when you said we will catch us some Kelpies?' Avery inquired.

'He was referring to the water horses!' Glen exclaimed with excitement as he appeared right behind Avery. 'I always wanted to see them but never dared to dream of riding one – much less living to tell the tale.'

'Blimey Glen, where did you come from?' Avery uttered, overjoyed.

'Well, straight from Elfame!' giggled Ursula as she jumped out behind Glen.

'Ghilli Duh brought us back to help you! You would be lost without us!' Glen added as he embraced Avery.

'Aye, right! I am so happy you're back. We have so much to tell you, Glen.'

'No need, Ursula filled me in,' Glen responded with a broad smile and winked at Ursula.

'I don't like to break up this happy reunion, but we better hurry down to the beach to catch ourselves a ride! Follow me!' Darion interjected and led the friends further into the forest.

'What beach you are talking about, Darion? All I can see is a Dark, dying forest!' Avery declared, looking around impatiently.

'Well, mo ghràdh, my ancestors occupied many caves in Wemyss. And some of them have passages that lead straight to the seashore. Come on!' Darion explained and silently chuckled as he led the group to a large standing stone covered with strange symbols. He raised his left hand and placed his fingers on five indentations. He closed his eyes and began to recite a strange-sounding incantation. The friends stood rooted and listened to the melodic sound of his voice when suddenly, a large cloud appeared above them and blackened the sun.

'Take each other's hand and follow me,' Darion whispered, took Avery's hand, and led the group into the darkness. Avery was mesmerised and followed him into the abyss without hesitation.

The ground under their feet soon changed from a wet forest floor to soft beach sand. Every step led them deeper into the blackness and silence of the underground passage. Soon, the musty smell was replaced by the scent of the sea, and a faint, blue light appeared in the distance. It took almost an hour till the friends reached the cave's mouth and walked out onto a beautiful beach. The moon's soft light illuminated the night sky and made the wave's crest shimmer like silver. A crisp sea breeze filled their lungs and blew away the memories of the dying forest and the deadly battle.

'I am sorry to rush you,' Darion said, breaking the serenity of the moment. 'But we must find the kelpies and get on our way.'

'Aye, that's fine with me, Darion! But how will we find them and lure them to us?' Hugh asked, looking up and down the beach, searching for the magical horses.

'Oh, that is not hard to do, Hugh. All we have to do is have a good time, cheer, and laugh. Kelpies target mortals that are in a cheerful and slightly reckless mood.'

'Brilliant, this is not hard. Glen is naturally reckless,' Hugh replied with a broad smile tapping his brother on the shoulder.

The friends began to play silly games and run up and down the beach while looking for the beautiful jet-black horses.

'Here, they come! Be ready! Let them come right up before you grab their bridles. Once you have taken hold of the bridle, they have to submit and do as you wish,' Darion whispered, turning to face the group of Kelpies that came ambling up the seashore.

Avery and Ursula were taken aback by the horses' beauty and grace. They began to caress them by gently scratching their necks and combing their silky mane with their fingers. The men followed suit, and soon, everyone had gotten hold of a Kelpie's bridle.

'Be careful now! Watch them close!' Darion warned. As the horses raised their heads and began stomping and pawing the ground.

'Hold on tight and remain on their side! If they rear up and strike you, you'll be very fortunate to walk away with only a bruise. A strike from a Kelpie will shatter your bones, and if it lands a kick to your head, you'll be dead!' Darion shouted, holding on to the Kelpie's bridle with both hands.

The horses flared their nostrils and began to snort angrily. Then threw back their heads, raised their front legs high up in the air and started to kick violently.

'Pull their heads down! Don't be shy! Put your whole weight into it! Come on, folks!' Darion shouted when he saw his friends struggling with the water horses.

Avery released the tension on the bridle slightly and used the opportunity to swing herself onto the Kelpie's back as it lowered itself to slip out from under her grip. She held on to its mane tightly, squeezed its sides gently with her thighs and began patting its neck, calming it down. To her great surprise, it stopped fighting, and so did the other four. The horses obeyed and reacted calmly to their riders' commands from now on.

'Well, let's get on our way. We have quite a ride in front of us!' Darion exclaimed and nodded, satisfied as he galloped into the breaking waves. The four friends followed and soon found themselves speeding across the sea's surface and over towering waves.

Avery turned to take a last look at the tree-covered mountains of Wemyss before they disappeared in the distance. It was exhilarating to soar over the water with giddying speed on the back of these magical beings. A cold breeze picked up and blew across her face, tousling her long brown hair and filling her nose with the salty smell of the sea.

The hours flew by as quickly as the horses, and soon a radiant light appeared on the horizon, sending its light across the sky. The sun was born again from the Darkness of the night with the promise of a new beginning.

'We have reached Moray Firth. Look over there, can you see the dunes?' Darion exclaimed, pointing to one of the most spectacular sights the friends had ever seen. About five miles ahead of them lay a group of dunes that glowed like pure gold in the light of the afternoon sun.

'Aye, I see them! They are magnificent! But tell me, what do you call these crazy creatures?' Avery asked, laughing when surrounded by a large pod of jumping dolphins.

'Aww, they are here too! They are all around us!' Ursula cheered as she bent down to try to touch one that kept jumping out of the water close to her.

'They are Dolphins, and look at the group of Selkies over there. They all came to greet us,' Darion exclaimed, overjoyed!

The Dolphins accompanied and entertained the friends to the inlet of Moray Firth and only turned around as waves began to break close to the shore.

'Thank you for carrying me, my black beauty. I hope we will meet one Day again.' Avery whispered in the Kelpie's ear. She gently slid off its back and kissed it on the forehead as she let go of its bridle. In a blink of an eye, the Kelpies turned and disappeared in the breaking waves of the Northern Sea.

'Well then, here we are! What's next? Where are we heading?' Hugh inquired, looking at Darion with high expectation.

'I suggest we head towards that smoke! It might lead us to a fisherman's lunch!'

'Aye right Glen, as usual, all you can think of is food,' Avery replied and broke out in laughter.

'It may come as a big surprise to you, but I agree with Glen!' Darion said, smiling. 'Let's see if we can get some food before we make our way to the River Ness.'

After a tricky and strenuous climb across the dunes, the friends reached a vast plain covered with soft beach grass edged by shading trees. After a few steps, Glen had found a campfire nearby.

'Now that is strange!' mumbled Glen looking around for the fisherman.

'Not as strange as you think, my dear brother!' Hugh chuckled while exchanging looks with Darion.

'Right, there are no fishermen, Glen. Selena prepared the fire and the fish broth. She saw us coming and knew that we would need food. She and her family took care of our lunch.'

'Selena? Are you trying to tell me there was a lassie out there? I didn't see a boat. Did you see a boat?' Glen asked, looking at his friends with wide eyes.

'Selena is a Selkie! A shapeshifter! She can turn into a beautiful young woman. I am sure you heard of them. They are timid and cautious. Too many men have stolen their skins to enslave them. A very brutal boat builder caught Selena's mother. She endured cruelties for many years before I found her and returned her to the sea,' Darion explained.

'Since she died, her Daughter Selena provided me with fresh fish whenever I come to her shore. But enough of that, let's have a quick bite and head to River Ness,' Darion sighed, sitting down and helping himself to a bowl of fish broth and freshwater. The friends finished their meal, hid the cauldron, and put out the fire before they walked on to the mouth of the river.

'Well, you guys, I hope you are refreshed and well-rested.'

'Sure, but why you're asking Darion? Sunset is hours away, so I think this would be a perfect time for a nap,' Glen replied, spreading his blanket under a large weeping willow.

'There is no time for a nap! We have to prepare the boat for our journey. Come on! I am sure you had enough rest in Elfame,' Darion replied with a broad smile.

'Alright! What do you want us to do, master? The boat looks fine to me. All that's missing are our provisions and water.'

'Oh, Glen, you are terrible! What would you like us to do, Darion?' Avery inquired as she stepped into the boat.

'We have to make it invisible,' he answered.

'We what? How are we supposed to do that? We are no magicians!' Avery exclaimed, looking surprised.

'There is no need for magic, mo ghràdh! All we need are some branches and a reasonable length of rope. Come with me. I'll show you.' Darion responded, reaching out his hand to help Avery step back on land.

'I think we found the perfect disguise for the boat!' Ursula and Hugh shouted as they appeared from the nearby rush pulling a sizeable hollow trunk behind them.

'Take a good look at this beauty! The trunk will slide over the boat easily,' Hugh boasted as he rolled the trunk up to the boat.

'The web of roots will offer perfect protection against arrows.'

'Aye, and not to mention the Boobrie!' Glen added in a sarcastic tone of voice, doubling over laughing.

'Ah, you think you're funny, Glen! Well, you are not!' Avery hissed and stepped closer.

'Let's not fight! We need our strength for far more important things. Come on, let's get to it. It won't be long before the sun sets, and Ariana will arrive with her brothers,' Darion said, stepping between Avery and Glen. The friends settled down and created a masterpiece. After their work, the boat was no longer recognisable, and the tangled roots offered an impenetrable shelter.

'Well done! Maybe we are magicians after all! Just look at this. It will be as slow as a snail but will be invisible,' Glen teased, bursting into infectious laughter. Soon they were all laughing so hard that they did not notice Ashray's arrival.

'I'm sorry to interrupt, especially since you all seemed so happy! It's wonderful to hear you laughing!' Ariana whispered with a warm smile.

'My brothers and sisters are ready to accompany and protect you on your way through Loch Ness. The trooping Sluaghs will secure the skies while the Dryads guard the forest,' Ariana announced, pointing to the sky and the wooded shore. 'No corrupt mortal, hideous beast, or Dark magic will harm you on your journey while we are there,' she added.

'Thank you, Ariana! We're ready when you are,' Darion replied, ushering the group into the boat.

As soon as the friends took shelter under the canopy of gnarled roots, he signalled the Ashrays to move out. In an instant, the river began to boil as countless Ashrays started to pull the boat away from the shore. It took forty Ashrays to pull against the current that rushed past the boat, stony banks, and tall, beautiful bullrushes down to the sea. The cold and crystal-clear water was churned into the foam around them by hundreds of silver carp, river trout and salmon that tried to reach their spawning grounds.

'Hugh! Look at that! All we have to do is reach into the water to catch us some supper!' Glen exclaimed and was about to leave the roots cover to catch some fish.

'Are you bonkers, Glen? Are you trying to give us all away for some blimey fish? I swear your love of food will kill you one day,' Ursula hissed, grabbing his tunic and pulling him back down.

'What? There is no one anywhere near us. Don't get your knickers in a knot, Ursula,' Glen responded, red-faced.

'How can you be so sure about that, Glen? Just look at all the movements along the riverbanks,' Darion whispered, pointing to a group of shadows rushing through the thickets along the river's edge.

'Damn! How did they know we'd come this way? Do we have a traitor in our midst?' Glen asked, looking at Darion with a stunned expression.

'I am afraid something much more Dangerous gave us away!' Darion sighed while keeping a close eye on the riverbanks.

'What do you mean?' Hugh inquired, looking concerned.

'I was not sure at first, but I thought I heard the howling of Cu'Sith just before we entered the cave.'

'The howling of what?' Glen asked, looking perfectly terrified.

'Cu'Sith is a dog the size of a young bull with shaggy green fur. I am certain he followed Cait Sith and overheard our conversation. Which means Lord MacNab' is now aware of our plan,' Darion explained.

'Blood bas! That's bad, very bad! I better get my bow ready and tell Ursula to strap on her slingshot,' Hugh whispered as he crawled back to the bow of the boat to talk to Ursula.

'Do you think they'll attack the boat?' Glen asked, tensed.

'Not for now. I think we're too fast. But I'll feel a lot better once we enter the loch.'

'Aye, right, which should be just now. But we should inform the Ashrays about our suspicion,' Glen suggested. He leaned over the side to share the information with Ariana.

The friends were now alert and surveyed their surroundings with eagle eyes. Darion shot an arrow fetched with white feathers up into the sky to get the Sluaghs attention.

'Lord Darion, what's your concern?' Lian Cael, the leader of the Sluaghs, asked as he hovered over the boat.

'Lian Cael, we are being followed, and I am worried about the safety of our friends down at Achterawe.'

'Say no more, Lord Darion. I'll send some of my brothers to keep an eye on things,' Lian Cael replied in a deep, droning voice. Before he flapped his mighty black wings and shot back up into the night sky.

The Ashrays picked up speed and reached the loch quickly. Soon the wooded shore receded as they pulled the boat to the centre of the loch.

'Crivens, this was scary! Can we relax now, or are we still in danger, Darion?' Avery asked, sounding weary.

'We should be fine for now, at least until we reach closer to Achterawe. You guys can come out and take a breather.' Darion said while helping Avery crawl out from under the canopy of roots.

The friends breathed a sigh of relief and calmly gazed at the moon's reflection in the Dark blue water of Loch Ness. Everything seemed calm. The wooded shores around the loch remained still, and the trooping Sluaghs well protected the sky. The gentle bopping of the boat felt very soothing, so the friends had to fight to keep their eyes open.

'Wake up, you, guys!' Darion shouted in alarm, ripping them out of their Daze just before the boat capsized. Ursula gasped in shock as she hit the freezing water of the loch and had to fight hard to stay afloat. She had the feeling her armour was pulling her down, no matter how much she struggled. Just as the water closed over her head, a hand grabbed her wrist and dragged her to the surface.

'Damn, don't tell me that you can't swim, Ursula!' Hugh exclaimed, utterly horrified.

'I can! But the bloody armour was pulling me down like lead!' Ursula answered, spitting water.

'It wasn't your armour, Ursula!' Avery called out, pointing to a dead soldier floating close to her.

'What? How!' Ursula screamed and looked wide-eyed at Avery.

'I'll tell you later. There is no time now. Look at the boats! They are full of Lord MacNab's men. Swim ashore. I'll meet you there later,' Avery said and disappeared in the Dark water.

Avery joined the Ashray warriors as they circled the approaching boats, capsizing them one by one. Many of the armed men were unable to swim and drowned quickly. Others managed to stay afloat and swam towards Avery to grab her, when all of a sudden, the water got ice-cold and began to swirl faster and faster.

The Ashrays recognised the Danger instantly and soared through the water, grabbing AmaDa and pulling her away. Not a moment later, a gigantic black shadow appeared from the depth of Loch Ness. It breached the water directly next to them and crashed back down onto the group of swimming soldiers.

'Crivens, what was that?' Avery exclaimed in shock and surprise.

'That was Nessie! She came to your rescue. We would have lost many warriors if it wasn't for her,' Ariana replied and sighed with relief.

'Hm, Nessie. I heard of her but always thought it was just an old wives' tale,' Avery muttered nervously.

'Well, now, you know different. Nessy doesn't trust mortals and therefore stays in the depth of Loch Ness and Moray Firth,' Ariana replied, looking at the whirl of water in which Nessie had disappeared.

'Ariana, I must leave you now and join the others. I hope I'll see you again soon.' Avery whispered and swam to the shore of Achterawe.

Darion paced up and down the shore, tormented by thoughts of Avery being hurt or worse. His heart almost stopped moments earlier when Nessie launched herself out of the water, twisted in mid-air, and crashed back into the loch, taking the lord's men with her. He knew that Avery could breathe underwater and that Nessie would never willingly harm her, but he could not stop the distressing thoughts until he saw her walking out of the loch.

30 The Blue Glacier

Avery walked out of the water, feeling limp, cold, and bruised like a wet rag doll. I hope the others made it out alright before Nessie breached, she thought as she removed her scabbard and loosened her armour.

'Mo ghràdh, I'm so glad you're alright!' Darion exclaimed, pulling her into his arms.

'Aye, I am fine! Just a little bruised, but still in one piece, which cannot be said about the Lord's men. They have been smashed to pieces by Nessie,' Avery said and couldn't suppress a burst of laughter.

'Well, I saw it! And so did all the men. Soon everybody will know about her. Let's hope she will remain safe,' Darion responded. 'Speaking of remaining safe, William has some important news for us. Let's go and join the others,' he added, taking the scabbard from her hands and placing his arm around her for support.

Luckily, it wasn't a long walk to William's camp and the warm glow of the fire. Hugh and Ursula were sitting by the fire warming themselves, chatting with Seamus and James, while Glen was busy cutting a chunk of meat from a boar roasting on a spit nearby.

'I am glad that you haven't lost your appetite, Glen!' Avery shouted, shaking her head in disbelief.

'Och, that will never happen! You know how much he loves to stuff his face!' William chuckled as he walked up to greet her. 'We've to talk,' he added, sounding very excited.

'I now know what the so-called Lord is after. Let's take a few steps and sit over there. It's not something we could share with everyone.' William added a low voice while leading Avery and Darion to a broken-down crofter's cottage.

'We should have some privacy here,' he continued, making sure no one could overhear them. 'Alright, the Dryads searched the area before we arrived and watch over us now from the surrounding trees while we get ready,' he explained.

'So, what do you need to tell us that's so secret that we need to hide in the bushes?' Avery asked impatiently, stepping from one foot to the other.

'I hope it will not take too long. I am cold and hungry,' Avery added.

'I am sorry, my bonnie lass. But what I have to tell you could change Scotland's destiny and that of Elfame,' William replied in a hushed voice. He went ahead to tell Darion and Avery what he had learned from his grandfather.

'So that is what he's after! What do you think we should do first? Return the stone or try to find that sword?' Avery asked, looking at William and Darion with great curiosity.

'We must return the stone to break his power before we can even think about the sword and its whereabouts, ' Darion replied, looking bewildered at the two of them.

'Aye, I agree! Our first and utmost concern should be to free this land from him and his

Dark creatures!' Avery responded with chattering teeth.

'Well, we have to get you into some dry cloth quickly so that we can head out while we have the help of the Sluaghs!' Darion responded. He wrapped his cloak around Avery and led her back to the camp.

'I like that thought. But where will you find dry clothes for me? I don't think that it would be something the troops would carry along,' Avery whispered while breathing on her hands to warm them.

'No, they don't! But we do!' responded a soft voice from the trees nearby.

'Oh, my goodness, Oren, is that you?' Avery exclaimed, surprised.

'Aye, Laratbogh and I brought you some new clothing,' Oren responded.

'And a helmet to make you invisible from above,' Laratbogh cheered.

'Come on, let's get you changed,' Oren exclaimed, pulling Avery behind a large clump of fern.

Avery was more than happy to get out of her wet clothes and very impressed by the beauty and comfort of her new outfit. She loved the helmet Ghilli Duh made from green dragonhide and embedded gold. She was quite a sight in her Dark green suede truis, tunic and jerkin. Her armour and braces had been cleaned and dried and felt so much more comfortable than before.

'Well, I am ready and hope you are too!' Avery said, spinning around to show off her new and improved outfit.

'You look stunning, Mo Chridhe,' Darion whispered, pulled her closer and kissed her.

'Love your helmet, Avery! You look as if you are wearing a crown,' Ursula exclaimed in admiration.

'Alright folks, enough of that! El Cael just told us that about two hundred armed men are heading our way. Let's move out!' William urged, signalling his men to get in the saddle.

'Two hundred armed men! How shall we get past them? We have no more than a hundred men,' Avery said, a look of despair washing over her face.

'Leave it to us! We'll split them up and lead them astray!' Oren chuckled and winked at Avery before she and Laratbogh disappeared into the woods.

'How? Do you think that they can lure them away, Darion?'

'Aye, they can! All they need is a little help from the Hinky Punk,' Darion responded, laughing.

'The what?' Avery asked, perplexed.

'The Hinky Punk, Avery,' Darion replied.

'Come along. I'll show you.'

'Hugh, we'll ride up that mountain to have a closer look. Keep an eye out for the Wulver. He should show himself at any moment now to guide you through the bog,' Darion shouted over to Hugh, who was busy checking the weapons. He then took the reins from Avery's horse and pulled it along.

The horses had difficulties climbing the Munro and staggered a few times before reaching the top. Avery and Darion slid off their horses and hid under a large ash tree, from where they could see the entire glen and nearby swamps.

'Oh dear, look at this! That must be far more than two hundred men. The riders alone come up to about fifty,' Avery whispered, sounding very distraught.

'Never mind, that will change just now. Hang on and keep looking. Do you see the flat area over to your left?'

'Aye, I do, Darion! What about it?' 'Well, that's where the bogs and

swamps begin. One has to be very careful not to leave the narrow path, as there is no coming back if you stray,' Darion said, lifting Avery's chin kissing her gently.

'I understand. That's why the riders carry torches for the men to follow,' she replied.

'Just keep looking mo ghràdh,' he said, wrapping her in his cloak to shelter her from a stiff breeze that came out of nowhere. Moments later, the breeze reached the marshes and blew out the torches. Avery was stunned and turned to Darion to ask him what would happen next. But he just smiled, placed his finger on her lips, and pointed down to the glen. Hundreds of small, blue, flickering lights appeared in the bogs drawing soldiers away from the safe paths.

Avery gasped when she saw that the men were following these mysterious lights and then disappeared in the marshes.

'There is no need to talk. I know how you feel, Avery. But remember, they have chosen a path of death and destruction. And that is what they found. Let's return to the others to give them the good news,' Darion said in a whisper as he helped her into the saddle.

Avery did not speak a word until they caught up with the troops, and even then, she left it to Darion to inform William and the commander. She knew very well that these men would not have hesitated to kill her or her friends. But she still could not manage to bring herself to see the death of so many men as a victory. She had just begun to tell Ursula about the Hinky Punks when a blood-curdling scream echoed through the glen. A moment later, one of Lord MacNab's men dropped from the sky directly in front of her. Her horse was spooked, reared, and began to kick violently. Avery wrapped her arms around the horse's neck and held on with all her might to avoid falling off.

'Ho, ho, my sweet! Calm down -! It's all right, sshh!' Darion said as he took the horse's reins to calm the horse.

'The Sluaghs just prevented an ambush from Lord MacNab's men!' William announced as he galloped past Darion and Avery.

'Alright, Avery, that means you, Ursula, Glen, and Hugh must ride as fast as you can into the forest!' Darion said. 'The Sluaghs must leave by sunrise, so we would be an easy target for the Boobrie, which I am sure is lurking somewhere nearby,' Darion added. He turned his horse around and followed William, James, and Seamus with flying huffs.

'You heard what he said! Let's get us some cover,' Hugh and Glen shouted! The two lads urged the girl's horses into a gallop and closely followed as they Dashed towards the forest. The horses' hooves barely touched the ground as if carried by invisible wings. The sky above them began to change from the twilight grey to a brilliant gold as the morning broke.

Avery's eyes were fixed on the sky, expecting to see the menacing shadow of the Boobrie now that they were without the protection of the Sluaghs. Just moments later, her worse fear came true as the cry of that murdering beast broke the silence. The girls exchanged looks and nodded to one another in silent acknowledgement. Ursula turned around in her saddle and lay down on the back of her horse with the slingshot raised and drawn, ready to fire.

Avery pulled her swords out and stood upright in her stirrups, prepared to slash the beast wide open. That's when she heard the call of the golden eagle. Ioroth had come to their defence. The Boobrie was so startled by the arrival of the magnificent king of the sky he fled.

A few more strides, and we are safe, Avery thought as the edge of the forest came closer. She sheathed her swords as soon they reached the tree cover, dismounted her horse, and breathed a sigh of relief.

'Well, we made it,' she said, smiling. 'Aye, we did,' Ursula replied as she

slid off her horse. 'But where are the lads? I can't see them anywhere,' she added.

'Right here, Mo Lennan,' Hugh whispered as he stepped out of the thickets.

'You have to leave your horses. They wouldn't be able to make it through the forest,' Hugh said, taking control of their reins.

'Why wouldn't they make it? You're talking rubbish, Hugh. I won't abandon my horse,' protested Avery looking at Hugh with flashing eyes.

'Who said anything about abandoning? The Pixies will take care of them,' Hugh replied, pointing to four tiny faces peeking through a blueberry bush.

'Well then, let me introduce you to our four new friends. Alida, Sindri, Nolana, and Pooky,' Hugh announced, bowing to the group of Pixies.

'Honoured to meet you all,' Ursula and Avery exclaimed, smiling.

The Pixies did not say a word but giggled while beaming at the girls with their big brown eyes. A mischievous smile flashed over their faces as they took the reins and led the horses away.

'Aye, so that's taken care of,' Hugh sighed, relieved as he rolled up his sleeves.

'Fine, but what are you up to now?' Ursula inquired. 'Helping you up into the tree, it's high time we get off the ground,' Hugh answered with a smile. He bent over and formed a step with his hands to lift the girls to Glen, who sat on a branch above them, waiting to give them a hand.

'But why?' Ursula asked, pushing him away.

'Oh, come on, don't be so difficult,' Avery interjected, stepped into Hugh's hands, and disappeared into the tree.

'It will get horrid here in a moment,' Hugh said impatiently, grabbed Ursula's waist and lifted her. Glen was ready and pulled her onto a large branch where Oren and Laratbogh were waiting,

Ursula was furious. She honestly did not like to be manhandled.

'What did you do that for?' she hissed as Hugh swung himself up to a branch next to her.

'Goodness, Ursula! He had to do it! No one will be safe down there as soon as Ghilli Duh speaks his enchantment,' Oren sighed, rolling her eyes.

Not a moment later, the forest floor shuddered. Moss covered rocks broke through the ground as if pushed by invisible hands. The trees began to entangle their branches and pull their roots out of the earth to form tall arches making it impossible to pass.

'Oh, how bloody brilliant! Avery cried out in sarcasm. 'Why did Ghilli Duh do that? Now we'll never make it to the Blue Glacier before Lord MacNab',' she exclaimed in frustration.

'Sure, you will! The only ones who are slowed by this spell are Lord MacNab's men,' Oren replied and winked at Avery.

'They have to take the long route around the forest. That will buy you at least half a Day,' Laratbogh added, smiling.

'Avery, my dear, the only ones that would risk passing through this forest now are the Red Caps as they blindly follow your scent, not realising that they will meet their doom,' Ghilli Duh said in a voice that made Avery tremble. For the first time, she felt his immense power and determination to annihilate everyone and everything that Dared to threaten her.

'Alright, I understand it,' she replied. 'But how will we get through?'

'Oren and Laratbogh will guide you through the treetops. You'll reach the foot of Ben Nevis by midday,' Ghilli Duh explained before disappearing right in front of her.

The friends moved through the treetops like a breeze reaching the edge of the forest by midday. They bid Oren and Laratbogh goodbye and returned to the ground, where Asanopirh and Sorcha were waiting with their horses. After a brief welcome, the group decided to find shelter for a short rest and exchange information. Avery was relieved when Asanopirh told her Adelaide looked after her father and that her friends had returned to their families. She leaned back and had some water before sharing the sword's information with the group. The friends listened intently to Avery. She could tell they needed some time to deal with this new development, except for

Asanopirh. He stood a few steps away from the group and stared aimlessly into the distance.

'Asanopirh, are you alright,' Avery inquired, laying her hand on his shoulder?

'I am fine, Avery. What you said brought back beautiful memories of a time when mortals and the Seelie Fae lived peacefully side by side,' Asanopirh replied, smiling.

'Sorry to interrupt, but William and his men have arrived. It is time to get ready for our final battle. Let's go,' Sorcha exclaimed as she stepped up to Avery and Asanopirh, handing them the reins. The friends rode in full gallop to the foot of Ben Nevis and joined the others.

'Let's split up to provide cover for Avery and her comrades while they climb up to the Blue Glacier,' William ordered, threw Avery a kiss and joined his men.

'Alright, let's hide the horses. From here on, we have to walk,' Darion declared, dismounted his horse and tied it under a large oak. Hugh and Glen were already on their way when they heard Ursula's scream. Avery turned around in horror, swung herself back on her horse and rode to where she thought the voice came from.

Ursula's horse was hit by an arrow and fell on top of her. She was pinned down by the animal, unable to free herself. Avery jumped off her horse in full trot and landed on her knees right next to Ursula. The two tried to raise the horse's shoulders but did not manage to free Ursula's foot caught in her stirrups.

Avery stood up looking for help when she saw two Lord MacNab's men flying towards her with their lances raised, ready to impale her and Ursula. She could not pull her swords between the large boulders around them. There was no way out. Avery and Ursula were sure their end was near and braced themselves for the defeat. Suddenly, the saddles of their assailants slipped off their horses at the last possible moment, sending them flying. The men hit the ground so hard their necks snapped on impact. The girls gasped for air, wasted no time, and frantically tried again to free Ursula.

'Shall we give you a hand,' asked a soft voice coming from the dust cloud. Four tiny Pixies appeared.

'Goodness, where did you come from?' Avery said, looking at them in disbelief.

'We jumped on to the horses of these buffoons as they passed the oak,' the four blurted out, giggling and slapping their knees.

'Well, and then we cut their saddle straps,' screamed Pooky dropping to the ground laughing.

'I don't know how to thank you,' Avery sighed as she helped Ursula stand. 'But we have to go now. You better return to the forest. It is too dangerous for you out here,' she said before she and Ursula returned to the oak tree, where they hoped to find Darion and the lads.

'Crivens, where are they,' Ursula exclaimed in panic when she discovered the men were not there.

'Calm down, my bonnie lass. They are safe,' Bilobeal called from a gap between the tree's roots. 'Come on and mind your head. We had to go underground to shake off this bloody scum,' he whispered, holding out his hand to help the girls. Once again, Avery found herself in total Darkness and had to trust the one that led her. The girls had to stoop down low to make it through the tunnel and were glad when they finally saw the light. Darion waited at the end of the tunnel and sighed, relieved when Avery appeared.

'Well, it's high time to make it up to the Glacier. Lord MacNab and his men are drawing close. Some of the Red Caps escaped Ghilli Duh,' Sabaltalab informed the group as he and his brother Phaervlon carefully hid the tunnel's entrance.

The friends tightened their bootstraps and began their ascent. It was a strenuous climb from rock to rock while avoiding loose stones. Moments after the friends left, the tree cover rain began to fall and soon became hail. Thousands of little icy balls hit their faces, making it impossible to check their surroundings. Once in a while, the wind carried the battle sound from the glen up to them. But there was another sound, one that was eerie familiar. Avery recognised it right away as the sound of the Boobrie. Before the friends could take him out in the sky, another scream filled the air. But this time, it was Glen's scream. The Boobrie had caught him by surprise and grabbed him with his sharp talons. Moments before the beast was able to disappear in the clouds, Ioroth shot through the sky like a lightning bolt. The eagle circled him once to assess the situation before he turned and attacked the beast. He sunk his talons deep into the Boobrie's eyes, blinding him and sending him into a mad flapping frenzy. The creature had lost his sense of direction and flew straight towards the rock wall when Ioroth returned for another attack. In its attempt to escape Ioroth's attacks let go of its prey. Glen was now falling fast and seemed to be lost when at the last moment, Ioroth returned and caught him just before he hit the ground. When Ioroth returned him to his friends, he was as white as snow and trembled uncontrollably. They all had tears in their eyes as they wrapped their arms around him and sighed.

'This was too Damn close!' Glen said in a trembling voice.

'Too Damn close indeed! But I think that this was the last attack from the Boobrie,' Avery replied, pointing to a black heap of feathers at the foot of Ben Nevis.

'Bloody brilliant! Let's hope it was the last of our worries,' exclaimed Hugh with a faint smile.

'It won't be, Hugh. We are not there yet,' Darion said, pointing to the snow-covered peak of Ben Nevis. 'But at least we no longer have to watch the sky,' he chuckled and pulled Avery closer.

The friends unrolled their blankets and wrapped them tight around their shoulders before approaching the snow line. But when they reached, they realised it wasn't just snow but ice, which made it very difficult even to make slow progress. Frozen to the bone and out of breath, the group finally reached the cave's entrance atop the Blue Glacier.

'We have done it, Avery,' Darion called out and stepped aside to make way for Avery. She stood perfectly still like an ice statue and gazed into the blue cave in awe. She was happy but couldn't deny that she was reluctant to meet the almighty Goddess Cailleach.

'Go mo ghràdh, Lady Cailleach is waiting,' Darion said encouragingly.

'Give me a moment! I have to let it sink in that I have reached the Blue Glacier before I can return the Sapphire to the Goddess,' Avery sighed.

'Oh no!' she screamed in terror. 'I don't have the stone! Asanopirh never gave it to me.'

'Calm down, Avery. You had it all along. Take off your helmet and take a look,' Darion uttered, looking at her with the softest smile.

Avery removed the helmet and was stunned when she saw blue Sapphire.

'I had it all along,' she exclaimed as she removed it? The stone felt amazingly warm to the touch and tingled with energy.

'Oh no, you won't, you bloody bastard!' shouted a small voice behind her.

Avery spun around and saw a Red Cap in mid-air. Pooky had tripped him so that he fell into his pikestaff. Half blinded by the plum of yellow ashes, Avery saw how a second Red Cap raised his pikestaff and killed Pooky. She was horror-stricken and filled with burning fury as she drew her sword and slashed the Red Cap. Avery could no longer suppress her rage and released it with a scream that echoed through the cave-like a clap of thunder. She fell to her knees, picked up the tiny lifeless body of the Pixie, and held it close to her heart.

'Leave him to me, my sweet bairn! I will take him to summer land where he will be with his ancestors, happy and free,' whispered a voice behind her. Avery looked around but could not see anyone.

'Follow me!' said the voice, as a blue light appeared in the distance. Avery got up and followed the light into a cathedral-like cave. It took her a moment to adjust her eyes to the bright light before she noticed a crystal bowl that floated above the Blue Glacier.

'Return the Sapphire to its birthplace and release your light, Daughter of my beloved sister Murigen,' the Goddess whispered.

Avery lowered her eyes and saw Pooky was gone, and the Sapphire she held in her hand emitted a bright blue light. She stepped up to the bowl as if in a dream and released the stone. Her heart felt as if it would burst at any moment, and Avery had to take a deep breath. She had expected the air to be ice cold, but it was pretty warm, to her surprise. She slowly calmed enough to gaze at the blue ice surrounding her. She raised her arms as if in a trance and was engulfed by a bright white light that melted the Glacier and created a magnificent river.

'The water you freed returns the life to all that was once dead and releases the Sword of the mighty King Somerled,'

the voice of the Goddess echoed through the cave as the Sword appeared.

'Take it, Mo Ghràdh, it is a gift from Lady Cailleach. It will help us to free your mother,' Darion urged.

'But we must first return to Ursula, Hugh and Glen first,' Avery replied.

'No need, Mo Ghràdh! Lady Cailleach returned them to Kilchurn Castle along with William and his men. They are now reunited with Adelaide, Julia and their families,' Darion explained. He took her hand and led her through a sphere of radiating white light to a fragrant garden. Avery recognised the garden from the night on the loch where she heard her mother's voice for the very first time.

'Avery, you have returned.' It was her mother that spoke. Avery spun around and saw her mother for the first time. She looked like an ivory statue with long silver hair. Her gentle green eyes reminded Avery of Cait Sith.

'Let us join your father before you both go and rest,' Murrigen said in a whisper. She took their hands and led Avery and Darion to a beautiful palace, where Gregor awaited their arrival. The once frail man had not only completely recovered but regained his youth and strength.

'Welcome, Avery and Darion. We are so glad the time of trials has ended, and we are reunited. There is much to tell you and much to hear, but there'll be time after your rest. But before we part, I must give you a message from Adelaide,' Gregor explained, handed Darion a small roll of parchment and walked away.

Darion unrolled the parchment and read it out to Avery.

Avery and Darion,

We thank you from the bottom of our hearts for what you have done for us and the sacrifices you had to make. We would have loved to have you here with us at Kilchurn Castle to celebrate your great victory over Lord MacNab and his Dark magic. But we understand that you need time to get to know your parents and recover. William and I agreed to travel to Touraine to bring Anne, Lucie, and Harris back home, now that William has taken over the Lordship of Glen Orchy and Argyll.

We send you all our love,

Adelaide.

Darion rested the parchment down, took Avery into his arms, and carried her to their bed where they finally could rest and dream without fret or fear.

Thanks for reading my book ! If you enjoyed this adventure and the inside to Scottish Mythology, stay tuned for the continuation of our story in book two. I'd be very grateful if you'd post a short review on Amazon. Your input truly makes a difference.

Thanks again for your support!"

Ursula Williams

Legends from the kingdom of Alba

Some Scottish expressions

Aye - Yes
Aye, Right!!- You're saying something Unbelievable
Baltic – very cold
Dreich – very wet
Blood Bas - Expression of surprise
Blood Basm " "
Bonny – pretty, nice
Crivens - An exclamation of astonishment/horror.
Dinnae – don't
Madainn mhath- good morning
Mo Leannan – My lover
Mo Chridhe – My sweetheart
Mo ghràdh – My love
Mòran taing – a lot of thanks
Nay - No
Ken- Know
'Fàilte mah
Feck- Fuck
Eejit - Idiot
fret - worry
Haud yer wheesht! – Shut up.
Bairn – Child
Lass – girl
Lad- guy
Slainte Mhath – Cheers, good health
Slàinte mhòr agus a h-uile beannachd duibh!'
Great health and every good blessing to you.
Wee – small, tiny

The Celtic Mythology

Seelie Court

In Scottish folklore, the Seelie Court (more benevolent but still dangerous)

The Seelie Court was described as the realm of fairies who would seek help from humans, warn those who have accidentally offended them, and return human kindness with favours of their own. Still, a fairy belonging to this court would avenge insults and be prone to mischief.

Unseelie Court

The Unseelie Court (more malevolent).was used to describe the darkly inclined fairies. Unlike the Seelie Court, no offence was thought necessary to bring down their assaults. As a group (or "host"), they were thought to appear at night and assault travellers, often carrying them through the air, beating them, and forcing them to commit such acts as shooting at cattle.] In Scotland, they were seen as closely allied with witches. Some of the most common characters in the Unseelie Court were bogies, bogles, boggarts, abbey lubbers, Boobrie Read Caps, Cu' Sith and buttery spirits.

Goddesses

The Goddess Cailleach Na Beira Dubh created Scotland when she roamed the world long ago as a giant woman. She has been called many names: The old Hag, Winter Witch, Queen of the Weather or Bridgid, but I call her the Cailleach, and that is how you will meet her in this story.

The Cailleach has a staff of power, and she can tap the earth and freeze it, and if she plunges it into the earth and pulls it forth, water will spring free, and it will run down the side of the valley, and her animals will drink from it. But sometimes, she rests and lays back on the mountains she created, surveying her work, and she will fall asleep, forgetting to shut the well. And so, the water runs down and gatherers in the valleys, and that's how Loch Lomond, Loch Awe and Loch Ness were created. She wears a great plaid, and once a year, she takes it off and washes it in the Ayrshire Bay. It creates a sea storm that is so loud you can hear it in Glasgow, and when she is finished, she lays it across the land, and we see it as the first snow of winter. She has a hammer of power, and she can use it to smash into the landscape. She sculpts the mountains, the coastline and islands and crafts the land we live in today. One side of the hammer is a lightning bolt, and when she hits the earth with it, lightning springs up into the heavens. She was the original Thunder God, but many of you have forgotten her.

Brigid is the Goddess of spring, fertility, and life. She was known as the master of both healing and smithing. Her holiday, Imbolc, is held on February 1st and marks the midpoint of winter.

Coventina is the Goddess of rivers and streams.

Momo is the Goddess of wells and hills and streams.

Arianrhod Is the goddess of the moon. Of time, karma and retribution. Keeper of the silver wheel of stars, a symbol of time and karma.

Murigen Is the Goddess associated with the deluge legends. Rules Over: Water magic

Other Mythological Creatures

The Loch Ness Monster, or Nessie, is Scotland's favourite creature. It lives in Loch Ness in the Scottish Highlands and has been described as a large, long-necked creature not unlike a colossal sea snake.

Kelpies are water fairies that are said to have the strength and endurance of 100 horses. They roam Scotland's beaches as beautiful horses and often entice unsuspecting humans to ride them and take them into the water and to their death.

Selkies are beings that could shape-shift from human to seal and back. They can slip off their soft seal skins and take on a human form. They are powerful and seductive and can easily capture human hearts.

Ghilli Dhu Is a powerful male faerie and lives deep in Scottish forests but prefers sunlit birch groves, where he lives alone most of the time and camouflages himself with clothes made of leaves and moss and only comes out at night. This wild tree spirit is kind to children lost in the woods.

The Brownies are good-natured mythical little people. The tiny brown elves live in country houses, workshops and kitchens of the old Castles across Scotland. If they like their hosts, they will do the household chores while people sleep, but disappear if poorly treated or if their host is dishonest and greedy.

The Wulver *is* a creature, half man and half wolf. He is covered in a layer of thick brown hair. Unlike the werewolf, he was never human but took the form of a man with a wolf's head. He is benevolent and friendly and is known to have left fish on the windowsills of poor and hungry families

Cait Sith CAIT SITH: is a fairy cat as big as a dog, and wholly black apart from one white spot on it could be deadly when seen face to face.

Dryads could shapeshift between the form of a human or a tree. Dryads live exceptionally long lives and always carry a seed of the host tree to be reborn in the young tree when planted. Dryads are protected by the gods and goddesses and punish any mortals that harm their trees or forests.

Ashrays are translucent water creatures like sea ghosts. They are male and female and live only underwater. If one manages to capture an Ashray and expose it to sunlight, it will melt and leave a puddle of water.

Pixies are childlike benign mythical beings that love to dance and cause mischief. They can be found around stone circles, barrows, dolmens, ringforts, or menhirs.

Jack-o-Lantern/Will-o'-the-wisp are mysterious lights that can be seen at night over bogs, swamps, and marshes. They are said to lead unexpecting travellers astray and into the bogs and marshes, never to be seen again.

Drows are short, strong elves that live in Scotland's mountain caves. They are said to be master crafters and blacksmiths,

Unseelie Court / malevolent creatures

Red Caps Red Caps are murderous goblins that soak their caps in the blood of their victims. No mortal can outrun a Red Cap. They are extremely fast, even with the heavy pike staffs they carry and their iron-tipped boots. But it is said that they turn to yellow ashes when struck with an elven blade

Boobrie lives near water. It can transform into a horse and canter across water and land or change its appearance to a gigantic waterbird or a water bull. But most of the time, the Boobrie appears as a giant savage bird that will devour anyone who dares to cross his path.

Cu' Sith is a malevolent dog the size of a young bull with green matted fur that hunts Scotland's forests.

Main characters (mortals)

Amanda
William
Maighread
Adelaide
Harris
Ursula and her parents, John / Annette
Hugh, Glen and their parents, Balthair / Madge
Jonathan, Amanda's grandfather
Gregor Amanda's real father
Lord Clyde MacDougall, William's grandfather
Lady Sarah MacDougall/Campbell William's mother
King Somerled William's grandfather
Lady Julia MacArthur/Campbell Duane Campbells mother
Colin Campbell, first Lord of Glen Orchy, William's father
Duane Campbell, son of Lady Julia and MacNab
Angus Guild master
Ross MacDuff butcher, Peter, his son, a soldier
in Duane's army
Gavin Baker
Leerie lamplighter

Servants of Kilchrun Castle

Kenneth stable hand
Alan men servant
Rhona kitchen maid

Dunollie Castel

Dunbar Clyde's men servant
Commander James
Cadets Seamus & Fergus

Jenny kitchen maid
Marseille
Tavish Treasurer
Magnus blacksmith, his son Rory his wife Caitlyn
Allister captain

Opponents
Ruadhri
MacNeil's of Barra
Brian boatswain
Draws
Bilobeal, Pharvelon, Sabaltalab-
Dryads
Laratbogh,
Faerydae, Aislinn,
Oren, Hazel -
Ashray
Ariana-
Brownies
Nissa, Lala, Ben, Fen-
Selkies
Selena, Darach, Una. Silie
Pixies
Pooky, Alida, Sindri, Nolana
Sluagh
Lian Cael, Rupert

Main character immortal
Lady Cailleach
Lady Arianrhod
Lady Brigid
The Morrigan

Queen of Elfame
Lady Murigen Amanda's mother
Ioroth Golden Eagle

Information on King Somerled
www.undiscoveredscotland.co.uk /us
biography/s/somerled.ht

ABOUT THE AUTHOR

Ursula Williams is a born traveller with an insatiable thirst for new experiences and not afraid to take risks. She left Germany and a successful career in marketing many years ago to start a new life on a small island in the Caribbean. Ursula worked for more than 25 years as a designer, business coach, tutor, crisis counsellor and even directed her very own TV show.

She explored the rainforest, found ancient settlements, and organised their archaeological excavation. Ursula met and befriended Taino and Calinago chiefs and medicine men who shared their herbal cures and mythology knowledge with her.

Ursula returned to Germany when her children left the island to study abroad. She travelled through Europe and visited ancient sites in Northern Africa, Ireland, and Scotland.

Scotland stole Ursula's heart and inspired her to start a carrier as an author. Her undying love for Scotland and everything mystical shows in her descriptions of Scotland's scenery, its forests, lochs, and glens.

Her narratives are so vivid that the reader can see the sites, feel and almost smell them. Her protagonists are so lifelike, likeable, or feared that their speaking patterns or actions make them easily recognisable.

Contact

https://authorursulawilliams.blogspot.com/

https://www.facebook.com/FantasyAuthor

UrsulaWilliams

https://twitter.com/UrsulaW25897746

Printed in Poland
by Amazon Fulfillment
Poland Sp. z o.o., Wrocław

11664811R00179